SOME MONSTERS NEVER DIE

Monsters and Mayhem Book One

E A COMISKEY

Scarsdale Publishing, Ltd

TRADEMARK ACKNOWLEDGMENTS

The Taco Wagon
Hyatt Hotels
Morgan's
Coke
Top of the Hill
Walmart
Al's Breakfast
Entertainment Weekly
Dairy Queen
The Weather Channel
Boy Scouts
Spearfish Regional Hospital
Salvation Army
Wray Municipal Airport
Wray Museum
Dollar General
Miralax
Big Nose Kate's Saloon
HBO
The Emporium

Crystal Palace
The Longhorn Café
Six Gun City
Circle K
O.K. Cafe
Mack Truck
Velcro

For my dad, the original Curmudgeon.

CHAPTER ONE

Richard

OLD AGE WAS THE MOST VICIOUS OF BULLIES. LIFE HAD already scorned him, knocked the books out of his hands and beat him to a pulp. Now, here came Old Age to kick sand in his face. It wasn't fair. All his life, he'd been promised a retirement from hardship—a handful of golden years before Death's bony hand reached for him. Now, when it was far too late to do anything about it, he realized the whole blasted world had conspired against him.

There were no golden years. Only a lonely descent toward oblivion.

Everest Senior Living Facility was not the nursing home of his nightmares. As a younger man, in his seventies, Richard had woken in a cold sweat with visions of dirty, closed-in rooms, abusive nurses, and seeping bedsores. The reality of his old age was nothing like that.

The old-folks home was bright, full of sunlight that streamed through enormous, plentiful, spotless windows. Perky young girls who smelled faintly of coffee bustled about with rhinestone-studded stethoscopes draped around their necks.

The food was bland and mushy, but at least as good as what he'd lived off in the years since his sweet Barbara had died, and they served ice-cold prune juice at every meal, so his guts kept moving like they were supposed to. Thanks be to the Holy Lord above, there were no olive loaf sandwiches. He'd eaten enough olive loaf to last a dozen lifetimes.

All in all, Everest was as good a place as any to be abandoned by your family while you waited for death.

Well, it would have been, if it weren't for Stanley Kapcheck. Stanley with his shiny bald head and perfect teeth that were all his own. Stanley had a flat stomach and a British accent. He wore a leather coat.

Honestly! What kind of respectable senior citizen wore leather?

Pretty nurses, young enough to be his grandchildren, giggled and blushed when Stanley spoke.

Richard loathed Stanley.

Was it so much to ask for a man to grow old and die the way nature intended? Something was weird about a man Stanley's age who still wore well-shined lace-up shoes that he tied himself.

Consequently, the sight of Stanley's pristine wingtip tapping on the white tiles of the dining hall floor was chipping away at the core of Richard's soul. And if that weren't enough, the pompous old peacock had an extra helping of chocolate pudding on the table in front of him. That new girl with the wild black curls had brought it to him, offering it like she was presenting her dowry.

Richard used the back of his chair and the edge of the table to push himself to his feet. He held on for a moment to make sure his balance was good and steady, and then moved his hands to his walker and shuffled in Richard's direction.

The insufferable old fart smiled at him. "Good evening, Dick! You're looking well. How's that hip of yours?"

How dare he act like they were friends? And, Lord, but how he hated being called Dick.

Richard lifted his chin and looked down his immense nose at Stanley. "I see you have two puddings."

"Yes, a little indulgence is good for the soul, don't you think?"

"No. I disagree completely. I think this world is a sick and broken place where people indulge all too often and abstain not nearly often enough."

"Oh, come on now." Stanley reached forward and patted the round paunch of Richard's stomach. "It seems perhaps you've enjoyed one or two indulgences over the years."

That was it. That was going to be the comment that sent his blood pressure so high something inside would finally burst. He pointed a shaking finger at the other man and tried to get a word out, but his lips were pressed into a thin, tight line of fury and he couldn't quite seem to remember how to get them to move.

"Mr. Bell," the wild-haired girl said. "Did you want to have dessert over here with Mr. Kapcheck? Here, let me move your pudding for you." In a flash, she scooped the little bowl away from his seat and plopped it down across from Stanley. "There you go. Now you can sit with your friend."

She trotted away to refill the teacup Mrs. Wiler was holding in the air and left Richard standing there, red-faced and trembling with rage.

"Your shoes are ugly!" Richard spat the words out of his mouth with all the force he could muster.

Stanley threw his head back and laughed.

Richard spun on his heel—or, well, he turned around with pathetic, tiny, careful little steps and did his very best to stomp out of the room. It was difficult since he lived in mortal fear of falling again and therefore never lifted either foot more than an inch or two off the ground.

Back in his room, he lowered himself into the soft brown arm chair and clicked the TV on, just to have some noise. He sat there, staring at some stupid nature documentary. After a minute or two, he realized that he never enjoyed a single bite of dessert, but he'd left Stan Kapcheck sitting in the dining room with three bowls of chocolate pudding laid out in front of him.

The unfairness of life was a burden nearly too great for someone as old as him to bear.

CHAPTER TWO

Finn

Finn was one hundred percent certain that cigarettes were the only thing keeping him from ballooning up to three hundred pounds. If he was smoking, he wasn't shoveling potato chips into his mouth.

He lit a Marlboro and leaned back, making the soft leather of the enormous desk chair squeak. Outside the window, a hummingbird flitted around the red plastic feeder and buzzed away again. The smoke curled up in his lungs, sank into his blood, kissed his soul, and made its way back out of his body as he exhaled.

On the computer screen, the little black cursor flashed against the blank white page.

He'd done an internet search for tips on how to conquer writer's block.

Exercise. Take a walk. Get a change of scenery.

What a joke.

Another long inhale filled him up so completely he thought maybe he could float right out the window and fly away.

Letting it go, the weight on his shoulders returned twice as heavy.

The blank page mocked him.

He breathed in.

Upon exhale, he whispered to the empty room, "Dear God, send me a Muse. " Slick tendrils of smoke wrapped around the words and carried them toward heaven.

With the cigarette dangling from his lips, he stood, grabbed his keys from the hook next to the door, and headed out into the brilliant sun. Joe's was open, and the owner would serve him a cold beer any time of day, no questions asked.

A little pink Vespa was parked outside his front door. A girl, presumably the owner of the preposterous scooter, sat on the hood of his car, her smooth, tanned legs crossed like a school child's. For all that, she sported every attribute of a grown woman. At the sight of him, she flashed perfect white teeth. Tiny dimples formed on her round cheeks. "Hi there!"

He plucked the cigarette from his mouth. "You're sitting on my car."

"I didn't want you to leave without me," she said.

"Why's that?" It had been years since the first fan had approached him on the street. He'd been so flattered then it left him cocky for a full week. After a while, fame lost its appeal. They all asked the same questions. Half of them wanted him to make them famous writers, too. The other half expected him to be one of the characters in his books. None of them really cared who he was, outside of his life as a writer. This girl, though, had the distinction of being the first groupie to seek him out at his home. It seemed a level of stalkerly ambition worth a decent conversation, at least.

Plus, the t-shirt stretched tight across her pert, unbound breasts created an interesting diversion from the all-consuming thoughts of self-pity he'd battled the past few weeks.

"Can I have a cigarette?" she asked.

He fished the crumpled pack from his pocket and offered it to her. She let him light it for her and inhaled like the smoke was salvation. "I haven't smoked in forever."

"If you can go this long, you should probably keep up the clean streak."

She inhaled again and blew the smoke out in a long, thin stream through the purse of her full pink lips. "Where you goin'?"

"Have we met before?"

"Maybe you've seen me around. Everybody around here knows each other, right? So, where you goin'?"

He studied her face. She didn't look the least bit familiar. "I would remember you."

She hopped down and stepped over to him. The cigarette fell to the ground and she crushed it under the heel of her white sandal. "Where you goin'?"

"I'm going to Joe's to get drunk."

"It's cheaper to get drunk at home."

"Only alcoholics drink alone."

She grinned up at him. "So, you're looking for company?"

She was Venus on a half shell, offering herself up for his pleasure. How could he resist? Why should he resist? Damn! Remember that. It would be a perfect line in the new novel. Twenty words down, seventy-nine thousand, nine hundred and eighty to go. "Care to join me?"

She bounced on her toes. "I thought you'd never ask. I would love to join you for a drink."

"You are old enough to drink, right?"

"In all fifty states," she promised.

It seemed like there should be some voice in his head listing reasons why it was a bad idea to invite this tiny, adorable stalker to go to the bar with him. He listened hard. The voices were as silent as they had been when he'd stared at the computer, so he reached around her and opened the passenger door.

She slid in and ran a hand over the gearshift. "I adore this car. You have amazing taste."

He watched her fingers glide over the molded plastic. Still, there was no voice, but there was more than a little seismic activity south of the equator. "What's your name?" he asked.

"Tell you later," she said, looking up at him through lashes so long they surely had to be fake.

The door slammed a little harder than he meant for it to. His boots thumped against the pavement and the car sank under his weight when he dropped into the seat. He crushed the cigarette out in the car's ashtray. "Tell me now."

She pouted. She had a perfectly bite-able bottom lip.

"Please," he said.

"Sara."

He had to ask. "What do you want, Sara?"

"I want to drink a beer with you at Joe's."

He lit a fresh cigarette, put the Mustang in gear, and headed toward Joe's.

CHAPTER THREE

Richard

THE LIGHT TAP ON THE DOOR CAME LIKE CLOCKWORK, JUST after the start of the eleven o'clock news.

"It's open!" Richard called out, as if it weren't always open. Doors at Everest didn't have locks. A pretense of privacy was maintained, but the charade wasn't lost on him. Strangers washed his underpants and strangers cleaned up under his bed. Strangers asked about his morning stool and peeked in on him while he slept. Privacy was a privilege afforded to those who could still contribute to society.

The door swung open and a child with a shiny blonde pony-tail on the very top of her head bounced into the room. "Evenin', Mr. Bell. How you feelin' tonight?"

Over her shoulder, Richard caught a glimpse of Stanley leaning against the wall in the brightly lit corridor. He wore jeans and a lilac button-front shirt. His legs were crossed at the ankles. He caught Richard's eye and smiled. Jerk. Looked like a darn wrinkled up old gigolo on a street corner.

The little girl peeked into the bathroom. They always did that. What were they looking for, anyway?

"That hip bothering you at all?" she asked.

"Only when I sit or stand," Richard told her. When he'd fallen off the curb in front of his house and shattered his hip, the doctors had assured him that the newfangled titanium implant would be better than the original. They'd lied. They always lied. Medical school probably had a course—Effective Falsehoods 101. He hurt all the time. It wasn't just his hip, either. Since they'd officially declared him an old man, he hurt in every joint of his body.

The girl was undeterred by his gruff attitude. "Time to lay down then?" she asked.

"I'll be layin' down for eternity soon. I'd like to sit up and watch the eleven o'clock news now, if you don't mind."

She giggled as if he said something funny and took his wrist between her slim fingers. Glancing at the TV, she told him, "I really love her. She's so much more relatable than the woman who was on there before."

The woman who was on there before? Was she talking about Barbara Walters? Of course, Barbara Walters wasn't relatable. She was iconic. She was untouchable. She was exactly what a TV personality should be. These pretty young things in short skirts were more concerned about looking like the latest celebrity than in finding incorruptible sources. Not that he had anything against pretty girls in short skirts, but there was a time and place and the nightly news was not that place.

Nurse Ponytail let go of him and gave him a long look. "Can I ask you a personal question, Mr. Bell?"

That was new. Not once, since he'd moved into this place, had anyone asked permission before getting personal. Out of curiosity as much as anything, he said, "You can ask. Don't promise I'll answer."

She tugged on the ends of her lavender stethoscope. "I just... You seem pretty unhappy."

He stared at her, waiting for something more than a statement of the obvious.

"Do you still enjoy life?"

It took a moment to even process the question. Enjoy life? Images flashed in his mind. He was a boy on the farm, swinging from a rope in the hayloft and landing in a pile of fresh, sweet-smelling straw. He was racing in the State track and field championships, the crowd screaming his name. It was his wedding night and he learned about the astonishing secret power that women held over men. He held his newborn child in his arms and thought his heart would burst with pride and joy. His wife lay in a hospital bed. His company gave him a gold watch and a pat on the back for forty-two years of loyal service. He buried his best friend. His daughter told him she just didn't have time to give him the care he needed and she was having him moved to a rehabilitation facility.

To his astonishment, hot tears pricked his eyes for the first time in decades. "I..."

"Yes?" She leaned in toward him, listening with unusual intensity.

"I don't..."

A loud banging startled him so badly his heart gave a painful squeeze. The door swung open and there stood Stanley.

"Dick! Thought I'd stop in and see if you'd like to join me for a nightcap in the cafeteria. Of course, they don't serve alcohol, caffeine, or sugar, but we might be able to sweet talk the ladies into some sugar-free cocoa."

Richard's mouth fell open and he snapped it shut again. If Nurse Ponytail had proposed marriage, he'd have been less surprised than he was by the invitation from Stanley.

"Come on, my friend!" Stanley insisted. "If we're not there

by eleven thirty, they'll have all the peanuts packed up and we'll miss out on that perfect combination of salty and sweet."

Nurse Ponytail giggled and patted Richard's arm. "Sounds like you boys are gonna have fun. See ya later, Mr. Bell."

Stanley stepped into the room and held the door for her, giving a courtly little bow of his head when she bounced past him. He let the door fall shut behind her and turned toward Richard. "Are you all right?"

"What in tarnation are you talking about?"

"Did she hurt you? Take anything?"

Richard glared at Stanley. "You havin' a stroke or something?"

Stanley seemed to relax. "Great. You're all right." He looked over his shoulder, like he was checking to make sure the door was still closed tight, then came to sit on the corner of the bed so he was practically knee-to-knee with Richard.

"That woman is not what she seems, and I'm quite certain she has her sights set on you as her next victim."

Richard felt the hot blood in his face. "I know you take me for some kind of fool, Stan Kapcheck, but I tell you I'm no man's stooge. Get out of my room. Play your stupid jokes on someone else."

Stanley had the audacity to look truly hurt. "Dick, I...."

"Just get out of my room!" Richard bellowed.

Stanley's lips pressed into a tight, thin line. "All right, then. That's fine, Dick. I'll get out of your room and you can deal with that creature by yourself when she comes back for you."

"I'm sure I can manage five feet of blonde ponytail."

"Very well, then," Stanley said, rising to his feet.

Just after the door clicked shut, Richard growled back, "Yes, it is very well."

It irked him to his core that Stanley moved so fluidly when he rose from the bed and left the room. He was as graceful as any athlete—as graceful as Richard himself had been in the years before life became all about soft food and nurses who called him cute. With a sigh, he clicked off the television and shuffled into the bathroom to wash up before bed.

He never would have known anyone had come in, except that the door made a tiny, high-pitched squeak that caused his hearing aid to give feedback. He dropped the washcloth on the edge of the sink and spun around. "Dagnabit, Stanley Kapcheck, I told you..."

The creature stood before him, five feet of pink scrubs with bat-like wings, red eyes, and long, dripping fangs.

Richard stumbled back, tripped over the toilet and fell against the wall. The jolt ran through his bones like an explosion. "Jesus, Mary, and Joseph!"

"I will have your memories, Richard Bell. I will devour the sweet, rich memories full of the glory days," it hissed at him.

The door swung open again and Stanley appeared behind her shoulder.

She launched herself toward Richard as he cowered against the cold tile wall, but Stanley's arm lashed out in a flash. The pointed end of a broken stick burst through the thing's chest and, with a wheezing exhale carried on a plume of black smoke, she dissolved into a pile of ash on the floor.

Stanley stood there, panting.

Richard's lips took on a will of their own and started forming a series of incoherent sounds. Maybe he was having a stroke. This was how a stroke had always felt in his imagination.

Stanley skirted the pile of filth, keeping his wingtips shiny, and extended a hand. "I told you she was coming for you," he said.

"I...she...teeth..." Richard managed.

"Yes," Stanley agreed. "The teeth are horrible. And those big, batty wings. Dreadful creatures. We should go before the others realize what we've done here."

Richard blinked up at him. He allowed himself to be helped up. "Others?"

"The strigoi never exist in solitude. They move in packs."

"Strigoi," Richard squeaked in a weirdly feminine voice.

"Strigoi," Stanley said. "No doubt about it. Get your coat. We have to move quickly."

"Coat?" Richard asked.

Stanley crossed the room and knelt in front of Richard's walker. He took the fanny pack from the top of the dresser, strapped it around the front handles, then filled it with a tiny water pistol, a crucifix, and a baggie full of garlic, all retrieved from his own pockets. Then he took the yardstick that lay on the table next to Richard's jigsaw puzzle and snapped it in half over his knee. He slipped both jagged pieces into the long, narrow pouch meant for an oxygen tank. Thankfully, Richard wasn't yet so far gone as to need to lug one of those around. Then he stood, retrieved Richard's Wellington Plastics jacket, and held it out. Richard let Stan tuck him into the garment just as if he were a girl on a date.

"Don't hesitate to use that squirt gun if you need to. Holy water won't kill them, but it will slow them down long enough so we can do what we need to do." He positioned the walker in front of Richard.

Richard stared down at the little bag's unzipped compartment. The toy gun's red plastic handle was just barely visible. "It's a joke," he muttered. It pleased him to hear that his voice had returned to a masculine tone, even if it remained somewhat tremulous.

Stanley gripped him by the shoulders. "Look at that pile of ash, Richard. Does that look like a joke to you?"

Tiny black tendrils of smoke still rose from the ash. It smelled like burnt eggs. His stomach turned.

"We need to get out of here," Stanley said.

Richard nodded and headed for the door, but the other man

grabbed his arm. "Don't be foolish, man! We can't go that way. They're not going to let us just waltz out the front door."

"Well, what do you suggest then?" Richard asked.

Stanley gestured toward the window.

"You've gotta be kidding."

"Really, Dick, you must learn what a joke looks like. It's time to go, and that's the only way out if you intend to save your wrinkled old hide, because this place is crawling with more just like her and they're not going to be happy to find her remains in your room."

Richard glanced at the mess one more time, grasped the handles of his walker, and headed toward the window.

CHAPTER FOUR

Finn

Neither the empty bar nor Joe asked any questions. It was perfect.

Sara waited for him in a shadowy booth in the corner of the restaurant farthest away from the front door. He set two frothy mugs of beer down and slid into the ugly vinyl booth across from her.

"Thank you, Finn."

He drained half his mug and wiped his lips with the back of his hand. "How do you know me?"

She sipped her drink. "Everyone knows you, Finn O'Doyle. You're famous."

"Not very," he said and finished his drink. "Joe, can I get another?" he called out. A moment later, Joe arrived with a full glass. He set it down, glanced at Sara's full mug, took the dirty cup, and walked away. He was Finn's favorite bartender in the whole world. When the man was gone, Finn leaned forward with both arms resting on the table. "I would very much like for you to tell me who you are and why you're here."

"I'm Sara. I'm here because we're having drinks."

He laughed and leaned back. "So, it's like that, is it?"

"Yup. Just like that. You overcomplicate things. It's one of your greatest stumbling blocks."

"Good to know." Did she know that her breasts jiggled fetchingly when she rested her arm on the back of the bench like that? He suspected she did, so he made no attempt to hide his glances in that direction.

"You know what else?" she asked, leaning her elbows on the table.

"I bet you're going to tell me."

"You need to remember how to have fun."

He smiled his most charming smile. He knew it was charming. It was a fact proven by his ninety-five percent success rate with women. "Oh, I'm fun."

She wagged a finger at him. "You used to be fun. You have always been powerfully full of life force. A wave of vitality washing through the world. You're just a little lost these days."

Her words struck too close to the truth. He took a long drink to cover his discomfort. "And you know this, how?"

"Drink your beer, Finn." She pushed her glass across the table. "You can have mine, too."

He raised an eyebrow at her. "And you accuse me of not being fun?"

"I guess my tummy just isn't ready this early in the day."

Draining both mugs presented no challenge. Not until the bottom of the second one did he even start to feel the familiar warm fuzziness that he'd come to think of as the best part of the day.

"Let's take a walk," Sara suggested.

"It's cold."

"It's sixty degrees and you're wearing long sleeves. Geez. Man up a little, for goodness sake."

The comment stung more than he wanted to show. "I'm plenty manly."

She laughed. "No doubt. Come on, then, Rambo."

He thought he must surely be mad to be following this strange woman around town. He thought of the email from his publisher, saying how excited they were to hear when his next book would be out. He thought about her enormous blue eyes. He reached for the mug, remembered he'd already emptied it, and sighed. Unable to come up with any reason why they shouldn't walk, he dropped ten dollars on the table and stood. On the way out, he called, "See ya, Joe."

"Yup. See ya, Finn. Have a good one."

Sara preceded him out the door and he noticed how her jeans fit across her tiny little backside. Who could say? Maybe for once, he actually would have a good day.

CHAPTER FIVE

RICHARD

THE MUDDY FLOWERBEDS UNDER RICHARD'S WINDOW WERE slicker than snot on a doorknob. Without the walker, he'd have fallen for sure, but maneuvering the thing through the muck was a Herculean feat. The two men stayed close to the wall and picked their way toward the back of the building.

Stanley peeked over his shoulder and whispered something in Richard's general direction.

"What?" Richard whispered back.

Again, the infuriating man's lips moved, but no sound reached Richard's ears. "What's that?" he asked, louder, fiddling with the control on his hearing aid.

Stanley stopped so abruptly that Richard almost bumped into the back of him.

"Watch it!" Richard said. His feet were cold and wet. Already, the horror of what had happened in his room had started to fade, replaced by annoyance at the absurdity of this disruption to his routine.

Stanley leaned much too close and whispered, "We have to be quiet, Dick. We can't be shouting at one another out here or they'll—" He gasped. "Run!"

Richard frowned. "They'll run?"

"Run!" Stanley shouted again.

Two of the creatures crept around the end of the building, headed in their direction.

Pushing the walker before him to keep himself upright, Richard stumbled through the mud toward the grassy field that separated the back of the Everest Senior Living Facility from US-223.

A third monster dropped from the sky and landed in front of them, its red eyes glowing in the dark night.

"Eep! Argh! Blechnech!" Richard shouted incoherently before yanking the toy pistol from the pouch and shooting the thing in the face.

The tiny stream of water arced across the space that separated them and hit the monster square in the eyes. Its inhuman shrieks filled the air for an instant before Stanley slammed a broken yardstick into its chest, causing it to fall to ash and smoke.

Growls rose up behind them and Richard remembered they were outnumbered. He turned and shot the gun toward the other beasts. One of them screamed when the water touched its face. The other launched itself into the air.

Stanley ripped the last broken yardstick from the bag on the walker and stabbed the one that had hesitated. He snatched a pistol from the small of his back, aimed carefully, and fired a single shot. The creature diving toward them exploded, sending bits of soot raining down on them.

For the first time in decades, Richard ran. Well, he shambled along in fits and starts, pushing his rattling aluminum walker in front of him like a bulldozer. Every time his foot struck the moist earth a shock of pain jolted through his body.

Air wheezed into his lungs in huge bursts that stretched his chest, enlivening parts of him he'd thought long dead.

It was fantastic.

At the edge of the highway, Stanley stopped and looked over his shoulder. He tucked the gun behind him again and glanced back at Richard. "Shells full of wood chips soaked in Holy water," he said.

Richard stood slumped over his walker next to a 55-mph sign, gasping for air. "We should get somewhere public, right? That'll be safer." He raised a shaking hand and pointed. On the other side of the road, an enormous yellow sign outside of a diner read, "Always Open."

"Perfect."

They waited for two semi-trucks and a Volkswagen Beetle to pass by, crossed the road, and staggered across another grassy field into the parking lot of the restaurant.

As they hurried, Richard glanced back over his shoulder. Spots of red gleamed in the dark sky not so very far away. He redoubled his speed, kicking up little bits of mud as he went.

When Stanley yanked the door of the little diner open, Richard couldn't recall a single thing in his entire life that had felt so good as the blast of warm, slightly greasy air that washed over him. They lurched forward into the bright fluorescent lights and a young girl with purple hair and a gold ring in her nose looked up at them with an expression of boredom so complete it was surprising she was still conscious.

"How many?" she asked, apparently taking the sight of two disheveled, mud-splattered, breathless old men bursting into the restaurant in the middle of the night as par for the course.

"Good evening," Stanley said. He wiped his mud-covered shoes repeatedly on the rough fabric of the entrance mat.

It did Richard's heart good to see the filth on Stan's shoes and the cuffs of his jeans. What kind of a senior citizen wore jeans anyway? Those were for children and cowboys, not for old men in retirement homes.

"It will be just the two of us this evening."

"'Kay," the girl said. She pulled two menus from a wooden rack on the wall. "Over here."

They followed her past a table of drunken men in county road crew uniforms, two teenaged girls, what appeared to be a homeless man hunched over a half-full cup of coffee, and a young couple so engrossed in one another, the restaurant could have burned down around them and they would never have noticed.

"Don't people have anywhere better to be in the middle of the night?" Richard wondered aloud.

"Life doesn't stop when the sun goes down, old boy. All the best fun happens after dark."

"My mother always told me nothing good happens after midnight," Richard said.

"Well, Dick, that certainly explains a great deal about your life."

Just as they slid into the booth, a scrawny kid with a buzz cut appeared, asking for their drink order.

Richard ordered a glass of milk.

"I'd like some of your strongest coffee, black, and you can bring us an order of your fantastic fried cheese sticks right away while my friend and I look over your menu."

The kid grunted in assent and slunk away.

"You're going to have coffee and cheese at this hour? Are you crazy?"

Stanley shook his head. "You have to learn to live in the moment, Dick."

Richard hated being called Dick. After eighty plus years of jokes made in bad taste, he had no use whatsoever for the word. He crossed his arms in front of his chest. "So, we're in public. Spill the beans."

"The things I have to tell you are rather fantastic." He stopped and leaned back to let the boy serve the drinks. When he'd skulked away again, Stanley continued. "You're going to accuse me of teasing, but I assure you, on this topic, I am always serious."

"Go on, then," Richard said.

"When I was a boy, I lived in Lowestoft, England. It's a town on the sea, and I adored being on the beach. At every opportunity, I begged my mother to take me and, thinking I was terribly clever, I'd often sneak off on my own.

"One such day, I was scouring the coastline for all the interesting things that wash up and I found a small statue made of black stone. It was stunning, and obviously quite old. I held it in my hand and stood where the water just lapped at my ankles. After a moment, I had the strongest feeling I was being watched. Well, I looked around and noticed I had the attention of every creature for a mile. Every creature, Richard. There were starfish at my feet and gulls standing on the sand watching me. The people on the beach stared. None of them moved at all, not even when I waved my arms at the birds.

"I shouted for the foul beasts to fly away." He took a sip of the fragrant coffee and continued gazing into the depths of the black brew. "I had a deep fear of gulls. 'I don't want you near me,' I said, and they died. Every one of those birds. Just like that. They fell over and died.

"The people on the beach didn't move at all, but then a single man emerged from the crowd and came toward me. He was a strange fellow, dressed in bright robes like a creature from a fairytale. He walked toward me, hunched forward like he pressed through a gale, though all around me everything was as still as glass. When he was close enough to be heard, he called out to me."

Richard watched him sip his coffee and look around the

restaurant for a moment, then sputtered in frustration, "That's it? You're not going to tell me the rest of the story?"

Stanley shrugged. "I'm afraid I can't."

"Somethin's wrong with you," Richard said, pointing a gnarly finger at the other man.

Stanley nodded. "We are a broken race, my friend."

"So that's it? You dragged me to this greasy spoon in the middle of the night to tell me the first half of some crazy story?"

"It was you who suggested this restaurant, Dick. I merely saved you from certain death. I would like, very much, to tell you the rest of the story, but can't. I physically can't."

Richard scowled. He no more trusted the man than he trusted his own digestive system to cooperate on a consistent basis. "Why's that?"

"Because knowledge is meant to be sought out."

"Eh?"

"I can't tell one who isn't seeking."

"You won't tell me unless I beg?"

"I am literally unable to offer any further information on the subject unless you ask for it."

"If you want me to beg you to feed me some cockamamy tale about—"

"I promised you the truth, Dick. Surely, you'd like to know the truth about what you saw tonight."

What had he seen? Enough to scare the binky from a baby's mouth, that's for sure. A pretty girl had turned into some sort of a monster and dissolved into ash. A monster the size of a large man had fallen to the ground in pain when sprayed with a bit of water from a toy gun. Beasts with wings and red eyes had flown through the night at him.

Then his memory carried him to another time and place.

His beautiful Barbara, lying on a clean white sheet, tears

rolling down her pale cheeks. At thirty-two, she'd appeared to be ancient—her skin, dry parchment, her eyes, watery and gray.

He'd brushed her hair away from her face, trying not to wince when several strands came off in his hand. The doctors had no answers, only a grim prognosis.

The boy she cared for so deeply sat in a chair by the bed. How sad he looked. He'd finally found a mother figure to care for him and a mere moment later she was at death's door. In a way, it seemed a worse pain to endure than what their infant daughter would experience. She would never miss what she had never known.

Suddenly, for some reason he could not name, he was certain that the bizarre, wasting illness he'd watched his wife suffer through half a century earlier was related to the night-mare he'd lived through tonight.

"Tell me what you know, then," he said. "I'd like to under-stand what in tarnation is going on, and you better not be yanking my chain."

Was that relief that washed over Stanley's face?

"The man called out to me. He asked if I'd like to know what it was I had found. I told him I would like that very much.

"He said he was a hunter of beasts that had no place in the natural order. Just such a beast had possessed a man who lived long before anyone kept track of the years, and influenced the creation of the totem."

The waiter dropped a little plastic basket on the table between them. "Here's yer cheese sticks. Want somethin' else?"

"Not now," Richard barked.

The kid slumped off to a corner and pulled his phone out of his pocket.

Stanley waited for the kid's thumbs to start tapping the screen before he went on. "The totem gave its holder power over life and death, but such power was never meant to be held by humans. It would destroy me, he said, and I could feel that it was true. It was like holding a live electric wire."

"So, you threw it into the sea?" Richard guessed.

"I tried, but I couldn't let go. It had fused itself to me. I panicked, and the more upset I got, the more agitated the life around me became. They were murmuring, thrashing, falling to the sand and, of course, that only served to fuel my fear.

"Then the man pushed forward again. 'Reach out to me, child,' he said, and so I did. He took a crystal knife from a sheath on his belt. He held my wrist in one hand and stabbed the center of the thing with the other.

"It was as though an explosive had been detonated. The force threw me into the water. Sand blew into the air all around us. When I got my feet under me once again, I saw him kicking sand over a puddle of blood. 'Return to the earth,' he said and then he looked at me.

"He told me I would need a teacher, and for many, many years he fulfilled that role in my life. That I am alive at this ripe age is a testament to the fine job he did."

"Who was he?" Richard asked.

"I told you. He was a hunter," Stanley said. "And now, so am I."

Richard realized that he'd been leaning forward over the table, listening anxiously to the other man's story, and he forced himself to lean back against the bench and cross his arms. He'd be no man's fool. "A hunter, eh?"

"Yes. Like my mentor, Busar, I hunt those creatures who have no place in the natural order."

"Like what we saw tonight."

"Precisely." He took a cheese stick and nibbled off the end. "The strigoi feed on memories. They devour them until a person has nothing left. Then, with no will to go on, the person dies."

An image of the halls at Everest came to mind—mindless

shells of humans sitting in wheelchairs, staring into space. He'd noticed how many of them came in fairly lucid but, weeks later, were lost. A shiver crawled along his spine at the thought that he could have been next.

"Are you going back to get the rest?"

Stanley finished his cheese stick and dabbed at his mouth with a paper napkin. "The rest?"

"Well, yeah. You said you're a hunter. You can't just leave them there."

"First of all, I didn't come to Everest to kill strigoi. I came to find you, Dick. Second, I'm fairly certain we eliminated the entire nest."

Richard looked around to make sure no one listened. Surely, this conversation, overheard, would be enough to have them both committed to a mental institution. "I saw 'em. Chasin' us."

"Are you certain?"

"Red lights in the sky," he said.

"Following us?" Stanley asked.

"Well, not exactly. They were more, like, hovering behind the building."

Stanley smirked. "Those were radio towers, old boy," he said.

"What?"

"Radio towers. Not strigoi."

Richard threw up his hands. "What in tarnation were we running for?"

"We were running toward a fine cup of coffee and some excellent fried cheese."

Every arthritic ache Richard had ever experienced, and at least three new ones, flared up at once. He mumbled a name under his breath that his sweet Barbara would have admonished him for.

"What was that, Dick?"

"I despise you," Richard said.

Stanley chuckled. "Would you like to know more?"

Again, the memory of Barbara came to him. Undeniably, he hated Stan Kapcheck more than flies in his oatmeal, but, in all these years, who else had he ever been able to voice his belief to? The belief that her death was tied to this bizarre night grew like a cancer in his mind. Hesitantly, he said, "You say those things feed on memories."

"Yes."

"Well, is it possible... I mean, is there such a thing...a different thing maybe..." He sighed.

"What is it, my friend?"

"This is stupid. I know it's stupid, so you don't need to tell me it is, but...well...soon as you started talking, I started thinking 'bout it.

"My Barbara, she was as pretty a girl as you ever saw, and so full of life, I swear I thought she'd outlive me by fifty years. She was the best mama a baby ever had. Spoiled that child rotten, carrying her around all day long. She even took in some homeless boy. Musta been about fifteen years old. She adopted him like he was a puppy left on her doorstep. Kid followed her around like a puppy, too. Barely let her out of his sight. Hung on every word she said.

"Then one day, I noticed she was a little tired, and not a month later, I put her to rest, a wrinkled old woman too frail to draw her next breath."

"But it wasn't cancer," Stanley said in a matter-of-fact way that Richard was grateful for. He might have been tempted to hit him if he'd gone over the top with sympathy or, worse, pity.

"No. Not cancer. Not a virus. It was nothing at all, so far as a bunch of worthless, overpaid doctors could tell. She just wasted away overnight."

Stanley hesitated a moment before saying, "Fate plays strange games with us."

"Don't talk to me about fate, you old coot. It wasn't her fate to—"

"I'm not speaking of your wife's fate. I'm speaking of yours." He produced a small leather-bound journal from his pocket and placed it on the table, laying his hands upon it with an air of reverence. "I didn't come to Everest to be cared for in my old age, Richard. And I didn't come to battle the strigoi. I came to find you." He opened the book and turned the thin, crinkling pages until he seemed satisfied and then pushed it across the table.

Richard stared at the ink drawing of a vaguely humanoid form with long, skinny arms and legs and a head too big for its slender body. Wrinkled skin hung from the thing and long wisps of hair hung lank around its head.

Skinwalker, he read. *Twelve cycles of twelve new moons will wake this beast that dwells primarily in the American southwest. Skinwalkers are thought to be the earthbound souls of ancient witches; able to take on any form, they will almost always choose to appear as a beautiful human. They feed on the life force of humans.*

Cross reference incubus/succubus: related, not equivocal.

He closed the book and pushed it back toward Stanley. "In English?"

"My mentor's greatest motivation was to find and destroy the skinwalker who killed his father when he was a boy. The creature only appears once every twelfth, twelfth moon cycle—about ten years—for a single month. If it finds a human of fantastic vitality, it will feed on that human's life force and that will be enough to carry it through its period of hibernation. While it's awake and murdering its victim, it'll cause as much trouble as it can, just for the fun of it. Twelve moon cycles later it will wake and feed again. The trick is to figure out where it is, get to it, trap it, and destroy it all within a single month. Not even a month, really. A moon cycle. Twenty-eight days."

"You think one of these skinwalkers killed my Barbara?" A

leaden weight settled in his stomach. The words had the taste of truth.

"That is precisely what I think. Richard, I found you when I came across some old records on another case. It's another long story, best told some other time, but if I've done my calculations correctly, it's been a little over forty years."

Richard swallowed around the lump in his throat. "Forty years last winter."

Stanley's blue eyes twinkled with excitement in the bright light of the diner. "Where were you then?"

"Tombstone, Arizona." He could still smell the sweet alkaline scent of the desert, feel the warm, dry air blowing his hair away from his face, hear the country music spilling out of the saloons. The very name of the town carried the weight of magic in his memory. The best years of his life had been lived in Tombstone.

"Tombstone?"

"That's right."

Stanley shook his head and chuckled. "We got as close as Phoenix. We reasoned that there are more people there. It would be easier to blend in."

"You ever been to Tombstone?" Richard asked.

"Not once," Stanley admitted.

"It's the most alive place I've ever been. There's an energy there...different from anywhere else. Overwhelming sometimes. Drives people mad. Can't tell you how many handsome, hardworking young men come to that town and can't ever bring themselves to leave. A year later, they're hooked on drugs and alcohol. There's something wonderful there, but there's evil, too. Barbara and I both thought so. We spoke of leaving, moving east. We worried about raising a kid in that environment."

"All this time," Stanley marveled. "And now here you are,

telling me what Busar and I couldn't figure out in two lifetimes."

A devil of skepticism nipped at Richard's mind. "You're not pullin' my leg?"

"I have never been more serious," Stanley promised. "I was on a hunt in Ann Arbor and I came across some personal records from a certain Dr. Aldrich. He'd been treating my client for a malaise that had no physical cure, so far as he could find. He was doomed to lose her. Her disease was caused by a minor demon who'd latched on to her and only a powerful exorcist could have saved her. But in his record, he made a note that, though the two cases were different, it reminded him very much of a particular case when he'd been a fresh graduate from the University of Tucson College of Medicine."

"He was Barbara's doctor. I don't think the man slept the whole time she was ill. He tried everything."

Stanley nodded. "He's a good man, but blind to that which he cannot label scientifically."

Richard pushed the book farther away. "This is nonsense. Rational people don't chase monsters."

Stanley leaned forward. "If Barbara was killed forty years ago, at least three more people have died since then, and a fourth is in danger. You have the chance to help me stop this thing. You have the chance to do something with the time left to you. Something that matters." He sat back again and sipped his coffee. "Of course, you also have the right to go back across the street and settle into your armchair and live out whatever time is left. I won't stop you. The strigoi are dead. You should be perfectly safe and well cared for there."

Richard sat with his arms folded, watching the other man's face, trying to read his expression. He'd attended the First Presbyterian Church and paid his tithe every week for the whole first half of his life. He'd prayed the Sinner's Prayer and kept the faith in the promise attached to that until Barbara died. After that, he'd never held out for mumbo jumbo spiritual stuff. Truth was, he wasn't sure he'd believed it back when he attended, either. There were no monsters in the closet. There didn't need to be a devil. Humans were monstrous enough without help. Life was horrific, even without demons chasing you in the night. Still, he couldn't ignore the ring of truth. Hadn't he, after all, made a tenuous connection between what he'd witnessed tonight and what had happened to Barbara, even before the Brit told his fantastic tale?

He rubbed a hand on his rough, stubbled cheek. "All right then. What do we do now?"

"Well, if you're right, and I have no doubt at all that you are, my friend, then we need to get to Tombstone. By my calculations, our monster is awake and on the move. We have twenty-seven days to put an end to his terror."

Reality crashed down upon Richard. "We're too old to go traipsing all over the country. I have a doctor's appointment on Tuesday. And we got no car and no cash. Heck! We don't even have a change of underwear! How the devil do you expect us to get all the way to Tombstone, Arizona?"

Stanley cocked his head. "You're a pessimist."

"I'm a realist, and you're a darn fool."

Stanley picked up his book and slipped it back into the inner pocket of his jacket before leaning both arms on the table and looking directly into Richard's eyes. "Tell me you haven't felt more alive in the past hour than you have since you were a boy. Tell me there wasn't a joy you've never known before when you witnessed the destruction of evil. Tell me you don't think the skinwalker murdered your wife, and that you have no desire to get revenge on that beast. Tell me, and you'll never hear from me again."

Richard swallowed the lump in his throat. "We're too old."

"We're not dead yet, Richard. We can do this. Our resources are not as limited as you imagine. I have found that the Universe always provides for those who are on the side of good."

Skepticism raised its head once more. "Give me one example of the universe providing anything."

Stanley grinned. "That's easy, my friend. Just when I thought I'd reached a place where I was lost and without direction, the universe sent me you, Dick. I've been reminded that I still have life and I still have purpose."

"Hmph," Richard grumbled. "You still ain't told me how the heck we're gonna get from here to Tombstone, Arizona."

"We'll drive, of course."

Richard mumbled about crazy men with ridiculous notions, but at the same time, he couldn't help but notice those pains had lessened up a little and he felt something deep inside he hadn't felt in a very long time.

Richard Bell was excited to participate in life's next great adventure.

CHAPTER SIX

Finn

"SO, WHAT DO YOU WANT TO DO FIRST?" SARA ASKED. SHE walked with a peculiar bounciness that was difficult to keep up with, despite the fact that his legs were nearly twice the length of hers.

Finn held his hands out. "I thought this was your show."

"You said you know how to have fun." She stuck a pouty lip out at him and that urge to take it between his teeth came to him again.

"Well, I was having fun at Joe's." He paused to let a horse-drawn stagecoach rumble through the intersection before crossing the street and stepping up onto the boardwalk that ran the length of the historic district or, as he thought of it, Tourist Hell.

"That wasn't fun. That was self-pity."

"I have fun pitying myself."

She turned abruptly and dashed into a store that sold Victorian era costumes. A floor-length purple dress with an elaborate bustle hung on a display just inside the door. Holding it in front of her, she gushed, "Oh my goodness! Look how pretty this is. We should dress up like Wyatt Earp and Big Nose Kate."

"Adults shouldn't play dress up."

"I adore role playing. I live for it!"

He slid his hands into his pockets and grinned at her. "Big Nose Kate was a whore who spent time with Doc Holiday, and there's not a chance in Hell I'm dressing like Wyatt Earp. Besides, they'd have to cut half that skirt off to make it the right length for your tiny little legs."

The hanger made a loud click when she dropped it back over the bar. "I'm insulted. I'm not that short."

"Nah. Not short. Just fun sized."

Her smile lit her whole face. "You made a joke, Finn!"

"I told you I'm a fun guy."

"Uh huh." She rolled her eyes. "Come on then, party pooper. This isn't the right place for us if you're not gonna play dress up with me."

"Definitely not the right place for us." He let her lead him back onto the boardwalk. The town was still quiet, the streets not yet busy with the tourists that would show up in time for a night of dinner and dancing. A warm breeze carried the scent of the little rosewood blocks sold in the gift stores and, somewhere beneath that, drifted the crisp alkaline smell of the desert. Finn inhaled deeply, letting the fresh air fill his smoke-tortured lungs. How long had it been since he'd taken a walk?

"The rock store?" she asked.

"Boring. What do you do with rocks?"

"Candy?"

"Surely not." He scowled at the thought of the sticky, overly sweet confections.

She stood on tiptoe to kiss the cheek of a cigar-store Indian and then pointed at the door of the shop. "Fine tobacco products?"

He cocked his head to one side. "I might find something worth wasting money on in there."

Grinning, she bounced through the door into the dimly lit, richly fragrant store. A man behind the counter with a silk top hat and a beard down to his chest nodded in their direction. "Afternoon."

"Good afternoon," Sara answered.

Finn walked the perimeter of the store. "Fine tobacco is a lost pleasure." He opened a glass jar and inhaled, wishing for the sense of smell he had before twenty years of smoking. Ironic, really.

"Do tell," she said.

"Commercial cigarettes—the pre-rolled things you buy at the gas station—they're full of garbage. This stuff in here, this is the real deal. It's fragrant and flavorful and won't kill you nearly as quickly."

"But it will still kill you."

He raised an eyebrow at her. "Everybody's gotta go sometime."

"How do you want to go, Finn?" She closed the distance between them and pressed her palms against his chest.

His body responded to her touch as though he were fifteen and in the backseat of a car for the first time. He swallowed hard.

"This isn't really how you have fun, is it? I can think of a thousand things we could do that would be better than hanging out in the tourist district."

He swallowed again and sent up a silent prayer that his voice wouldn't crack like an adolescent boy's. "Are you some kind of author stalker?"

"Does it matter?"

"Are you married?"

The corner of her mouth twitched upward. "No, Finn. I'm

not married. I'm over eighteen, and all I want in the whole wide world is to see you give in to your desire. I want you to be wild and free, to embrace life the way you did before you started worrying about deadlines and film options and all the rest." Her hands slid upward around the back of his neck and into his hair. "Tell me what your desire is."

"You terrify me a little."

"It's part of the allure."

"You two buyin' something?" the man behind the counter asked.

Finn stepped away from her and smiled at the man. "Yeah. Give me four of the cigars on the counter there." He paid for his purchase and stepped back out into the bright desert sun. It was like stepping into a different world. "I think I should eat something," he muttered, wondering if he would have had his arms around a strange woman if not for the beer.

She slipped her hand into his. "Perfect. Burgers at Murphy's?"

He shuddered at the thought. "You have to take two steps down to get into Murphy's. One to step down off the boardwalk and one step down in status."

She giggled. "You don't seem like a guy who cares about status."

"I'm a guy who cares about not getting food poisoning."

"Taco Wagon?"

He studied her enormous blue eyes for a long moment. The wind tossed her dark curls around her face. Her full lips were curved in a hint of a smile. He slid his free hand into her hair and pulled her close enough to bend down and kiss her. Her body molded against his. Her lips tasted like cherry chapstick. Before he could capture her lip, she caught his lower lip in her teeth and he struggled to stifle a moan.

"We could eat at your place," she whispered into his ear.

He stepped back. "The Taco Wagon will be fine."

She bit her lip. "I *will* get you to have fun," she said.

"I believe you." Why did the thought of having the kind of fun he was thinking of with this beautiful woman send a tingle of fear down his spine?

CHAPTER SEVEN

Richard

RICHARD LET STANLEY PAY FOR THEIR DRINKS AND THE cheese sticks with a few of the crisp bills he kept in a gold money clip. It seemed only fair, somehow.

They stepped out into the night and he glanced back toward Everest. Six radio towers blinked in the distance. He was thankful for the darkness that hid his warm face. "Now what?" he asked.

"Now we walk to that gas station over there and find a ride."

The gas station shone in the night like a castle in a dystopian fantasy. Lights glared down on the tarmac, chasing away any hint of a shadow. Even at this hour, a steady stream of cars and trucks passed in and out of the glow.

They waited for a lull in the traffic and set out across the wide highway.

"My hips are gonna be frozen stiff in the morning. My ankles are gonna swell up like a pregnant woman's," Richard complained.

Stanley clapped him on the back. "Take heart, old boy.

Perhaps you'll surprise yourself with how fit you are and, even if it hurts, there is joy in the pain. When the pain stops, your life is over."

"Weirdo," Richard mumbled.

They didn't go to the islands where cars were fueling up or toward the front doors of the store. Rather, they skirted the building and approached the truck parking.

A broad-shouldered man with shoulder length curls that spilled out from under his baseball cap was squatted down, checking his tire.

"Excuse me," Stanley said.

The man turned and Richard's eyes widened. "Not a man, but a woman with her shirt unbuttoned far enough to show her impressive cleavage. He focused his gaze on the side of the truck so as not to be tempted to stare.

"Do for ya?" the woman said in a voice that had been sanded down by tobacco and tar.

Stanley remained as courtly as ever. "Forgive the intrusion. It must seem silly to a young woman such as yourself, but my friend and I are on an adventure. We were wondering if you could give us a ride? We need to get to the storage units on M-50, just outside Adrian."

Her expression softened. Richard marveled. Was it the accent that made women love him?

"This a bucket list sortta thing?" she asked.

"Something like that," Stanley said.

"I respect that. Yeah. I can haul ya to Berry's. 'Taint more'n twenty miles from here and right on my way."

"Your kindness only enhances your beauty. I can't tell you how grateful we are."

The woman actually blushed.

Richard rolled his eyes.

"Go on in the cab, then. I'll be finished up in a jiff."

"Thank you," Stanley said. His elbow bumped Richard's side a little harder than necessary.

"What? Oh! Right." He made a face at the enormous woman. He hoped it passed for a smile. "Yeah. Thanks. 'Preciate it."

She eyed Richard for a moment, flashed a smile at Stanley, and went around the back of the truck to do some further maintenance there.

Richard gazed up at the door. It seemed a mile high.

"Don't worry. I'll give you a boost."

"I ain't worried," Richard declared. "And I don't need no boost from you, neither."

"You looked concerned. I just thought I would offer to help."

Richard held onto his walker with one hand and reached up with the other to grasp the handle on the door of the cab. The door swung open on well-oiled hinges. The shining chrome step was just a little higher than his knee. He wrapped his left hand around the metal bar that ran alongside the door and used his right hand to grasp his thigh and lift. There! He'd done it! His foot was on the step. Pulling hard on the handle, he lifted himself from the ground and, for a moment, believed completely that he was going to make it. Then that dagblasted bad hip locked up and he was tipping backward, losing his grip on the handle. The fall would be the death of him, for sure.

Stanley's hands smacked solidly into Richard's backside and the push propelled him into the cab of the truck. He righted himself and scowled down at Stanley. "Don't touch my butt."

"I won't make a habit of it. I promise," he said, snickering.

"And don't you laugh at me!"

Stanley held his hands up in surrender. "I wouldn't dare." He folded the walker and slipped it into the space behind the big bench seat before lithely jumping up onto the step and hauling himself into the truck.

They sat, side-by-side, waiting for the woman to join them.

"Well, Dick. I'd say we're on the verge of a great adventure."

"This is crazy," Richard replied.

"Are you loving it?" Stanley asked.

Richard wasn't about to admit that he was.

BERRY'S STORAGE CONSISTED OF FOUR LONG, LOW BUILDINGS in a row, with corn fields on three sides. The trucker, who gave her name as Trixie, pulled onto the shoulder and set the brake. The digital numbers on the dash glowed 1:23. "Here you go, boys. Awful dark out there. Sure you're gonna be okay?"

"We'll be quite fine, thanks in large part to your generosity, Trixie. We are grateful."

She looked doubtful about the wisdom of leaving the two seniors on the side of the road in the middle of the night, but she said no more.

Stanley pushed the door open and hopped down. He retrieved the walker, set it up and then offered a hand to Richard. Stubbornly, Richard braced himself with one hand on the door and one on the metal bar. He turned and slid his body down until both feet reached the step, lowered himself down, and managed to hit the pavement upright. The landing hurt everywhere, but at least it didn't wound his pride. He positioned himself behind the walker and the two men watched the behemoth roll away in a curling puff of exhaust. They stood alone in the light of the waning moon.

Stanley put a sure hand on Richard's shoulder. "Come," he said. "I think you'll be quite pleased with what I have to show you here."

They made their way across the deserted highway, the rattle of the walker on the rough asphalt startlingly loud in the still night. Stanley entered a six-digit code into the keypad next to the gate, and the chain link fence clattered open. Advancing slowly, to accommodate Richard's halting progress, they passed the first building and turned right. Halfway down a row of green garage doors, they stopped. Stan squatted and opened the padlock on unit number seventy-seven. He pushed the door upward and revealed a treasure that seemed just about priceless at that moment—a 1959 Cadillac convertible in mint condition. The red paint appeared to glow in the darkness.

"Jesus, Mary and Joseph," Richard whispered in awe.

"She's beautiful, don't you think?"

Richard abandoned his walker and walked next to the car, running a finger along the length of it with reverence. "This your car?"

Stanley slipped his hands into his pockets. "Technically, it's Busar's."

Richard stopped with one fingertip on the red flame-like taillight. "Where is Busar?"

A shadow obscured the other man's face, making it impossible to read his expression. "He's gone."

"Killed?"

"Gone." He stepped into the garage and came around to where Richard stood. "I'd rather not discuss it right now." Stan's silver key slid into the lock just below the Cadillac emblem and the enormous trunk popped open. A suitcase sat in the middle, slightly askew. Stanley lifted it out and set it aside, then raised a false bottom to reveal a hidden space beneath. A sword, three large rifles, two handguns, five daggers of different materials, a long silver rope, and a length of iron chains were nestled in little custom spaces in a foam pad. On the far right, a silver box the size of a tackle box was tucked into a rectangular nook. He took it out, opened it, retrieved a stack of twenties from the piles of cash contained within, closed it, and tucked the box back in. He replaced the false bottom, then the suitcase and closed the trunk with a dull thud.

Stanley met Richard's eye. "I thought maybe we could sleep in the car for a few hours and then hit the road. We'll stop in a hotel tomorrow night. There are a few things I need to take care of on the way west." He tucked the money into an inner pocket of his jacket and let himself into the car.

Richard stood there, mouth gaping like a fish. Surely, he'd died, and this was some bizarre, unexpected version of the afterlife. Real life couldn't be this weird.

CHAPTER EIGHT

Burke

BURKE'S GRANDFATHER WAS THE SINGLE MOST DIFFICULT human being she had ever had the displeasure of being forced to eat Thanksgiving dinner with. Her reaction, then, when her mother called at seven o'clock on a Friday evening to discuss the old man, was less than enthusiastic.

"Burke, you have to go to the home and talk to them about Grandpa."

She reluctantly set aside her copy of Anne Rice's newest book and made a mental note to never answer the phone again. From that moment on, even the Mom calls would be screened. Maybe especially those. In her calmest, most submissive daughter voice, she asked, "Why would I do that?"

"He's missing."

She rubbed her forehead, trying to stave off the oncoming headache. "Missing?"

On the other end of the line, her mother was weighing her words carefully. She could tell by the long, slow breaths she took before speaking. She could hear it in the weird, high-pitched voice she'd always reserved for unpleasant news and backhanded compliments. "Apparently, there was a bit of foul play. It seems there was a small fire of some sort in his room and he and another man have disappeared."

Burke waited for more, but that's all she said. "He can't have just disappeared, Mom. Where in the world would he go?"

"Well, I'm sure I don't know. That's all the man told me."

"What man?"

"Doctor Payne."

"Doctor Pain?" Burke asked.

"Yes. Doctor Payne is the head of the facility. That's what he told me."

"Well, did they call the police?"

"He said they don't do that unless someone is mentally incapacitated."

Burke thought of a thousand things to say about the surly old man's mental state, but held her tongue.

"You have to go over there and find out what's going on. You have to find him, Burke."

"Why is this on me?" Burke asked. "He's your father."

"You would make me drive all the way down there from Rochester?"

Burke sighed. "Fine, I'll go in the morning."

"In the morning?"

"Yes. In the morning. During business hours."

"Tomorrow is Saturday, Burke. There's no guarantee Doctor Payne will be there on a Saturday, but we know he's there now because he just called. This is no joking matter, you know. He's gone mad and he's a danger to himself and others. He could be out wandering the streets causing mayhem until he freezes to death. You have to go find him, Burke Dakota. You have to."

Upon her mother's use of her middle name, Burke felt the quicksand of family drama rising up around her legs. "Fine, Mom. I'll go over there right now and talk to Doctor Payne to see if I can figure out what's going on." She glanced at the book. It was really good. She'd been pretty excited about binge-reading it in one sitting. So much for that plan.

"Good. That's good. But"—her mother paused. This silence carried a different weight. It held the gravity of maternal judgement—"you're at home in your pajamas at this time on a Friday night?"

"Mom—"

"Well, really, Burke. It's no wonder you haven't found a man. I mean, if you spend your life holed up with a book, what else can you expect?"

"I had a man once, remember? He left me for an underwear model."

"He was probably lonely because you always had your nose in a book."

There it was. The sand had sucked her in and she was officially in over her head. "Gotta go, Mom. Wouldn't want Grandpa to end up in jail for bludgeoning some poor, defenseless stranger."

"Do you think he would do that?"

"I gotta go, Mom."

"That's a good girl. Let me know when you get him back and all settled in."

Burke mumbled something that was, hopefully, unintelligible, and dropped the phone next to the book. She wasn't sure if she should laugh or cry, so she just lay there with her head resting on the soft microfiber pillow, staring at the ceiling.

An image came to mind: Her grandfather, shivering in the snow, shaking his cane at passing cars and shouting obscenities at the drivers. Fantasy Grandpa slipped on the ice and fell on his bony butt.

"It would serve you right, you miserable old fart."

With a sigh as immense as a tidal wave, Burke heaved herself off the couch and went in search of proper pants.

CHAPTER NINE

Richard

THE CADILLAC'S WHITE WALL TIRES SANG ON THE WIDE, FLAT expanse of highway. Their music was accompanied by the low thrumming roar of the engine, a powerful beast in a metal cage.

Richard closed the leather book and slid it into the glove compartment. Very deliberately, he removed the reading glasses from their perch on the end of his substantial nose, folded them, and slipped them into the breast pocket of the button-down shirt Stanley had purchased for him that morning at a Walmart outside Chicago. The printing in the book was tiny, smudged in places, nearly illegible in others. His progress through the pages had been slow, yet so much information was packed into each sentence his brain felt heavy and full with new and preposterous information. "You've been doing this your whole life?"

"Since the day I told you about."

"Busar wrote about that day in the book."

"He did." Stanley, his eyes covered with stylish black sunglasses, never turned away from the road. Traffic was increasing as they drew near to Minneapolis. It didn't help that it was the time of day when the masses migrated from their workplaces back to the suburbs where they lived. Stan wove between the cars fearlessly, ruling the road in the impressive automobile.

"It looks like someone else made the earliest entries."

"Busar had a teacher, just as I did."

"And you made the most recent notes."

"That's right."

Richard rode in silence for a while, staring out the window at the cars they passed. The awe-filled gazes imbued him with the delightful buoyancy of pride. Even being a passenger in a car like this was a privilege. It would figure that life gave such a vehicle to friggin' Stan Kapcheck. Wasn't that always the way?

Stan turned off the highway and wove through increasingly narrow, maze-like streets until they reached the Hyatt hotel. Stanley told the boy who tried to take his keys that he would prefer to park the car himself after they checked in, and they entered the massive lobby with its book-lined wall and roaring fireplace. Richard followed Stanley to the long, black front desk.

"Can I help you?" asked a lovely young woman with skin like smooth brown silk. Did fancy hotels ever hire ugly people? Seemed the ugly clerks worked at the kinds of places he had been subjected to the few times in his life he'd bothered to travel.

"We need a room for the evening," Stanley said. He removed a Minnesota driver's license and an American Express Black Card from his wallet and placed them on the counter.

The young woman examined them for a second and then glanced up through her lashes. "It would be my pleasure to help you," she said, her voice a smidge more breathless than it had been a moment before.

"I appreciate that."

Richard rolled his eyes.

She went to work, tapping her keyboard and asking all the standard questions, and then held up the ID, the credit card, and two room keys in a little white envelope. "Here you go, Mr. Turlington. I put you in an accessible room. There are bars in the bathroom that may be helpful for your father. Is there anything else I can do for you? Anything at all?"

"You're very kind, but I think we're all set."

Hot blood flooded Richard's face. "Young lady! I'll thank you to—"

"Oh, that's very nice, Dad. But I've already thanked her. Come on, now. I'll help you up to the room."

Richard yanked his arm out of Stanley's grip and turned toward the elevator on legs that trembled with rage. "How dare you?" he said, once the shining golden doors had closed, effectively separating them from the lobby. "And who in tarnation is Turlington?"

Stanley chuckled. "Just a little joke, Dick. Life's too short to be so serious all the time. And Turlington is an unfortunate chap who met up with a Zoroastrian demonic spirit two years ago."

"So, you just helped yourself to his ID and credit card?"

Stanley raised an eyebrow. "I borrowed his name. Not his bank account."

"And the car, the guns, the money? That's all stolen, I assume?" He couldn't claim to have lived a perfect life, but he'd never been a thief and he wasn't about to start now. He felt like a fool for not having realized sooner that Stan Kapcheck was a thief as well as a detestable coxcomb.

"I didn't steal any of it, Dick. For a man who doesn't move very fast, you certainly are quick to jump to conclusions."

A bell chimed and the door slid open. Stanley held one hand in front of the sliding door and motioned Richard to go ahead of him.

"I won't be a part of illegal shenanigans, Stan Kapcheck. If that's even your name."

Stanley tipped his head in acquiescence. "I'd never dream of luring you into shenanigans, Richard." He held out one of the room keys. "I believe you'll find our suite at the end of the hall. I'm going to park the car and then I'll join you."

When Stanley returned from his chore, Richard was stretched full length on the single most comfortable bed he'd ever laid on. He'd tried to resist, but the thick white coverings were too great a temptation. The last time he'd pulled anything close to an all-nighter, an actor from California was running the nation. The struggle to even stay awake long enough to ask the question that he'd been considering since he'd closed the leather journal was a mighty battle. "Why are we here? In Minneapolis? It's not on the way to Tombstone, at all. Is there some kind of magic here we're gonna need to fight the skinwalker?"

Stanley shed his jacket and shoes, striped down to his pristine white boxers and t-shirt and slipped beneath the covers of the unoccupied bed. "We are hunting a good night's sleep, Dick. I'm exhausted, and of all the hotels in the US, not one has more comfortable beds than this one."

Not sixty seconds later, he was snoring softly. Richard wanted very much to stay awake and be angry with Stan, but it really was a fantastic bed and sleep was too sweet a mistress to resist any longer.

CHAPTER TEN

Finn

FINN ROLLED ONTO HIS BACK AND STRETCHED, A STARFISH IN the center of a king-size beach, covered in Egyptian cotton. The sunlight, filtered through the heavy golden curtains, lent the room a soft, mystical air. The clock next to the bed told him it was almost ten in the morning. He'd been asleep for twelve hours. Had he ever in his life slept for twelve hours? If so, he couldn't remember it. How bizarre then, that, after all that rest, his body still felt spent, his mind clouded and slow.

He threw back the covers and headed for the bathroom. In the shower, he breathed deeply of the steam, letting it soothe his abused lungs while he thought about the past few days.

Friday, he'd ended up spending the entire day with Sara. Sara, who was just as much a mystery to him now as she had been when he'd first seen her perched on the hood of his car like a mischievous little bird.

They'd played tourist again, this time in Bisbee, eaten too much greasy food, and spent the evening playing pool at Morgan's and avoiding questions from Bruce. The bartenders in

Tombstone were more gossipy than a bunch of old women at church. Except Joe. Joe could be trusted.

There wasn't a doubt in his mind that Sara would have joined him in bed if he'd given the slightest invitation, but he'd been exceedingly careful not to. Pressed for a reason, he'd never be able to give one. Every time he looked at her, he was caught in an adolescent fever of desire.

She's a scary little witch. An adorable, tiny terror. Like a gremlin who's been fed after midnight.

There. He admitted it. She scared him.

He had never thought being an author could bring him the kind of fame that would inspire a stalker, but what else do you call a girl who shows up uninvited and knows all about you but who won't tell you where she came from or anything about her past? He'd seen *Misery*. He knew there was a good chance she was a total psycho.

Still, she was undeniably beautiful.

And he did have fun with her. He used to be a fun guy. He was the kind of man who lived every day to the fullest, who seized the moment, and consequences be damned. Somewhere along the way, that all changed. The last time he had fun was probably shortly after the last time he slept for twelve hours straight.

Friday night he told her he really did need to work on Saturday, so he wouldn't be able to see her again.

She'd shown up at dawn with a bag of donuts and two enormous cups of coffee. "You won't know I'm here, Finn. I'll keep you fed, and stay in the shadows, and never ever say a single word."

"I told you I have to work. I'm supposed to drive up to a big conference in Phoenix today. I'm the keynote speaker."

"Tell them you don't feel well," she said.

Feeling utterly spineless, he opened the door and let her pass. The idea of calling in sick to the conference appealed to him. His agent would be mortified, but she wasn't going to drop her most profitable client. He wanted to stay home. He'd finally gotten some momentum on his new book. Stopping now would be a nightmare.

To his delight and surprise, she really did disappear into the shadows, and he really did work. Or, at least, it seemed he must have. He distinctly remembered looking at the clock around four in the afternoon and being ferociously hungry. He'd written nearly ten thousand words.

Like she'd sensed his need, Sara appeared with a bowl of spaghetti and meatballs and a glass of Coke. He devoured the food in minutes.

"Has it been a good day, Finn?"

The twin specters of dread and desire woke up, twisting his insides into an uncomfortable knot.

"It must have been a very boring day for you, Sara. Why are you hanging around here, anyway?"

She giggled. "It was a good day, right?"

He stood and stretched his fingers toward the ceiling. His spine crackled and popped. "Yes, actually. It was a great day. Very productive. I wrote more than I have in a long time."

"I'm glad I inspired you."

Had she inspired him? He thought of the character he'd centered his story on—a young woman rising to power by manipulating the men around her. "It was good progress," he said.

"Want to go out?"

"I'm exhausted. My eyes feel like I washed them with bleach." As he said the words, he realized he was telling the truth. He was so tired he could hardly think straight.

"Aw, Finn. Are you blowing me off? Do you want me to go away and leave you alone?"

"No!" The word flew out of his mouth, practically of its own volition. He rubbed a hand over the day's growth of beard. "No. I'm sorry. I'm just tired, okay?"

"That's what happens when you work too hard."

"Yeah, right. Look..." What did he want to say? Did he want her to go away? What if she left and took her inspiration with her? What if, after she was gone, the words dried up again? No. He definitely didn't want her to go away. "I'm just a little worn out, okay? Why don't we plan on lunch tomorrow? Top of the Hill? At noon?"

She hesitated for a long moment and a feeling of panic rose in him. What if he'd blown it with her? Finally, she answered, "Sure, Finn. Lunch sounds great."

"Deal," he agreed. As soon as he said it, he shivered. *Don't be stupid.* He needed a beer.

Sure enough, a drink or four later he was calm as could be laying on the sofa with his head on her leg. Not long after that, he drifted off to sleep and dreamed about all the things he hadn't dared to do in real life. Somehow, he'd made it to the bed, but he couldn't quite remember that part. Nor was he sure whether or not he was alone.

Sunday morning, showered and shaven, he found himself hoping she'd spent the night in his house. The dreams had been all good, and the after-effects lingered in his mind.

He found her waiting for him at the kitchen table. She beamed in greeting. "Good morning, sleepyhead. Still up for lunch?"

He slid his hands into his pockets and offered up a charming smile in return. "I'm famished. Also, I'm glad you're here."

"Why, Finn? Do you enjoy being with me?" Her blue eyes were wide and sincere.

"I'm a hermit and I like it that way. I must be twenty years older than you, and there's something... You're not the usual Tombstone bar girl. But, yes, Sara. I do enjoy being with you. More than I probably should."

"I'll take that as a compliment."

Finn let her wrap her arms around his neck and draw him close for a kiss before leading him out to the car.

Walking into the restaurant, he smothered an enormous yawn. How was it possible to feel tired after so much sleep?

"Coffee?" the waitress asked.

"Yes, please," he answered.

Across the table, Sara grinned at him, looking as young and fresh as a spring flower.

CHAPTER ELEVEN

Richard

AFTER MORE THAN TWELVE HOURS OF SLEEP INTERRUPTED only by the occasional bathroom break, Richard woke to sunlight peeking in around the edges of the heavy hotel drapes. He stood in the powerful spray of the shower, letting the hot water work magic on the kinks in his muscles, and dressed in a fresh change of Walmart clothes.

Stanley arranged for a cab to take them to a place called "Al's Breakfast."

"Don't understand why we gotta go traipsing all over town. They got coffee and muffins right here in the hotel," Richard said.

"Coffee and muffins are for businessmen dashing off to their next meeting. After a certain age, it becomes important for a man to properly nourish himself."

The elevator dinged open and they entered the lobby. A powerful scent of roses filled the air and Richard paused to inhale deeply. Each of his senses seemed more acute than they had been in a long time, as though the adrenaline of the strigoi attack had blown the cobwebs out of his pipes.

"We should hurry," Stan said, glancing around the lobby.

"If you're in a hurry, we can get coffee and muffins right back there."

"No, no. I just..." he trailed off, seeming distracted. "I don't want them to run out of food, you know. They're quite popular."

"You make about as much sense as boobs on a man."

Stanley roared with laughter. "Come on, my friend. You'll love Al's. I promise."

He was right. Richard nearly moaned in pleasure over the thick Belgian waffle smothered in cream cheese and strawberries. He hadn't had a breakfast like this since the accident that led to him being hospitalized for hip surgery and then sent to Everest. The food was even more delicious than he remembered. How could he have ever taken cheese for granted? Cheese was a gift from God.

Stanley smiled at him over his fancy omelet. "Al's never disappoints."

Richard couldn't quite bring himself to admit out loud that Stan had been right. Coffee and muffins didn't hold a candle to this. This kind of food did more than nourish the body. It gave a man a reason to stay alive until his next meal. He settled with, "I still think we need to get a move on."

Stanley was scanning the restaurant.

"You lookin' for somethin'?"

Stanley met his gaze. "No, of course not. Just admiring the industry of this diverse group."

Richard frowned. He had the feeling there was more going on than he knew, and being made to feel foolish always put him in a surly mood. Still, it was hard to stay angry when sweet star-bursts of joy exploded out of ripe strawberries and into his mouth. He sipped the dark coffee, letting the flavor of the slightly bitter brew mix with the sweetness of his food.

The noise level in the restaurant shifted, drawing Richard's attention to the door. A stunning young woman stood just inside. It seemed every eye in the place fixed on her, and it was no mystery why. She must be nearly six feet tall, with a glossy blonde braid that hung over one shoulder and almost to her waist. Her black pants could have been painted onto her long, shapely legs. A sliver of tanned skin separated her belt and the bottom of the t-shirt that stretched across her ample bosom.

"Daggum! That girl's a tall drink o' water on a hot summer day," Richard mumbled, not really meaning to say the words out loud. An inexplicable tingle ran down his spine. It was the sensation his mother would have described by saying a ghost walked over her grave.

Stanley slapped a few bills on the table hard enough to make him jump. "Time to go."

"What? But I still have—"

"Dick, there's no time to waste. I need to reach Spearfish, South Dakota, by nightfall if we're going to keep to the schedule."

Richard found himself sputtering and protesting in confusion at the quick change of pace as Stanley pressed him toward a back door between the lavatories.

"This makes the walk to the car shorter," he said before Richard could ask why they were going that way. "No time to waste."

They made their way through a narrow alley, around the corner and into a parking garage where Stanley told Richard to wait by the entrance while he went for the car.

Once in the car, Richard focused his gaze on the other man. "You want to tell me what the devil's going on?"

The tires squealed on the smooth concrete when Stanley hit

the gas. "The Devil is exactly what's going on, my friend. Some beasts weren't meant to be hunted, even by hunters."

"You senile?"

"If I was, I don't suppose I'd be aware of it." He took a hard left onto a narrow street and banked right toward the expressway's entrance ramp.

Richard grabbed the dash and hung on for dear life. Thoughts of the fiery car crash that was sure to happen at any moment chased away his questions for a few minutes, but as the city skyline fell away, he asked again, "What's going on? What happened back there?"

Stanley sighed. "I suppose you know enough now that you might as well know it all." He glanced over at Richard, his expression hidden by the dark glasses that once again covered his eyes. "Any hunter will tell you that there is always something bigger and meaner out there, hunting the hunters. Everything has a natural predator."

Richard scowled. "You tellin' me somethin's after you?"

"There is something out there that is bigger and more evil than anything I'm capable of taking down on my own. It's not after me, specifically." He checked his blind spot, signaled, and moved into the left lane to pass a motorhome. "I don't think." He pulled back over to the right. "Well, maybe."

"Hmph. Well, that's comforting."

"Did I give you the impression I live a life of comfort and safety? Have I deceived you in some way?"

"Darn right, you deceived me. Leaving out important facts is as much as lying."

"I can't tell you all the facts, Dick. Not in two days. It took me the better part of a century to learn what I know."

"And what did you know this morning, when you insisted we go out for breakfast?"

A muscle jumped in Stanley's cheek. "I didn't *know* anything."

"Don't talk in technicalities. There ain't no loopholes in honesty. Truth is truth. What did you suspect?"

His knuckles were white on the steering wheel, his lips pressed into a thin line. Richard didn't really expect he was going to get an answer, but after a moment, Stan said, "Every living creature carries a certain energy. Something that makes you feel good, calm, relaxed, angry, fearful, or sad in their presence. Your wife—could you feel her in the house, even when you couldn't see or hear her?"

Richard thought of those long-ago days when he would come home from the plastics factory and step through the back door. Every day, he was wrapped in the miracle of coming home. After she died, it was never home again. It was just a roof over their heads. "Yeah. I know what you mean," he said.

"There are creatures so powerful that their energy can change the energy of an entire city. This morning, when I woke up, I felt it. I knew she was in the hotel. I could smell her."

"Her?" The pieces clicked together. "The good lookin' dame at the restaurant?"

Stanley nodded.

Richard frowned and tried to remember if he'd felt threatened by her. He hadn't. Certainly not in the way he'd felt threatened by the creature in the nursing home. If he was to be honest, he'd have to admit he'd been drawn to her. Parts of him stirred that hadn't stirred in so long, he'd figured they were dead. But, at the same time, there had been that tingle of dread. *The fear made her that much more desirable, like forbidden fruit.* Well. That was one thought he wouldn't be sharing with Stan Kapcheck.

He reached for the water bottle that stood in the little cup holder on the seat beside him. A long drink helped clear away the lump in his throat so he could ask the next question. "Who was she?"

"She's The Devil."

Richard pursed his lips. "Fine. Make fun. Don't tell me."

"She's The Devil. Lucifer. Abaddon. Beelzebub. Satan. Prince of the Power of the Air. Call her whatever you want. That's what she is."

"But..." What was there to say? He blinked at the wide gray ribbon of road unrolling before them.

When Stanley spoke again, his tone had relaxed and softened. No trace of anxiety remained. His voice was seasoned with humor once more. "She's beautiful, isn't she?"

"A knockout."

"Nice, too. When she's not unleashing Hell, I mean. She'll say things that'll melt your withered old heart like butter. And she smells exactly like roses in summer."

Richard's hands rose up, seeming to grasp for some explanation, and then fell back into his lap. "But..." he said again.

"Precisely."

They were halfway to Sioux Falls before Richard even realized he was still sitting there with his mouth hanging open.

CHAPTER TWELVE

Burke

BURKE SAT ON THE SOFA IN HER QUIET LIVING ROOM WITH her legs curled under her, sipping coffee from her favorite mug. She couldn't stop thinking about her grandpa. As far as she could piece together, he had last been seen at dinner on Thursday night. It was assumed that he went back to his room. No one paid any attention when he didn't show up for breakfast as he had a habit of staying up late and sleeping in. When lunch was over, and someone checked a roster, it was noticed that he had missed two meals in a row and someone went looking for him. A few hours later, when every corner had been searched, one of the staff called the director. He insisted on searching again before they called Burke's mother.

By the time Burke got there last night, it was possible that he'd been missing for a full twenty-four hours. She'd suggested calling the police to put out a "silver alert," but the director of the facility had discouraged her.

"The thing is, Ms. Martin, he's an adult and he's never

shown any sign of being less than fully cognizant. Also, he's not the only resident who's disappeared."

"What do you mean?"

The doctor fiddled with a shiny gold pen on his desk. Sweat beaded the bridge of his nose. "Stanley Kapcheck is gone, as well."

"Who?"

"The resident who occupied the apartment across from your grandfather is Stanley Kapcheck. He's one of our most spry and active residents. They both seem to have disappeared around the same time. As far as we can tell from a cursory glance, they both took their jackets and wallets. They're not ill, Ms. Martin, and they're not senile. This facility is a residential care facility, not an institution of some sort. As far as we can tell, Mr. Bell and Mr. Kapcheck decided to leave, and they are completely within their rights to do so."

"My mother said something about a fire."

He carefully placed the pen in its stand and folded his hands. "Yes. There seems to have been a small, controlled fire in your grandfather's room. There was very little damage—just a floor tile or two. Certainly, it wasn't enough to cause him grievous injury." He smiled, tilting his head in what appeared to be a very practiced gesture of sympathy. "Ms. Martin, I'm sure you are concerned about your grandfather, but the probability is he went somewhere with Mr. Kapcheck and they failed to notify anyone. I can understand your concern for his well-being, but I'll bet he'll turn up in no time. Why don't you give it a day or two?"

At home, Burke had repeated his words to her hysterical mother. She'd finally ended the conversation by saying, "Mom, if it were you, would you want me to call the cops on you?"

Her mother's shouting turned into quiet sobbing.

"Look, Mom. I'm off tomorrow. I'll see what I can do about finding him, but let's keep the cops out of it for now, okay?"

"You'll look for him?"

"Yeah. Sure, Mom." Burke sighed. She had anticipated such a good weekend, just her and her book.

Burke went to bed, determined not to let family drama tie her in knots, but after a few hours of fitful tossing and turning, she gave up any attempt at sleep. She stood in the scalding hot shower spray until it began to run cool, brewed a pot of strong, black coffee, and sat down on the sofa with no idea what to do next.

How could you find a grown man who decided to walk away from his life? It was a big world. On the other hand, he didn't have a car. He had money, but not an unlimited supply. He could have bought a bus ticket.

A fat green photo album under the coffee table caught her eye. She set her mug on a coaster and pulled the dusty book into her lap. The first pages showed a series of black-and-white photographs that featured a handsome, broad-shouldered young man with a wide smile. In nearly every shot, his attention was focused on the beautiful woman next to him. They wore shorts on the beach, snuggled up on a couch, danced at a party, toasted someone's wedding, showed off a tiny bundle in a long white christening gown.

Around the time the photos began to have a bit of color in them, the images changed. There were pictures of Burke's mother as a toddler, learning to ride a bike, and dressed up for a formal school dance. The woman was gone, and in the few photos where the man appeared, he looked angry and distant.

She went back to the beginning. There was something there that she wasn't noticing. The thought tickled her brain, but if she looked directly at it, it skittered away into the shadows.

Her phone rang and she fished it out of her pocket to check the caller ID. The red button beckoned, but she chose the green out of—what? Duty? Devotion? Sadistic tendency?

"Hey, Mom."

"Have you done anything yet?"

The plastic on the album crinkled as she turned the page. Her grandparents were newly married, standing in front of an adobe church. They leaned against a car shadowed by an enormous saguaro cactus. "I'm trying to figure out what to do, Mom. I'm open to suggestions."

Her mother sniffed.

Please, God, don't let her start sobbing again.

"Has Grandpa ever done anything like this before?"

"No! He never even missed a day of work in all those years at the plastics factory. Grandma Bell used to talk about a time when his car broke down on Charleston Highway and—"

She grabbed the thought that had been eluding her. "That's it!"

"What are you talking about?"

"You said Charleston Highway and that made me think of Tombstone and...well...don't you see?"

"See what?"

Burke closed the photo album and let her fingers dance excitedly on the surface. "The only time in Grandpa's whole life that he was happy was when you all lived in Tombstone before Grandma died. He's always been a surly old fart—"

"Burke!"

"Oh, like you don't know it's true," Burke said. "He has! But lately, he's been worse than ever. What if something finally happened that made him recognize his own misery and he decided to go spend his final days in the one place he was ever happy?"

"Tombstone is two thousand miles away!"

Burke's fingers tapped faster than ever. "I know."

"Well, how would he get there?" her mother asked.

"I have no idea, Mom. A bus? A cab to the airport and a quick plane ride?"

"He doesn't have the money to be flying around the country."

"Maybe not, but something tells me I'm right about this."

"Well," her mother's voice was shaky, but if she was crying, she had it under control. "What are you going to do about it?"

Burke's hands stilled. "What do you mean?"

"You have to do something, Burke."

"Why?" The more she thought about it, the more she agreed with the ludicrously named Dr. Payne. Grandpa was a man of reasonably sound body and mind. Why shouldn't he be allowed to go wherever he wanted without asking permission?

Clearly, her mother disagreed. The pitch of her voice was climbing again. "What do you mean, why? You can't let a man of his age traipse all over the country alone."

"Mom, there's nothing we can do right now but wait. I can't just go driving around the wild west looking for Grandpa. He'll turn up."

"Oh, Burke." The tears came now, fast and furious.

Burke slid the photo album back into its place under the coffee table and stood to pace off some of her pent-up energy. "I have a life, you know. I have an appointment, and I'm supposed to help with the local garden club fundraiser this week."

"The garden club?" She was approaching full-blown hysteria. "You're more worried about the garden club than your own grandfather? I see what family means to you. I don't know where I went wrong. I thought I raised you better than this, Burke Dakota!"

"There's nothing I can do, Mom!" Burke shouted back. She took a deep breath in an attempt to control her temper, then spoke in a softer voice, "Look, I'll tell you what. I don't see the sense in driving out there aimlessly, trying to find him, but if we hear anything, I'll go get him."

"Do you promise?"

Burke rested her forehead against a window. The cool glass felt good against her burning skin. "Sure, Mom. I promise. If we hear something, I'll go."

"And if we don't hear anything in a few days, maybe we can call one of those detectives or something."

"Yeah. Maybe. We'll see, okay?"

"Okay. Yes. That's good. It's good to have a plan." The tears had disappeared so quickly, Burke questioned their authenticity. "I have to go, Mom. I'll call you if I hear anything, all right?" She waited for a response and then clicked the phone off.

She thought of Tombstone. She hadn't been there since she was a kid. She'd been fascinated by the stagecoaches on Main Street, and the stores full of cap guns and plastic bows with suction cup arrows, and half in love with the dusty cowboys in the O.K. Corral gunfight show. There had been a candy store that sold roasted nuts that made the whole block smell like cinnamon and sugar.

Having successfully negotiated ownership of her day again, she grabbed a bag of baby carrots and headed for the sofa. Her book still waited on top of her "to be read" stack. She picked it up and her attention fell on the book beneath it, a best-selling psychological thriller by an author whom she'd read about in *Entertainment Weekly*.

Her heart tapped out an eerie little rhythm in her chest. It had to be coincidence.

Even though his books weren't her usual style, she'd been interested in his work because he lived in and wrote about Tombstone. She picked up the book and read the lines at the bottom of the back cover.

"Finn O'Doyle lives on his family's property in Tombstone, Arizona. He shares the estate with numerous wild animals and likes it that way."

He was strikingly handsome, with bright blue eyes and a mop of dark hair that fell across his forehead.

She shook her head. "It's just a weird coincidence," she said, but hearing the words did nothing to convince her of their truth.

Acting on nothing more than a wisp of instinct, she started packing. By midmorning, she was headed south on I-23.

CHAPTER THIRTEEN

Richard

AS THEY PASSED A LONG WHITE BUILDING WITH A ROW OF garage doors on one end and a veritable mountain of tires in the parking lot, Richard sat up and rubbed the sleep from his eyes. He stretched as best he could in the small space. He'd fallen asleep at some point west of the South Dakota state line and he must have fallen into a sound sleep because the muscles in his back and legs seemed frozen.

Stanley turned into the parking lot of a Dairy Queen. "We can pop in here, get a bite to eat, wash up a little, and make plans for tonight." He killed the engine, slid out, and stood next to the car, filling his lungs with deep breaths of air. "It's a beautiful day, Dick. Simply stunning."

Richard glanced through the windshield at the crystal blue sky. The sunlight stung his sandy eyes. Gingerly, he maneuvered himself out of the car. The pains of every one of his eighty plus years screamed at him. He arched his back, groaning. "I gotta pee."

"Let's go then," Stanley said, slammed his door shut. He

strode away toward the restaurant. "There's really no time to waste."

"I really hate him, "Richard muttered to no one in particular as he shuffled along behind.

In the restaurant, they found a tiny restroom with scalding hot water. Richard washed up and tried to tame his wispy, white, fly-away hair. His reflection stared at him with accusing, bloodshot eyes. "Ya gotta admit," he told the man in the mirror, "it really is better than sittin' around waitin' to die."

The tired old man in the mirror shrugged, unconvinced.

He found Stanley sitting cross-legged, reading the paper. His eyes were bright, his smile wide. The wingtips had once more been polished to a bright sheen.

Richard glanced down at his ruined, mud-crusted loafers. "Unnatural," he muttered, slowly bending toward the chair.

"I took the liberty of ordering some burgers and fries," Stanley said.

"I might have wanted chicken," Richard replied.

"Did you?"

"No, but I might have. Presumptuous of you to think you know what I would want for dinner."

Stanley folded the paper into a magazine-sized rectangle and pushed it across the table. He said, "Take a look at this."

The headline showing on the little section read, "Livestock Deaths Trouble Local Ranchers."

"Yeah, so?" Richard asked.

Stanley turned to face him directly and leaned forward across the table. "The DNR is saying that there are wolves killing the cattle, but that almost never happens. Wolves have developed a strong aversion to lingering near settled areas. Furthermore, they kill to eat, and this says these animals haven't been eaten, just killed in the night."

"Yeah, so?" Richard asked again.

"This is something else."

Richard bit into the burger. After months of grilled chicken and fresh asparagus spears, the greasy, cheesy mess was the single most fantastic thing he'd ever tasted.

"We need to take care of this before we go," Stanley said.

"You said we were in a big hurry. Twenty-seven days, you said." He shoveled half a handful of fries into his mouth and nearly moaned with pleasure. Oh, hot, salty delight!

Stanley nodded. "Twenty-four, now. There's not a lot of time to waste, but if I've learned anything, it's that when fate puts a beast in my path, no good will come from my stepping around my destiny. I've come to kill this monster, and kill it, I will. Then we shall carry on toward Tombstone. Twenty-four days is plenty of time, my friend."

"Only fools believe in fate," Richard said before chomping down on his burger once more.

"If I'd ignored fate, you'd be staring into space by now."

Richard couldn't think of anything good to say to that. The very picture Stanley just described had haunted him since Thursday night.

Stanley unwrapped his food. Holding his burger with one hand, he picked up the paper with the other and read it while he ate. Not a single drop of ketchup dripped to the table.

"Unnatural," Richard mumbled for the second time in less than an hour.

"What's that?" Stanley asked.

"Nothin'."

"Hmmm. We'll only be able to drive so far down the canyon. We can park at Bridal Veil Falls and hike from there."

"I can't hike!" A fry lodged in his throat and sent him into a coughing fit.

Stanley waited for him to pull himself together and then asked, "Why not?" as though such a statement was an absurd thing for an octogenarian to declare.

Richard huffed in impatience at the other man's blatant

stupidity. "I'm old. My bones ache. This hip joint is metal, screwed into my bones, for Pete's sake."

"Your bones ache because you've sat still so long you've begun to petrify, Dick. Time to loosen the joints."

Richard slammed a fist on the table. "Stop calling me Dick!"

A young couple with two small children glanced over, alarmed looks on their faces.

Stanley chuckled. "It's good to see your blood pumping again." He put the paper and the sandwich down and leaned forward again. "I'm telling you, there's a chupacabra in that valley and we are meant to hunt it. You and me. Destiny led us here. She's no fickle mate. If she wants us to do this, she'll provide you the strength you need and the tools to get the job done."

"What tools?"

"Well, el chupacabra isn't like the strigoi. Anything that will kill a wild beast will kill it."

"So, you need a gun?"

"Not necessarily. Men killed beasts long before guns."

Richard cackled. "You gonna spear it like a caveman?"

Stanley sat back and crossed his legs again. "You think I can't?"

"Oh, get off it. You might be James Dean with your leather jacket and all, but you're not gonna hike into that canyon and kill some wild animal with a homemade spear."

Stanley grinned, showing off his perfect white teeth. "Challenge accepted, my friend. I'll leave the guns in the trunk and do it the old-fashioned way. Finish your dinner. We'll take a rest and head out at sunset."

"You're a lunatic!" With the impact of a freight train, the ridiculousness of the entire situation smacked into him—chasing mythological beasts that came around every ten years, based on the moon cycles; el chupacabra; strigoi; the Devil, Herself... Lunacy! Richard said all that and more before wrapping up with a grand, "I'm calling my granddaughter to come and get me."

"Okay," Stanley said.

His total non-resistance completely took the wind out of Richard's sails. "Darn right, it's okay. It's what I want to do," he said in a much softer voice.

"That's fine." The Englishman shrugged. "I thought you wanted to avenge your wife's death, help make things right in the world, have a grand adventure before you shrivel up and die, but you just go right on back to watching the Weather Channel and eating boiled oats for breakfast every morning. I'm certainly not going to be the one to stop you."

Hot anger rushed to Richard's face. "Fine!" he exclaimed. "I'll go to the stupid canyon with you, but I'm sitting in the car. I'm too dang old for hiking."

Stanley smiled. "Have it your way, then, Dick."

FOR ALMOST AN HOUR, THEY DROVE VAGUELY SOUTHWARD down the steep grade into the canyon until they reached a point where one side of the road was a sheer rock wall rising into the night and the other side was a short, treacherous drop toward the relentless little river that had done its slow work of erosion there.

Just enough space existed on the edge of the road for tourists to pull over and stare at the waterfalls in the distance.

Stanley turned off the car and took a deep, fortifying breath. "Smell the night air, Richard! Come on, old chap. Walk a ways with me. The stars are bright in the sky."

Richard sat with his arms crossed. He refused to admit out loud that it was probably the most beautiful spring night he could remember. "Fine. I'll walk along the road with you, but I ain't doing no hiking nowhere."

As he followed Stanley across the road, Richard listed his woes, lest he get too complacent in going along with the madman's wild schemes. He was cold and his feet hurt. His stomach ached with gas. He'd bought a case of prune juice at the Walmart, but he'd forgotten to drink it and now the juice was locked in the trunk of the car and he was thirsty and tied in knots. He longed for a hot meal of easily digestible foods and a soft bed with a heated mattress. Obviously, he wasn't going to confess any of this to Stanley, who was strolling along at a jaunty clip. Anyone watching the Englishman in his fancy shoes and leather jacket would have assumed he was out for his evening constitutional.

Stanley strolled a few feet alongside the road, stopping every so often to examine a broken twig or some markings in the dust at their feet. Finally, three hundred yards from the car, he stopped and pointed at a meadow on the other side of the river. Two dozen sheep slept in the shrubby grass, enormous cotton puffs in a field of dry stalks.

"It's been working its way toward this meadow since I first heard of it. It will strike here after midnight."

"Somethin's wrong with you. You're a lunatic."

Stanley grinned. "Such a skeptic. Come on." He crossed the road and began picking his way carefully down the steep incline.

Richard stood on the gravel shoulder, clinging to his walker, and whispered as loudly as he dared, "I told you, I ain't hikin'. You'll break your neck out there in the dark." Speaking in his normal voice seemed obscene, like shouting at a funeral. The night was hushed and still.

"Stay there, then, if you're afraid," Stanley said. "It's nearly twelve already. It shouldn't be long."

"Fine! I will stay here," Richard whisper-shouted. "Not because I'm afraid. Just because I think you're an idiot."

"Very well."

Stanley appeared supremely unaffected by Richard's choice, which only served to heat Richard's blood to a near boiling point.

Richard found a boulder jutting out among the trees and plopped down on it. The stone hurt his bony butt. That ache was just another discomfort on top of the myriad of woes already plaguing him. He muttered as he watched Stanley cross the river by going heel-to-toe over a failed tree. "Unnatural."

Once across, he hopped down onto the rocky bank and squatted to examine something there before disappearing into the shadows.

The boulder was cold as well as rough, and Richard shifted in an attempt to find a more comfortable perch. He shivered. A crawling sensation started in his belly and radiated outward. He ignored it, shifted again, and grumbled incoherently. In his head, the muttering took on form.

If a car comes along I will flag it down and ask for a ride. Once I'm back in civilization, I'll call Burke to come and get me. I'm done with this fool's errand. Running all over God's green Earth with that blunderbuss, Stan Kapcheck. Stan friggin' Kapcheck! Bah! Why'd I ever listen to that danged fop anyway? I'm too old for this. The kid was right. I belong in an old folk's home, eating unsweetened applesauce and sugar-free chocolate pudding.

Overcome by thoughts of chocolate pudding, it took him a moment to hear Stanley calling to him across the water.

"Whadayawant?" he shouted back. His words echoed in the chilly night air and bounced back to him. He immediately regretted being so loud.

"What time is it?"

Blast Stan Kapcheck. That fancy diamond watch of his had probably stopped. Richard glanced at his sturdy Timex with the luminescent face and shouted back, "Twelve oh six." The weird echo wrapped all around him. *Dang it!* He'd forgotten to be quiet again.

The sheep stirred, probably disturbed by the ruckus.

A twig snapped behind him.

He froze. Maybe, if he didn't move or draw attention to himself in any way, whatever was there would leave.

A low growl, more felt than heard, vibrated in his bones.

Slowly, he turned to glance over his shoulder.

The beast stood twenty feet away, near the edge of the road. It appeared to be snakelike, as wide and solid as an adolescent black bear. Its two tiny arms lifted the weight of its head and shoulders off the ground as if it were doing a push-up with bad form. Muscles rippled beneath the scales that glittered in the moon's bright luminescence. It bared fangs as long as butcher knives. Red eyes glowed in the dark.

Richard had no idea what to do. He tried to think back to his days in the Boy Scouts, three-quarters of a century ago. How was a man supposed to remember such things? Some animals were frightened away by shouting. Some you were supposed to submit yourself to. Sometimes you were supposed to meet their eye, but often you shouldn't.

The thing swayed from side to side. It seemed to regard him with curiosity.

He raised his arms out to the sides and shouted at the top of his voice.

In response, the beast loosed an horrific shriek that shattered the tranquility of the night.

Richard left his seat and took off toward the bottom of the slope, leaving the walker behind, his aches and pains forgotten in light of this new emergency.

The cracking sticks, the rustle of leaves and the clatter of rocks dislodged by a heavy, slithering body followed him.

He splashed into the stream. The icy water soaked his pants up to his thighs and the current, fast with springtime snow melt, pushed him, slowing his progress. Glancing over his shoulder, he saw the creature slip into the water behind him.

Stan was running toward him, but he slipped and fell hard. A loud snap was audible, even over the beating of Richard's poor old heart.

"Cut the head off!" Stanley cried. Lifting his right hand, he expertly threw a machete that stuck into the soft soil at the river's edge.

The beast bumped hard into Richard's back, pitching him forward. He landed in the shallow water, sputtering, only inches from the blade that shimmered in the moonlight.

"The head! You have to cut off the head!" Stanley shouted again.

Richard grabbed the blade, flipped onto his butt and, sitting upright with his legs akimbo, swung at the thing's head as it launched itself toward him. The head flew into the water and was swept away by the current, but momentum carried the heavy body forward and the bloody neck slammed into Richard's chest, knocking him backward and pinning him to the rocky riverbed.

Stanley crawled forward, grunting with effort and pain, and managed to pull the thing off him.

He sat up again, covered in blood and soaked with near-freezing water. Already, he shivered from the extreme cold. Panting, he looked at Stanley. Perfect, always-well-groomed Stan Kapcheck sat covered in mud and red-faced with exertion.

A laugh built low in Richard's belly. It bubbled up, coming out first as a little chuckle, then a loud guffaw, and finally culminating in wheezing, gasping, tear-wrenching hysteria.

The sheep ambled to the other side of the pasture and went back to sleep.

Stanley's laughter joined Richard's. "You should have seen your face!" He gasped.

"Me?" Richard said, panting for air. "The head! The head!" He waved his arms over his head in mock panic and then he was overcome again, unable to talk between the terrible shivering and the uncontrollable glee.

"Well, well, well." A voice like rich melted chocolate reached out of the darkness, carried to them on the scent of roses. "Here I thought you might need a hand, and I find you having the time of your lives." The woman from the Minneapolis diner stepped out of the shadows. She stopped at the river's edge and regarded them, hands on her lovely rounded hips, bright smile shining in the dark. "I do love to see boys having fun."

The laughter died a sudden, violent death in Richard's throat. He could actually feel the tension radiating from Stanley. Her lovely, floral aroma roused his senses.

"I don't believe we've been officially introduced, Richard Bell. I'm Ashley DeVille."

"Ha!" Stan barked out an indignant sound. "Ashley DeVille? That's what you're using these days? Sounds like a stripper from Ohio."

"Stanley, I was hurt when you ran away from me in Minneapolis." She stretched one desirable leg out before her and took a step onto the water.

Not into it.

Onto it.

Richard's shivering rose to a whole new level.

Ashley, or whatever her name was, walked across the surface of the water. Her eyes flicked toward Richard. "Don't look so surprised, dear. Jesus wasn't the only one who knew a good parlor trick." She squatted down next to Stanley and lay one hand gently on the leg that was bent at a bizarre angle in front of him.

Stanley winced, sharp breath drawing in between his teeth.

"Why did you run away, Stan? We've had some good times, haven't we?" Her hand slid upward along his leg, toward his inner thigh.

"Get thee behind me," Stanley grunted through clenched jaws.

"You need help, Stanley. You can't walk. Your friend is hypothermic. Even if he weren't, he'd never be able to carry you out. No one will find you until sometime tomorrow. By then, your friend will be dead and you'll wish you were."

"I don't want anything from you," Stanley stated in firm, steely tones.

"Stan?" Richard managed through his clacking teeth.

They both ignored him.

"Tell me why you ran, Stanley," she insisted.

"Go back to Hell," he growled.

She shifted, placing one palm against his cheek. "I know you miss me, Stanley. I can see it in your eyes." A soft sound, far too complex to be called a giggle, emanated from her slender, elegant throat. "I can see it in your soul. We're good together, Stanley. What did I ever do but care for you, cater to your every desire?"

He swallowed hard.

"Tell me you didn't love every minute of it."

"I..."

"Tell me to go and I'll leave right now."

"Excuse me," Richard said.

No one looked at him.

"I want you back, Stanley. I want you back and," another soft, lovely laugh, "I admit it. I just plain want you."

Richard had had enough. He was freezing and hurting, terrified, and frankly disgusted. More than all of that, he was sick and tired of being so blasted passive about everything that happened to him. With lightning reflexes that he'd thought died with Reaganomics, his hand shot out and snatched the cell phone from the girl's belt. He tapped a few buttons and heard the sweetest sound in the world.

"Nine one one, what's your emergency?"

He clenched his eyes shut and spoke as fast as he could, waiting for the searing pain of a pretty, demonic fist ripping into his chest to crush his heart. "I'm in Spearfish Canyon, maybe a quarter mile east of Bride Veil Falls. My friend and I, we're elderly. We toppled down the hill. I think he broke his leg. I'm soaked through, freezing to death. We need help right away."

"What's your name, sir?"

"Richard. Richard Bell."

"Help is on the way, Mr. Bell."

Richard wasn't sure if he could make his muscles obey him and turn off the phone. He dared a peek in Stanley's direction.

The Brit sat there, mud covered and tattered, grinning like an idiot in the moonlight. "Well done, old chap. Well done."

Already, sirens wailed in the distance. They would die, to be sure, and probably not too far in the future, but it wasn't going to be tonight.

Richard and Stanley lay side-by-side in the emergency room of Spearfish Regional Hospital.

Stanley's right leg was encased in a medieval looking device of plastic and metal. He had refused pain medication and the sounds he made while they were setting his leg made Richard's stomach turn. Now that it was over, he lay quiet, his hands folded across his stomach. He'd asked a nurse for a cup of hot tea. Of course, she had brought it to him right away.

Richard couldn't bring himself to complain, though. The heated blankets wrapped around his practically naked body were a sample of the pleasures of heaven. Plus, he was alive. Just a few hours ago, he hadn't been so sure that would be the case. It was a pleasant surprise to find out that he still wanted to live.

Neither of them had spoken about the woman, or the beast

that Richard had pushed into the river to be washed downstream. Now, a doctor with bags under his eyes the size of steamer trunks sat on a tiny wheeled stool between the two beds, a stern, parental look on his face.

"You boys could have died out there. It was a very close thing. What you did was foolish. Beyond foolish."

They took the scolding in silence.

Then, the doctor dropped the bomb—the thing he'd obviously been building up to. "Tell me why I shouldn't call the police," the doctor said. "I'd bet my last dollar someone's looking for you two."

Richard glanced at Stanley out of the corner of his eye. Stan's face was a mask of serenity. His lips turned up the slightest bit at the corners.

Apparently, Richard's core was all warmed up, because heat flooded his face. "Just where do—"

"Tell me why you *would* call the police, doctor," Stanley interrupted.

The doctor narrowed his gaze on Stanley. "I'm sure your families are worried."

"I have no family, sir. My friend's daughter had him admitted to Everest after a routine surgery. Clearly, neither of us are senile or medically incapacitated to the point of not being able to tend to our own basic needs. Would you have a man answer to the rule of his children, simply because he is of a certain age? To my knowledge, there is no law prohibiting licensed senior citizens from taking a vacation. No rules dictate our need to ask permission of anyone."

His words had an obvious softening effect. The doctor sighed. His shoulders sagged. "Fine. I would like to keep you both overnight for observation. I won't call the police, but I ask you, as a man with a father in a nursing home"—he looked to Richard—"call home. Let them know you're safe." He stood and slipped the clipboards he held into the little pockets at the bottom of the beds. "Transport will be here in a few minutes. If you're feeling well enough tomorrow morning, you'll be free to go on your way."

"Thank you," Stanley said.

The doctor nodded toward him, looked at Richard one more time, and then disappeared into the bright, sterile hallway.

Once they lay in their private room with the door tightly shut behind them, the words that had been burning Richard's tongue burst out of him, "Will you tell me what in the name of Sam Hill happened back there?"

"Evidently, I was wrong about el chupacabra."

Richard snorted. "Yeah, okay. Let's start there. What in tarnation was that blasted thing?"

"A bowrow."

"There weren't no bowrow in that book."

"No, neither I nor my mentor ever encountered one. I'll have to make a note. They're not common in the Great Plains."

"Make a note. Ha! Yeah. You do that."

"You seem angry, Dick."

Richard fought the urge to pick up the ugly pink water pitcher on the table next to him and throw it at the man. "You lied again."

"I did no such thing."

"You...you..." Richard sputtered. "You told me that woman was The Devil."

Stanley nodded. A little sigh fluttered out of him.

"So, you'll deny you were shaking the sheets with her?"

Stanley rubbed his eyes. "Have you never made a poor choice, Dick?"

"You admit it!" He sat straight up in bed.

"Did I ever imply I was a saint?"

Richard fell back against the raised bed and stared at the black rectangle of the silent television screen.

After a long moment, Stanley said, "I won't hold it against you if you want to quit."

More silence.

"The skinwalker will be a thousand times worse than the bowrow."

It took a moment for Richard to process what he'd said. He hadn't been thinking about the bowrow much, at all. He'd once shot a rabid dog. The two experiences didn't seem terribly different. "She's following you," he finally said.

"It would seem so," Stanley agreed.

"Why?"

"She was right. We were good together. I've never in my whole life felt more vibrant and alive than when I was with her."

"You're just a man, right? What was in it for the big, bad Queen of the Damned?"

Stanley chuckled a little to himself, shaking his head. "I'm not *just* a man. I'm a hunter."

"You're human though." He paused. "Right?"

"Yes, I'm human, but as long as I was distracted, her little minions had free reign to do their damage. I'm not boasting when I tell you that I'm the finest hunter who ever lived. My work was diminishing her power." He shifted, carefully. "Every incarnation of evil I slay is a blow to her, but the skinwalker is something special to her. In its human life, it made a deal with her. Its soul is trapped in a cage of her design. She does not want it freed. She's trying to distract me."

"Why doesn't she just kill you?"

Stanley shrugged. "We were good together."

Richard's fingers drummed an anxious rhythm on the blanket folded back over his midsection, but he said no more. His brain whirled with thoughts and questions. They swam in a tangled mass under the foggy surface of the narcotic shot they'd given him in the emergency room.

"You said you would call your family," Stanley said some time later.

"So?"

"You have other children?"

Richard still stared at the black rectangle. It wasn't just dark. It was inky. It seemed quite possible that answers to all of life's biggest questions could reside within that void. "Just the one daughter."

"Are you going to call her?"

"No. She's a flake."

The sheets on Stanley's bed rustled as he repositioned himself. "You should call her," Stanley said.

"I told you, she's a dang flake, a dirty hippie. Ran off with a Negro man to sing to the trees or some such."

Did these long pauses between bits of conversation really exist, or were they just an effect of the drugs? Sleep weighted Richard's eyelids, but he resisted. Too many things existed in the world that could attack a man while he was vulnerable. Sleep was foolhardy, an invitation for disaster.

"The car is gone, Dick."

"What?"

"The car and everything in it. It's gone. She took it."

"The money?" Richard had thought a lot about that metal box full of twenties, most of the time trying to figure if they were genuine or counterfeit.

"And the guns, the swords, the crystal dagger, and the ceremonial athame. Even your prune juice and the clothes from Walmart. All of it."

It sure was a lot of money. Must have been ten thousand dollars or more in that case.

"We're trapped here, Dick. We don't have a ride."

Richard finally turned his head to look at Stanley. In his hospital gown, with his leg propped up on pillows, he looked very much like the old man he was.

"We don't have a ride," Stanley said, "and we have work to do. There's a hidebehind at the tri county state line, southeast of the Crow Reservation. I'm sure of it."

"And only twenty-four days to get to the skinwalker in Tombstone."

"Twenty-three by the time we get out of here."

Richard rubbed his eyes. His lids rasped like sandpaper. "Why did she disappear, Stan?"

"You took one of her tools and used it against her. The bigger the tool, the more damage it will cause. The phone wasn't much, but it got her to give us enough space to get help."

"She'll be back for us."

"I imagine she will, and probably not very happy about what happened."

Darkness pulled at Richard, even as the light of dawn slipped through the cracks around the window blinds. "I'll call my granddaughter. She's all right, all things considered." With a leaden arm, he reached over and lifted the handset from the phone that sat on the table between them.

His granddaughter answered on the first ring. "Hello?"

"Burke?"

"Grandpa? Where are you? Are you okay?"

A little tendril of comfort wrapped around his heart. Maybe they hadn't visited much, but they were worried when he was gone. "Yeah, yeah, I'm fine."

"Where are you?" she asked again.

"I had a little accident in—"

"An accident? What kind of accident?"

"I'm fine, kid. I'm fine. I need a ride, though."

"Okay. Just tell me where you are."

"Well, I'm..." he looked around the hospital room. No denying it. "I'm fine, but I'm at the Spearfish Regional Hospital."

Her soft gasp reached through the line, but to her credit,

she stayed calm where her mother would have been hysterical. When she spoke her voice was steady, "Spearfish, South Dakota?"

"That's right." Had he ever been so tired? Why did people crave these drugs? They made a man feel like he was drowning on dry land.

"Okay. I'll be there as fast as I can. Promise you're okay?"

"Fine, fine."

"All right then. I'll—"

"Burke?"

"Yeah?"

"Nevermind." How could everything be explained over the phone? He didn't have the strength for it. Better to tell her in person after a nice long rest. "Thank you," he said.

After a long pause, she answered, "You're welcome, Grandpa. Stay put. I'll see you soon."

He was so tired, he fell asleep with his hand still on the phone after he hung up.

When he woke, Stanley was watching the midday news. A bowl of cold boiled oats and a cup of apple juice waited for him. He looked over at the other man. "You might have to help me convince her to take us to Tombstone."

A wide grin crept across Stanley's face. "I've always been good at talking women into things."

CHAPTER FOURTEEN

Burke

TRAFFIC IN THE CHICAGOLAND AREA HAD BEEN SPECTACULAR. It was always congested, but that day it came to a dead stop. Every few minutes, the entire line of cars would inch forward like an injured serpent. Horns blared. For what purpose? Where did they want the other drivers to go? The highway was a tar pit and everyone in the city was stuck in it together.

The entire time she sat there, her thoughts spun like so many electrons around the nucleus of her grandfather. He really was a terrible person. He was mean and hateful, racist, demanding, and rude. But in those old photos, he had appeared to be so full of joy. Maybe he had been a different person in his youth.

Everyone goes through hard times. What excuse did he have for reacting to his difficulties in such a way? Sure. He lost a wife. Burke had lost a husband, but she didn't treat people like something unpleasant on the bottom of her shoe.

Especially not based on their race. For decades, he'd been cold toward his own daughter for choosing to marry a Black man. It didn't matter that the Black man was well-educated, kind, hard-working, and faithful. He was good for one of his kind, but his kind could never be good enough for Richard's daughter.

The daughter he barely spoke to anymore.

And if he hated her father for his skin color, what did that say about her own place in his heart? She should let him go to Tombstone and die in the desert alone. She'd put up with enough abuse in her life from the world at large. Why should she put up with abuse from her own flesh and blood? What was the value of a grandfather who couldn't see past her tawny skin and recognize his own blood running through her veins?

His own blood.

He was family. Family doesn't give up.

Every time her mother signed a Christmas card or picked up the phone to call him, she'd told Burke again, "Family doesn't give up. He wasn't always so bad, Burke. He's had a hard life."

In those old photos he had looked so open and kind.

By the time she got to the other side of the city, her energy was gone and her nerves were shot so she decided to rent a room at the Fairfield Inn in Joliet. The hotel was nothing special, but it was clean and she could stretch to her full length on the bed. There wasn't much more she wanted after being in the car all day.

The next day was enough to convince her that everyone east of the Mississippi lived in the greater Chicago area. Between Chicago and Des Moines, the road was virtually deserted. She'd planned to spend the night in Iowa, but as she watched for the blue signs telling her which hotels were ahead, her phone rang. She tapped the green button and immediately switched it to speaker.

"Hello?"

"Burke?"

Her heart stuttered in her chest. Gratitude, relief, annoyance, and anger exploded out of her, making her voice sound uncomfortably similar to her mother's. "Grandpa? Where are you? Are you okay?"

"Yeah, yeah, I'm fine," he said, but he didn't really sound so good. His voice held a tremor and his words were almost slurred. Was he drunk?

"Where are you?" she asked again, calmer now. This was infinitely better than crossing North America on a hunch.

"I had a little accident in—"

Fear trumped everything else. Her mother had been right. He couldn't take care of himself, and she was the one who'd put off searching for him. If he was hurt, it was her fault. "An accident? What kind of accident?"

"I'm fine, kid. I'm fine. I need a ride, though."

She took the exit for a rest stop and pulled into the first spot she came to. "Okay. Just tell me where you are."

"Well, I'm..." He paused. "I'm fine, but I'm at the Spearfish Regional Hospital."

His words sent a shiver down her spine. *Thank you, God, for keeping him alive long enough for me to have another chance to do the right thing*, she prayed silently. A petulant little girl in the back of her mind added, *even if the old man never does*. Aloud, she asked, "Spearfish, South Dakota?"

"That's right."

"Okay. I'll be there as fast as I can. Promise you're okay?" Des Moines wasn't exactly on the way from Michigan to South Dakota, but she was a lot closer than she would have been.

"Fine, fine," he agreed in that soft, sleepy tone.

She did a quick calculation and figured she could make it by morning if she could manage to stay awake that long. "All right then. I'll—"

He interrupted her. "Burke?"

"Yeah?"

"Nevermind. Thank you," he said.

Family doesn't give up. In her entire life, she had never heard the old man thank anyone for anything. He demanded. He expected. He didn't thank. He especially didn't deign to thank Black folks. She swallowed hard. "You're welcome, Grandpa. Stay put. I'll see you soon."

The sun was just turning the sky pink when she pulled into the parking lot of the little regional hospital. She found her grandfather and the other man who'd been missing sitting up in their beds watching the news.

"You got here fast!" her grandfather exclaimed.

She took a seat in the ugly green vinyl chair in the corner and would have gladly slumped down and slept there for the rest of the day, given the chance. "I was already driving. Mom was a mess. You should have told us where you were going."

He had the grace to look ashamed. "I should have."

"It all happened rather fast," the other man said in a charming British accent that warmed something in her feminine heart she never before realized was chilly. "I take full responsibility."

"I appreciate that, Mr. Kapcheck, but my grandfather is a grown man. He should have known enough to pick up the phone and spare us all a good deal of grief."

"We'll tell you the whole story," her grandfather promised. "You'll understand then."

"I can't wait to hear it," she said. "In the meantime, I'm going to let Mom know you're still alive." She pushed herself to her feet and trudged down to the waiting room to make the call on her cellphone. Her mother was teary with relief.

"Let me know as soon as you're headed back this way," she said after Burke assured her at least ten times that Grandpa was not at death's door.

"I will. I gotta go. I'll call you later," Burke promised.

She got back to the room just as the nurse was dropping off the discharge papers.

CHAPTER FIFTEEN

Richard

"No," Burke said. "Absolutely not. You're out of your minds."

Richard exchanged a glance with Stanley. For the past thirty minutes they'd been sitting in the same Dairy Queen they'd eaten in a little more than twenty-four hours earlier. Burke had listened respectfully while her grandfather told her about the strigoi, the skinwalker, the bowrow, The Devil Herself, and the need to make a quick swing through the general vicinity of Wray, Colorado.

The incredulity in her expression was clear from the start and only grew as he talked, but to her credit, she didn't say a word until he wrapped up his speech with, "And...so...there it is. The car is gone and we need a ride."

Now it was time for Stanley to take over. "Miss Martin—"

"Mrs."

"Of course. My apologies. Mrs. Martin, I promise you neither your grandfather nor I have taken leave of our senses. I know how it must sound to you—"

"It sounds like you were completely accurate when you said this is entirely your fault," she said. "My grandfather was safe and well cared for until you got him mixed up in some crazy cross-country quest."

"It is my fault," Stanley agreed, still smiling his most charming smile.

"No," Richard said.

They both turned to stare at him.

"It's not Stan's fault." He scratched at his cheek. He hated talking about feelings. Men weren't supposed to talk about feelings. Men were supposed to take action. But it occurred to him in that moment that he was helpless to take action unless Burke agreed to go along with their plan, and the only way he could think to convince her to do that was by telling her how he felt. "I was dying in that place," he managed.

Her eyes widened. "Mom said she checked them out. They're really well rated."

He waved away her words. "It was a fine institution, Burke. Well, if you don't count the monsters. But it wasn't Everest. It was...being old."

"Grandpa—"

"No! Blast it, you need to hear me out. I'm old. I get that. I'll be lucky to see another ten years." He grunted. "Heck, it would be a miracle to see another ten years. Luck would only buy me five. I'm not talking about a number. I'm talking about being treated like an old person. After I fell, your mother put me in that place. She put all my things in boxes and gave it all to the Salvation Army. She gave away your grandmother's things, Burke. Things I'd saved for longer than you've been alive. She gave away my mother's books. A whole lifetime of belongings swept away like so much rubbish."

At the sight of the tears in her eyes, he felt a lump in his throat and looked away. Talking about feelings was one thing. He wasn't going to start crying like a little girl. A few deep breaths helped the feeling pass and he went on. "Everything that ever defined me was gone. My wife. My child. My job. My home. Even the ratty old underwear I was used to. It was all gone, and I didn't get a say in any of it. Then I was tucked into a nice soft bed and told to relax."

He slammed a fist on the table, causing the girl to flinch. "I don't want to relax. What does that even mean? Sleep until I die? Do nothing? Life is hard. Pain and growth go hand in hand. Nothing good ever came from relaxing. Not a single darn thing, but what else was I going to do? I had no purpose. Society had no use for me. I was just sitting there, sucking up resources."

"That's not true, Grandpa."

"It is true. Stan will tell you." He turned to the other man for support. "You know how it is to be treated like an old man, right? I mean, you must be..." he trailed off. "How old are you, anyway?"

Stanley's eyes widened a little. They darted toward Burke and back again. "Oh, I'm not sure my story is relevant here."

But now that Richard had thought of the question, he was really quite curious. Stan looked like an old man, acted like he was in his prime, and dressed like a juvenile delinquent with a trust fund. "No, really, how old are you?"

"One hundred, forty-six," Stanley said before picking up his coffee and sipping it.

Richard and Burke just sat there, staring at him.

He shrugged. "I've lived an unusual life."

Richard forced his gaze back to Burke. "Uhm...so...like I was sayin', I'm glad for this adventure. This quest, as you call it. It's dangerous. I hurt like I ain't hurt in all my life. I never been so tired, and my bowels are tied in a knot because the doggone Devil stole my prune juice, but blast it all, I'm alive."

Her tears broke through the dam of her will and spilled down her smooth cheeks, forming little rivers in the curve of her nose. "Oh, Grandpa." She sighed. "Mom is going to be so angry."

Again, the men exchanged a little glance. This one, triumphant. "She's been angry all her life, kid. Nothin' you were ever gonna do about that."

She rolled her eyes. Richard resisted the urge to tell her that her eyes looked like two oysters in a bucket of snot. Best to keep quiet as long as she was going along with the plan.

"Fair enough." She wiped away her tears on the cuff of the pink sweatshirt she wore, and a long, slow breath seemed to fortify her. "Okay. So, how far is it to Wray, Colorado?"

"If we leave now, we should be there by nightfall," Stanley answered.

Burke nodded. "Okay." Another long breath. "Nightfall. Okay. And what are we going there for?"

Richard stood up and gathered his trash. "He can tell you about it in the car."

She nodded again and began to stand. "I'm going to get some coffee. I'm going to need it if I'm driving all day again."

"Dick?"

He stopped and looked at Stanley, still seated. The crutch they'd given him at the hospital remained untouched. He held the stolen phone in one hand. "There's something I want to show you before we hit the road."

Richard returned to his seat and took the little device. The screen displayed a picture of a handsome young man with a shock of dark hair that fell across his forehead and a smile similar to Stanley's. No doubt, the boy had his pick of the ladies. He passed his finger across the screen and came to the article.

"Grandpa! You know how to use an iPhone?"

"I'm old. I'm not an imbecile. Babies in the grocery store play on these and no one thinks a thing about it. An old man picks one up and it's front page news."

She held up her hands in surrender and he looked back at the screen. The article discussed a supposedly famous author from Tombstone, Arizona. How famous could he be? Richard had never heard of him. The man had apparently missed an important appearance, having reported that he was too ill to attend.

"It don't mean anything," Richard said. "Tombstone ain't a big town, but he's one of a few thousand."

Stanley nodded. "True, but Finn O'Doyle isn't just famous for writing books. He's also a rancher and a world class marathoner. The kind of guy who's just full of life, don't you think?"

Burke dropped back into her chair. "Finn O'Doyle?" she asked. She must have been more upset than he realized. Her voice trembled when she spoke.

"Could be coincidence," Richard said.

"Could be," Stanley agreed.

"Finn O'Doyle?" Burke asked again.

"You know him?" Richard asked.

"Of course. He's huge. Do I want to know what all this has to do with him?" Burke asked.

"We've got seven hours. We'll fill in the gaps while we drive," Richard said, rising again.

He thought of his Barbara, a gifted painter, an avid equestrian, one of the busiest women he'd ever known. Even when she stopped to rest and watch TV, her fingers were busy with a crochet project. She was the kind of woman who was just full of life.

The three of them climbed into Burke's rented SUV and she pointed the car toward the highway. Richard wondered if Stanley noticed the scent of flowers carried on the breeze that passed through the open window on the way out of town, but he didn't ask.

One thing at a time. First thing first. The skinwalker was going to die. If he went down with it, so be it, but that thing would be stopped for good.

CHAPTER SIXTEEN

Burke

BURKE HAD WORRIED THAT SHE'D BE TOO TIRED TO DRIVE after having pressed on through the night, but the mention of Finn O'Doyle had been like a shot of adrenaline straight to her heart. She couldn't keep her fingers from tapping on the steering wheel. If there'd been a way, she would have started pacing. Sitting still was torture.

What kind of insanity had she and her grandfather stumbled into?

Monsters? Demons? The Devil Herself? Nuts!

And out of seven billion people on God's green Earth, it had to be Finn O'Doyle? The man whose book prompted her to get in the car and start driving in the first place?

Nuts!

She waited for someone to explain what was going on, afraid that if she spoke she would scream. *I won't be hysterical*, she told herself. *I will not act like my mother*.

She waited in silence while the odometer continued its monotonous count of the long miles

CHAPTER SEVENTEEN

Richard

THE BIG WHITE SUV WAS NOT HALF AS COOL AS THE Cadillac. No one looked at them as they puttered along in the right lane. Burke kept the speedometer at a steady sixty-five miles per hour, guaranteeing everything from sports cars to school buses blew past in a blur. Her long, painted fingernails tapped out a rhythm against the steering wheel.

Stanley sat in the back seat with his leg stretched out on the seat beside him.

Richard stared through the windshield, his mind, a stormy black sea. Every so often, a lightning bolt of thought crashed through the rest of the murk, bright and luminescent and powerful. Then the idea was gone as fast as it came, leaving him even more blind than before. He could hold on to none of the fleeting images.

They crossed the state line into Wyoming.

"You said you would fill in the blanks," Burke said. "I don't hear anyone trying to fill."

"There's a great deal of ground to cover. Perhaps it would be easier if you asked specific questions," Stanley said.

Burke's thick black curls were an effective shield. Her fingers stilled. "Okay. First, I want to know who you are and how you got mixed up in all this. And no lies from either of you or I drive straight to the nearest airport and we all go home. That includes lies of omission."

Richard looked over his shoulder at Stanley. "Lies of omission. That's what I was thinking of earlier. This kid has a vocabulary like Daniel Webster. If you hear her talk on the phone, you'd never even know she was half Negro."

Burke took a long, deep breath. "Grandpa, why don't you just let Mr. Kapcheck talk for a while, okay?"

He shrugged. "You don't have to take that tone. It makes you sound like your mother. I was just payin' you a compliment."

"I assure you, we will be completely honest with you, Mrs. Martin," Stanley said from the back seat. "It would be foolish of me, though, to imply that I will be able to pass on every detail of the situations surrounding us in the time we have."

"Do your best," she said.

"My name really is Stanley Kapcheck. I was born in Great Britain. When I was a boy, I stumbled into a situation involving forces one might refer to as 'supernatural.' A man named Busar helped me. Saved me. I was eleven years old. From that day on, Busar was my mentor and caretaker."

"And exactly who, or what, was Busar? What did he mentor you in?"

"Busar was a hunter. He taught me his craft, trained me to be his successor."

"A hunter. Like a demon hunter? Like Van Helsing?"

"More or less, yes."

"So that's what you do. You travel around the world looking

for boogeymen. And...what? You got lonely? How did you get my grandfather wrapped up in all this?"

"In the course of one of my investigations, I came across the records of Mrs. Bell's doctor. I recognized the signs of a skin-walker attack. There is only one skinwalker remaining in the American southwest, so far as I know. Busar was passionate about destroying it, but he was never able to do so. It wasn't difficult to track down Mr. Bell at Everest. My original plan was simply to meet him and speak with him, but then I noticed the strigoi."

"To hear you talk, a person would think there's a monster on half the street corners in America," Burke said.

Stanley chuckled. "I suppose it can sound that way. The truth is, there are fewer now than ever before. Fate has a way of bringing hunters toward their prey."

"So, you noticed these things were at Everest and, instead of just destroying them, you checked yourself in and waited a few weeks?"

Richard felt his eyebrows shoot up. He'd never thought about that. Why hadn't Stanley just taken care of the strigoi on day one?

"I was certain there were strigoi at Everest, but they're clever devils. It took time to identify them. Once I did, well, you know the story from there."

Burke made a non-committal sound. Apparently, she wasn't convinced that she knew the whole story from there. "And now you want to go to Wray, Colorado."

"My primary goal is to get to Tombstone and stop the skin-walker, but Wray is more or less on the way and it would be no small thing to rid the world of a hidebehind."

"And what is a hidebehind?" she asked.

"You're taking to all this with a remarkably open mind," Stanley said.

"I'm not convinced of any of it. I'm going along for now because..."

They waited for her to finish the sentence, but she said no more.

"Well," Stanley continued after a long moment, "the hidebehind is a beast of the forest. It's a sort of shapeshifter, in as much as it can stretch itself to the exact shape of any tree."

"And hide behind it," Burke said.

"Precisely. It hides until it finds a human, alone, and then it attacks, eating the victim's entrails while they're still alive. When it has finished eating, the creature uses its club-like tail to break the body into untraceable pieces."

"Can ya shoot him?" Richard asked.

"Yes, with iron rounds."

"Which you have, I presume?" Burke asked.

"Well, no," Stanley admitted. "But I know where we can get some."

Burke's head gave a funny little twitch. "I'm playing along as best I can here, Mr. Kapcheck, so allow me another question."

"Of course."

"How is a man with a broken leg going to hunt a creature that lives in the forest?"

"I couldn't possibly, of course."

"So, you expect that my grandfather will do this, alone?"

Richard spun to face Stanley. "What? Alone?"

Stanley smiled, "No, Richard. Not alone. You'll have help. I assure you."

"You talkin' all your fate and destiny mumbo jumbo?"

Stanley just smiled, shaking his head.

Richard leaned over the back of his seat to stick his finger in Stanley's face. "Listen to me, you smug old—"

"Grandpa!"

"What?"

"Sit down and put your seatbelt on. I have another question."

"Tell me what to do," Richard mumbled, but he obeyed, crossing his arms like a petulant child.

Burke's fingers betrayed her agitation once more. Richard almost wished for the hysterics of Burke's mother. It might have been better than the hard, deliberate silence that filled the air between him and his granddaughter.

In the backseat, Stan Kapcheck hummed softly to himself.

The humming bumped against the back of Richard's skull like a tiny woodpecker.

He was grateful when Burke took the exit for a truck stop that advertised, "Cigs, Souvenirs, and Fried Chicken." That any trucker lived past age forty was proof that miracles existed.

He couldn't wait to get out of the car. Not only was he near exploding, he was about to suffocate in the tension of the close space. And yet, when the SUV was tucked neatly into the box of white lines and the engine had been silenced, no one moved.

"You gonna go, or what?" he asked.

She turned to him. It was the first time he'd seen her face since they left Spearfish. Her eyes were red and swollen. Tear tracks lined her cheeks. "I have never been so scared in all my life."

"Scared of what?"

A half-crazed, incomprehensible sound of exasperation burst out of her. "This is crazy! It's all too crazy! Why am I doing this? I'm crazy. You're crazy. The story is crazy. And you," she turned, jabbing a finger in Stanley's direction. "You're the frickin' King of Crazyland."

Richard stared at her, wide-eyed and frozen with uncertainty. Eight decades had taught him nothing useful about how to deal with crying women.

Stanley leaned forward and placed a hand on her shoulder.

"Burke—" She jerked away, but he reached forward again. "Please hear me, Burke…Mrs. Martin."

She sniffed and wiped her face on her sleeve.

"I know this is all—"

"Crazy!" she said. "It's insane. All of it."

He nodded. "Yes. I know. I really do, but I implore you. Look into your heart. You know we've told you the truth. Our words have not been born on delusion, but upon fantastic experiences outside the norm."

Almost imperceptibly, she nodded.

"Is that what you're frightened of, truly?" Stanley asked. "That all those monsters you were promised existed only in fairy tales really do exist?"

If he hadn't had his hearing aids in, Richard never would have heard her soft reply. "I always knew they were there."

Stanley patted her shoulder. "As did I. Now that your suspicions have been confirmed, what will you do, Burke?"

She swallowed hard. "I have to use the bathroom," she said, and without a look back, she opened the door and left the two men alone in the car.

"I gotta pee," Richard said. "You need help getting out of the car?"

"Why, Dick, I'm impressed. You're becoming downright thoughtful."

"Oh, go suck an egg," he spat back. He had half a mind to let the insufferable old dandy sit there and suffer, but his conscience wouldn't quite leave him to do it. He helped the Englishman out of the car and walked at his side toward the garishly colorful building.

Presumably, the walker still waited for him on the shoulder of the road back in Spearfish canyon. At the hospital, he'd not asked for another. He found that, with all the exercise and movement, his legs weren't quite so stiff as they had been and, even if his balance was a smidge uncertain, it felt good to stand tall and walk like a man once more.

US HIGHWAY 385 TOOK THEM PAST SIGNS FOR THE WRAY Municipal Airport, which, based on what could be seen from the road, must have been little more than a flat stretch of field with a big barn at one end that they called a hangar.

They turned left on Third Street, passed a liquor store and a little brick building with big enough aspirations to sport a sign of large black letters spelling out The Wray Museum. One block farther on, they took a right into the parking lot of The Rocky Mountain Motel.

Burke turned the key to silence the engine. "There's a gun store across the street."

"Yes, that's true," Stanley agreed.

"Coincidence?" she asked.

"I believe in many, many things, but coincidence isn't one of them."

She flashed a look at her grandfather. "You stay here," she snapped. Then she got out and stalked off toward the office.

"What did I do?" Richard asked aloud.

"Of all life's mysteries, women are the most enigmatic," Stanley answered.

"Who asked you? I was just thinkin' out loud. Criminy."

CHAPTER EIGHTEEN

Burke

THE TINY BRASS BELL ABOVE THE DOOR JINGLED, MERRILY announcing her arrival. A woman with a bun of white hair on the very top of her head sat at the counter with her nose two inches from an open book. She dropped it on the counter and scrambled to her feet. "Good evening. Can I help you?"

Burke forced a smile. "I'm hoping for two adjoining rooms."

"Well, dear, that shouldn't be hard. You can just about have your pick of rooms this time of year. 'Cept for number seventeen. The Yellow Duck stays in there and I don't reckon he'll ever check out."

Burke blinked slowly, struggling to make sense of that sentence, but before she made much progress, the lady slid a registration form across the desk.

"I suppose we should switch to computers like everybody else, but this has worked for fifty years. Seems silly to fix what ain't broken."

Burke filled out the information and slid it back across with sounds of agreement. What she really wanted to say was that she had never been so tired in her whole life and, at this point, she would have chiseled her name on stone and slept in a cave as long as there was a sturdy lock on the entrance. That seemed a bit much to dump on this old woman, though.

The lady fussed with pamphlets and maps and gave enough information to satisfy the curiosity of a visiting town historian. Burke kept her smile plastered on her face, but her thoughts were not with the bison statue or stone artifacts in the local museum.

She was angry at her grandfather. She was angry with Stanley. She was downright furious with her mother for calling her in the first place.

Under all that, a slick, fast current of excitement raced through her spirit.

Stanley Kapcheck had sucked her grandfather and her into a world full of mystery and danger. Any unexpected thing could happen in this new world. Any sort of adventure was suddenly possible.

But before adventuring, there would be sleeping. Alone. Away from the two old men who had thrown her thoughts into turmoil. Maybe if she had some space and got some sleep, she'd be able to make some sense of all this.

Maybe if she made sense of it, she'd turn around and go back home. After all, that did seem the rational response.

As she reached across the counter to take the keys from the old woman, her attention fell on the open book, face-down next to the telephone. Finn O'Doyle's devilish grin beamed at her from the back cover.

Rational responses be damned. She wanted to see what all this was leading up to.

With as few words as possible, she got the men settled in their room. She double checked that the locks on the outside door as well as the one between the rooms were engaged, kicked her shoes off and fell asleep fully clothed.

CHAPTER NINETEEN

Richard

They'd been checked into two adjoining rooms with wood paneling and brightly colored bedspreads. The vertical stripes, next to the plaid on the blankets, did nothing to help Richard's balance.

Stanley had ordered pizza and spicy chicken wings that left him tossing and turning with raging heartburn all night long. They were delicious, though. Given the chance, he'd eat them again.

Early in the morning, Burke showed up with egg sandwiches from the Subway shop down the road.

Stanley sat on one bed with his foot propped on a roll of towels.

Richard sat in a little brown chair.

Burke brought over her laptop computer and a chair from her own room and completed the haphazard little triangle with the food spread between them on the bed within easy reach of everyone. Next to the sandwiches lay two identical revolvers with long barrels of brushed stainless steel and hardwood grips, and a little brown paper bag full of hand-made .44 caliber rounds.

Stanley had called the gun shop using The Devil's iPhone. Richard listened to Stanley's end of the conversation, which wasn't much, at all.

"Do you always answer the phone so brusquely?"

Laughing.

"She loaned it to me."

More laughing.

"Right, right. Well, listen old boy. I got her phone, but she got my car. Yes, yes. The Cadillac. It's a loss, but we all must find the will to carry on."

A long pause.

"That's an apt deduction."

Another pause.

"Precisely that, but double it."

His face grew serious to the point of solemnity. His eyes flicked to Richard and away again.

"I'm not certain. Perhaps."

Laughing again.

"All right then, I will. Yes. Room six. Yes. Thank you."

Richard knew, when the young man showed up with a delivery, what the call had been about, but he would have given a great deal to have heard the other end of the conversation.

Too bad he didn't have a great deal to give. He didn't even have his ugly new Walmart clothes anymore. He supposed, at some point, he'd have to let Burke know they needed to stop for socks and underpants, but how did a man ask his granddaughter for a thing like that? Better to wait.

He focused on the screen of the computer, where she pointed. "You're right," she said. "There are an unusual number of disappearances in this area, right where the Colorado, Nebraska, and Kansas state lines intersect, but you said that a hidebehind is a forest creature."

"That's right," Stanley said.

"That area isn't forested. There aren't many trees, at all. In fact, there isn't much of anything other than nothing and more nothing. We can drive right up to the state lines on this little road, here." She pointed. "But unless your hidebehind is hiding behind a few rocks and shrubs, that's not what's taking people."

"There are trees here." Richard pointed. "Looks like a river."

"Is that enough coverage for your monster?" Burke asked.

Stanley rubbed his chin with his fingertips. "It's unlikely, but possible. I can't think what else might be doing this. The attacks have all the signs of a hidebehind."

"If you're uncertain, is the mission off?" Richard asked. The idea caused equal measures of relief and disappointment.

"No," Burke said. "Thirteen people have disappeared in that area in the last ten years. If we can stop it from taking another life, we have to do it."

Stanley beamed at her. "I like your spirit, young lady."

She scowled at him. "I'm still fairly angry with you."

He waved away her words. "It'll pass, my dear. It looks like your best bet is to take that road to the edge of that stand of trees right there. We can park around twilight and then we'll begin the hunt."

"You mean I'll begin the hunt," Richard grumbled. "Old man going into the woods alone to hunt a monster. Must be nuttier than a squirrel turd to be goin' along with all this."

"You're not going alone, Grandpa. I'm coming with you."

Stanley continued staring at the map and rubbing his chin. The discussion seemed to have no effect on him.

Richard stated the obvious, "You can't come with me."

"Why not?" she asked.

"Because you're—" He gestured toward her body. "You know..."

She set the computer next to Stanley and leaned back in the

chair, crossing her legs and arms and lifting her chin a little. "I'm what?"

Richard was in trouble. He wasn't sure why, or how much, but he had enough experience with women to recognize that particular narrowing of the eyes. "I just... It's not safe, you know. And hunting, it's...well...it's a man's domain."

"Oh, a man's domain. I see."

He had to hold his ground. To do otherwise would invite disaster. "Yes. That's right. A man's domain. Your generation just lets everyone do what they want, all higgledy-piggledy, and it's a mess. Men need to be men and women need to be women and right now you need to let the men sort this out."

"Fine." She stood up. "Good luck sorting it out without a car, gentlemen."

"Do you know how to use a revolver?" Stanley asked, effectively stopping her from walking away.

"I'm a quick study."

"Good. Come here and I'll show you both."

Richard glared at Stanley. "I shoulda figured you'd side with the girl."

Burke threw her hands in the air and let them fall with a smack against her legs. "Seriously, Grandpa. Don't you ever have anything good to say? Look at me and tell me you see zero advantage in having me with you on this hunt."

Taken aback by her brusque tone, he did what she asked and looked at her. She stood before him, young and tall and slender. She wore sweatpants that stretched over muscular thighs. Her arms were toned and strong. Vaguely, he remembered his daughter telling him that Burke had become obsessed with physical fitness after her divorce. The reality was, he now realized, she was probably stronger and more fit than he was, but he wouldn't have admitted that out loud for all the tea in China. Instead, he groped for something nice to say that would not reflect so poorly on his own condition. "I suppose your dark skin will give you good cover in the night."

She closed her eyes and stood still as a statue.

"What? I'm just sayin' that's one advantage you have over me."

"Yeah. Okay. Fine. Thanks, Grandpa." She sat down again, facing Stanley. "Show us what to do."

Stanley nodded, lifting one of the guns from the bed. "This is the safety," he began.

Richard paid close attention, but every so often, he peeked over at his granddaughter. It struck him that he didn't really know her, at all.

BURKE'S TRIP TO THE DOLLAR GENERAL STORE YIELDED clean socks and underpants, and a Denver Broncos sweatshirt. None of it was what he would have chosen, but it fit. She'd tossed the bright yellow bag on the bed without saying a word.

Richard showered and dressed in similar silence, and no longer smelled like he slept in a gutter. Now he stood in front of the streaked mirror, shaving with the cheap disposable razor he'd found tucked in among the clothes.

"May I make an observation?" Stanley asked from his perch on the bed.

"Can't stop ya," Richard said.

"There's obviously bad blood between you and your daughter and her daughter."

Richard's hand trembled. He gripped the razor tighter to stop it. "You don't know nothin' 'bout it."

"That's true."

"Then you ain't got no place to say nothin'."

"Fair enough, it's just that—"

"Just what?" Richard asked, tossing the razor onto the

counter and wiping his face with one of the small, scratchy towels. "You think you know everything about everything. You think you're so much better than me you can tell me how I should act with my own family? Maybe you spent your life savin' the world and all, and you think someone like me is just some backwoods hillbilly factory worker who don't know Adam from a hole in the ground."

"I was going to say, it's just that I'm a little envious of you."

If he'd punched Richard in the gut, he couldn't have silenced him more effectively.

He went on, "When I was a boy, I was given a job to do. For years, I assumed I would do it, and then some day it would be done. By the time I realized it wasn't that kind of job, it was too late. Everyone I'd ever loved was gone. I was too old to have a family of my own. I'm alone, Dick. I've always been alone. I will always be alone, until the day I die, and I suppose when that day comes, I will die alone.

"I envy you a great deal for having had the chance to make a family, live a life. I don't know what happened, but whatever it was, it's not too late to fix it. You have a fantastic opportunity that I will never have. You have the opportunity to love and be loved."

Richard walked over to the second bed and sat on the edge. "You don't understand how it is." Thoughts and memories flashed through his mind, too fast to process.

"It all has to do with Barbara?"

He nodded. "Yeah. She...she was everything." He forced a sad little laugh to cover up the crack in his voice. "I don't know what she ever saw in a fool like me. She coulda had anybody she wanted. She coulda, but she picked me. Picked me over all the others. Can you imagine?"

"She must have loved you very much."

"I loved her. I never knew I could love like that. When she got sick, I woulda given anything to save her. Anything, at all. I woulda died in her place without a second thought. 'Course, life don't work out that way, does it?" He sniffed and squared his shoulders. "She went on to a better place and I was father to this little girl. What did I know about little girls? I didn't give her half of what she needed."

"I'd be willing to bet you gave her the very best you could."

"Well, what's that to a kid? My best wasn't ever gonna be enough. At my best, I couldn't be a mother. I thought maybe I should marry, just to give her a mom, but I couldn't bear the thought. My wife was gone, and I couldn't imagine anyone else by my side.

"She grew up and married the first dirty hippie she met in college. She coulda done better. She weren't a bad girl. Flighty, but not bad, but she settled. Wanted a real family, I suppose. Never brought the kid around much."

"That's not fair," Burke said, stepping through the door that adjoined the two rooms. Her wet hair was still wrapped in a towel. Her arms were crossed tight across her chest. "My father was a great man, not a dirty hippie. He was a soil conservationist for the US government. He was faithful to my mom, took great care of her, and was an amazing father until the day he died. Even after. He left that life insurance policy so Mom never had to worry about money."

"I still say she could have done better," Richard growled. It felt better to feed his anger than to admit embarrassment at having been caught pouring out his heart to frickin' Stan Kapcheck, of all people.

"Why?" she asked.

"What?"

"Why? What was wrong with him?"

"It ain't natural. All that hug-a-whale crap."

"You have something against the people who take care of the planet?" She took another step into the room.

"God gave man dominion over the earth."

"Right. God gave man the task of caring for the earth. Which is exactly what my father did."

"That may be, but that don't change the fact he was... "

She took another step. "He was what?"

Richard fought the urge to shy away from her. "He wasn't a good match for my daughter."

"Why not?" She was practically right next to him now, staring down at him. Was she taller than him? She must be. She seemed like a giant, at that moment.

"It's not natural, kid."

She gritted her teeth. "You have always hated my father because he was Black."

Richard was on his feet in an instant. "Hold on, now. That's not right. I never hated him."

"You just don't think he's good enough to be part of your family."

"It ain't a question of good or bad. It just ain't natural." He stood his ground, staring up into her dark eyes. She was taller than him. How had he never noticed that before?

"Not sixty seconds ago, you said he wasn't good enough for her."

"That's not what I meant. You're twisting my words." It would help if she got hysterical like her mother. This cold, quiet assault was terrifying.

"I just meant he weren't a good match for her. Not that he weren't a fine man, but he weren't the right man for her."

"Because he's Black." She glared down at him, teeth clenched so hard the muscle in her jaw jumped.

"Look what happens," he said, sensing he was in deep and desperate to dig his way out.

"I happened."

"That's right, and you don't fit in neither world. You married a white man, and what'd he do? He left you for a white woman. If you'd a married a Black man, the same thing woulda happened. You're a good girl, Burke, but your parents saddled you with a curse."

"You're a fool. You're cruel and you're hateful. The only curse I'm saddled with is the ignorance of my ancestors. Mom put you in that home because she wouldn't have someone in her house acting disrespectfully toward her family under her own roof."

"I ain't sayin' a thing against you, Burke!" he heard the plaintive tone in his voice.

Her cool facade shattered and flew at him in glittering words of fury, "Every word you say is against me. I can never be good enough. I can never be the grandchild you wanted. I can't change what you hate about me. I'm Black and that's all I will ever be in your eyes. I graduated valedictorian from an ivy league college—an ivy league college that my Negro father paid for, thank you very much. I made more developing software in my first year out of school than you made in your life, but you don't tell people about your granddaughter, the successful entrepreneur. You whisper to them about the melanin in my skin."

She tilted her head and closed her eyes, as though she couldn't bear the sight of him one moment longer. Then, with her voice modulated down to the silky softness of a feather, she said, "You say my grandmother was the most wonderful woman in the world. You say you lost your purpose, because you lost her, and never once did you stop to think that she lives on. If you could look past my dark skin, you'd see her features on my face, you'd see it's her great, analytic mind that allows me to do what I do. You would see that it's her powerful strength that pushes me toward success in a world filled with racist, bigoted jerks who would hold me down.

"But all you see is the daughter of a Negro."

She turned away from him and went back to her own room. The door separating them closed with a quiet, definite click.

Richard stood helpless against the tears that ran down his cheeks. He stepped into the bathroom and shut the door. He couldn't bear to see the pity that must fill Stanley's eyes. He was right that he'd lost everything, but it wasn't fate that had taken it from him. He'd lost it all because he was too stupid to hold on to it when he'd had it.

CHAPTER TWENTY

Burke

BURKE PACED HER ROOM, A TIGER TRAPPED IN A CAGE. HER heart would burst from the pressure. She would scream. If anyone walked in, there wasn't a doubt in her mind she had it in her to knock them out cold. Unable to stand the confinement of the ugly little room, she snatched the keys off the table and burst out into the wide-open space of the parking lot.

Her pulse slowed. By the time she had the SUV started, her hands were once again calm and steady. She made a large circle around the perimeter of the town, then serpentined up and down the little residential streets, crossed the North Fork Republican river half a dozen times, and finally found herself at the Creekside Tavern, only a few blocks from the motel.

The little place was clean and bright. Lunch was over and the early dinner crowd hadn't yet shown up, so only two of the sturdy, polished-wood tables were occupied. She sat at the bar between two tall brick pillars and ordered a glass of wine from a woman of indeterminate age with long silver hair tied back in a tight French braid, silver eyeliner, silver lipstick, and hints of glitter on her high cheekbones.

"Anything else?" the woman asked. "We've got amazing fries."

Burke smiled. "No, thanks, I'm good."

She went back to rolling silverware inside napkins. "You new in town?"

"Just visiting," Burke said.

The girl nodded. "I figured you weren't a local. Two thousand people in this town. I swear, I know every one of them, and they're all related."

"You ever get bored?"

Her smile was pretty in a strange, wide-mouthed sort of way. "What difference would it make if I did?"

Burke sipped the wine. It was cheap, too dry, and it burned her throat. "There are other towns."

"Not for me."

"Why not?"

The girl placed the last set of silverware on top of the pile in the black plastic tub and moved the whole thing to the end of the bar. She came back and leaned one soft round hip against the counter. "My family has been here a long time. We're sort-of tied to the land, I guess you could say."

Burke took another sip. The second one burned less. "Yeah. Home can be like that for some folks, I hear."

"Not for you?"

"I don't know." She swirled the crimson liquid in the glass. Maybe all the answers to life's problems would appear to her in the sloshing liquid. "I guess I've been restless for a while. Since I got divorced."

"Mmm." The girl nodded. "Makes sense."

"Does it?"

"Sure. Hard to start a new life in the same old place."

"Yeah," Burke agreed. Nothing had appeared in the glass

except little streaks of sugar that didn't look like anything but what they were. "No. That's not it." She drank deeply. "Can I ask you something?"

"Shoot. I don't have a thing to do until someone else orders a drink."

"What's your name?"

"People call me Wiper."

"I'm Burke. Nice to meet you."

The two women shook hands over the counter.

"So, tell me, Wiper, do you believe in the supernatural?"

The girl threw her head back and laughed. Her giggles sounded like a stream tripping over smooth stones. Something about it was soothing and peaceful.

"Sorry. I guess that was a crazy question."

She waved Burke's apology away. "No, no. Not crazy. Just... sorry. Some things strike me funny at the strangest times. Do I believe in the supernatural? What exactly do you mean by that?"

Talking about this was absurd. She'd be admitted to an asylum if she told anyone why she came to Wray.

"Come on, you have to tell me now. Don't leave me dying of curiosity."

Burke finished the wine but kept the stem of the glass between her fidgeting fingers. "I guess I just wonder if you think there's stuff out there that's...you know...bigger than us. Different than us. Stuff that goes bump in the night."

Her smile faded into earnest solemnity. "Abso-freaking-lutely, I believe. I believe there is so much more in the world than the average person ever sees...infinitely more. People are blind, ignorant, afraid of everything. I don't know about supernatural, though. The word implies that those things are above nature, or outside of it. I don't think that's possible."

"You don't think something can be unnatural?"

"Sure. Unnatural, but not outside of nature. Nature is

perfectly balanced. Every evil has an opposing good. Every darkness can be banished by light. There is always balance." She lifted the bottle. "More wine?"

Burke looked at the empty glass. "Sure. Why not?" She waited until it was full and asked, "What about magic?"

"Define magic," Wiper said.

She had to think about that. "Power that can't be explained. It could be anything. The power to make someone sick or restore them to health. The power to bring luck to a person, good or bad. The power to...I don't know...sense patterns in things."

"Patterns?"

"Yeah. You know. Like...signs from God. Patterns that point to something."

Wiper slipped her hands into the pockets of her baggy jeans. "A thousand years ago, you could have been burned at the stake for mixing baking soda and vinegar to make a bubbly fountain."

"So."

"So, magic is just the name we give to things we haven't named yet." She paused. "You can do this magic, right?"

"What makes you say that?"

The unusual, wide smile returned. "Because everybody can. Some people just forget the power within them."

"Say I was reminded of it due to...unusual circumstances." She drank and was surprised to realize she was already at the bottom of the second glass. "What do I do about that?"

"You embrace it, and you thank God for whoever brought you back to yourself. Kids, they know, but most people go through their grown-up life blind to who they are and whose they are. If someone gave you your magic back, you should be kissing the ground they walk on."

Hot tears stung Burke's eyes and she blinked them away,

tired of crying. "Okay. But what do I do with what I know now?"

Wiper tilted her head a little to one side, making the light dance on her glittered cheek. "You do like John Wesley?"

"The preacher?"

"That's the one," she confirmed. "You do all the good you can, by all the means you can, in all the ways you can, in all the places you can, to all the people you can, for as long as you ever can."

"That's good," she said.

"Yeah. Just imagine if the world took his advice."

Talking to this stranger was better than the therapy she'd paid thousands of dollars for after her divorce. She couldn't help but share one more thing. What difference did it make if she was acting like a fool? She'd probably never be in this tiny town again for the rest of her life. "You know, my grandfather is a racist. What do I do with that?"

"Fear and ignorance are the roots of racism, right? Love him. Teach him. What else is there to do?"

"He really pisses me off," Burke admitted.

She chuckled. "Sounds like a pretty normal family to me."

Burke found herself laughing along with her. "Do they teach you wisdom in bartending school?"

"Nah." Wiper blinked. One set of lids clicked together from the sides of her eyes before the second set fluttered. It was a motion so fast it would have been easy for Burke to convince herself she'd imagined if she hadn't come to this town to kill a creature that could shapeshift into a tree. "I've just had a lot of experience dealing with how to be happy while being different from those around me."

Burke swallowed hard. "Are you..."

The girl moved forward and took the glass from the bar. "I'm just another cog in the wheel, doing all the good I can."

She rinsed the glass clean and placed it in the rack. "This drink's on me. Go work your magic, Burke."

"Thank you."

She smiled and sparkled. "You're very welcome."

Newly fortified against her own wild emotions, Burke returned to the motel to find her grandfather locked in the bathroom.

CHAPTER TWENTY-ONE

Richard

THE TAP ON THE BATHROOM DOOR WAS SOFT. RICHARD ROSE and stood on numb legs.

With nowhere else to go, he'd plopped down on the closed toilet seat and cried like a little boy. Once the tears dried up, he wanted nothing more than to lay down and take a nap. His many years, a yoke too heavy to bear, pressed down upon his body and his spirit. But he couldn't go out there with Stan Kapcheck. To be so weak in Stan's presence was adding insult to injury. Now, the entire lower half of his body was full of pins and needles from sitting on the john so long.

He opened the door and Stan stood there. "Time to go, if we're going to do this."

Richard asked the question he'd been pondering for the past quarter hour or so. "Did being a hunter give your life purpose?"

"That's fair to say. I have seen terrible things, but in the end, I kept going out, again and again. Maybe, in all that, I saved the person who will find the cure for cancer or the key to world peace."

"I don't have a purpose anymore. I haven't had one for a very, very long time."

Stanley leaned on the crutch under his left arm, reached his right arm around his back, and produced the revolver from his belt. He lifted Richard's hand and slapped the gun into it, closing his hand over the other man's. "Welcome back, old boy."

Richard felt the corners of his mouth turn up. The weight of the weapon sent a surge of satisfaction up his arm, straight into his heart.

"Go get the girl," Stanley said. "You need her."

It took her so long to open the door at his knock, he wondered if she'd driven away without them. Finally, she was there, her face an emotionless mask.

"I'm a fool. I don't know how to change, but I'm willing to give it a shot if you're willing to help me. I need your help, Burke."

Her eyes sparkled in the dim light. "All right."

"Stanley says it's time to go."

"Let me get my sweater."

A tentative little finger of warmth poked his heart. The last time he'd felt hope was so far in the distant past he almost didn't recognize it for what it was.

CHAPTER TWENTY-TWO

Finn

HOT BLOOD PUMPED HARD THROUGH FINN'S BODY. HIS FEET smacked the ground in rhythm with his pulse, the slap of his sneakers against the pavement, a primal drumbeat in time with the breath of the universe. At the top of the hill, he slowed to a stop and stood with his hands on his hips.

"It's beautiful," Sara said. She'd kept pace next to him for ten miles without ever breaking stride. Once or twice he'd had the feeling she was deliberately slowing her pace to match his.

"I didn't know you were a runner," he said.

"There's a lot you don't know about me," she answered. "How do you feel?"

For days, he'd worried that he was getting sick, swinging wildly between fiery bursts of productivity and creativity and long stretches of coma-like sleep. Sara had fussed over him, watched him, fed him, and never once asked for anything other than his company.

That afternoon, she'd asked, "What makes you feel most alive?"

He didn't even have to think about it. "Running. When I run I..."

"What? Tell me, please."

"I feel connected to the universe. You ever see those religious fanatics? The ones who hold out their hands and weep and faint in church? When I'm running, I get it."

"You haven't run since I've met you," she said.

Of course, he hadn't run. He'd been in a downward, self-destructive spiral of writer's block when she showed up. Once she came, he began pouring out his soul into his new book, sleeping his life away, or drinking with her. As for the smoking, well... Backing off the cigs would probably go a long way toward feeling healthy again.

"I can run," she said, interrupting his thoughts.

"What?"

"I'm a good runner. Let's run."

"Sara..." The last race he ran was the monstrously grueling San Francisco Marathon. He'd come in third place. There was no way this little girl could keep up with him and he'd never find a good pace if he worried about her.

"Please, Finn? Just a little one?"

He had relented, and here they were, on top of the hill eleven miles from his house and she was barely out of breath. Maybe she wasn't an author stalker. Maybe she was a runner stalker.

"Who are you, Sara?"

She grinned up at him. "It's beautiful up here, Finn. Look around."

He did. It was. This was one of his favorite spots. From the top of this hill, he could see to every corner of his family's land. Sierra Vista sparkled in the distance. Across a wide stretch of desert, Sheep's Head Mountain watched over them. "Look at this," he said. Taking her hand, he led her down a little way, toward a thick grove of desert willows. A little pool, just big enough for two people, bubbled there, a hot spring pushed up to the surface of the dry desert.

She raced to the edge and squatted down to wiggle her fingers in the water. "Oh, Finn! It's perfect. No wonder this is your favorite place!" She stood again and tugged the sports bra she'd worn as a top over her head. Her full breasts, young and perfect, were bared to him. Before he could find the presence of mind to say anything, she kicked off her sneakers, dropped her shorts in a little pile with her bra, and stepped into the water. She sank down into it with a sigh of pleasure, turned to face him. "Come in with me, Finn. Why else would you have brought me to this place?"

He stood frozen. Every part of his brain screamed that this was a bad idea. He hadn't brought her to the spring intentionally. He'd run, and this is where his feet had carried him. But while his brain was screaming that he ought to turn around and start running again, his body wanted very much to stay.

"Sara, if I come in there, I'm going to make love to you."

She chewed on that perfect lower lip. "Why else would you have brought me to this place?" she asked again.

"I don't know anything about you. I must be twice your age. I'm clearly mad and probably dying from some weird disease that makes me sleep twelve hours a day. This is a terrible idea."

She cocked her head. "You talk too much, Finn. You're learning how to have fun again, remember?"

He couldn't exactly remember deciding to undress, but he found himself stepping into the silken warmth of the water. Then her hands were on his body, hotter even than the steaming spring. Finally, he managed to catch that lip between his teeth. It was exactly the delight he'd expected it to be.

CHAPTER TWENTY-THREE

Richard

THE HEADLIGHTS OF THE SUV PIERCED THE DARKNESS AND revealed miles and miles of fields. Hay gave way to corn. Corn turned into more hay. Occasionally a stand of marijuana would crop up. Richard didn't think he would ever get used to the idea that hash was legal. Strange times when a man could smoke a bone in public, but the lefties would throw a fit if he lit a tobacco pipe.

At half past midnight, Burke pulled the car to the side of the road and killed the engine.

The thick curve of the waxing moon peeked out from behind a cloud and hid its face again, leaving the world beyond their little bubble smothered in heavy black. Burke opened her door. A cool breeze crawled through the open door and slithered around the edges of the car's interior. Déjà vu swept over Richard.

They'd left the Cadillac on a gravel shoulder in Spearfish and walked off into the night and they'd nearly died twice over.

Burke said, "I'll leave the keys, Stan. Maybe you should move up here to the front, just in case."

"Thank you, dear. I'm quite comfortable. I'm sure you won't be long."

"I'm glad you're sure," she said. "I'm not sure of anything right now."

"You'll be fine," he assured her. "Stick to the plan and you'll be fine."

"Stanley, I don't—"

"You'll be fine," he said again. "We will *all* be fine. Just stick to the plan."

She clasped and unclasped her fingers around the steering wheel. "Okay. Ready, Grandpa?"

"Ready as I'll ever be." Richard opened his own door and heaved himself out. Not wanting to fall over and break his hip again, he held on long enough to make sure all the parts that were supposed to be working to keep him upright were going to do their job. Everything held. He nodded in satisfaction. "You keep outta trouble," he said into the car. It didn't sit well with him to be leaving Stan alone in this lonely place, but Stan had insisted on coming along and there was no way he'd be able to keep up with them.

"You do the same," Stanley said. The dome light twinkled merrily in his eyes.

The night seemed to eat the little snick of the door closing, so that the metallic click barely registered above the pounding of his own blood.

Burke retrieved two guns and two flashlights from the trunk and gave one of each to Richard. "Lead the way. I'll follow," she said.

Richard strode off in search of the monster. That was the plan. He'd go first. She'd stay back. It couldn't attack both of them at once.

His feet left the road, found their way, one in front of the other, across the uneven, sloping, rocky terrain. Trees loomed in the distance before him, velvet shadows on a black canvass. The heartbeat within his chest was not fluttering, but thudding fierce and strong.

He smiled.

Behind him, the earth protested Burke's steps with soft crunching noises. Her presence was a comfort. She hadn't left, hadn't given up on him. A chance still remained to right what was wrong.

Once they entered the canopy of the woods, he realized that the night sky actually had been offering some small gift of light. Now he slowed, struggling to make out what lay even a few inches in front of him.

It was very quiet. Too quiet. "Burke?" he whispered. "Burke are you still there?"

No answer.

Now his heart fluttered. "Burke?" He turned in a slow circle, but there was nothing to see but inky night. With a trembling hand, he lifted the heavy flashlight. The beam pierced the darkness. He swept it to the left.

Nothing.

He turned to the right.

A shadow dashed away from the glow, disappearing behind a tree.

With his man parts clawing their way up into his belly, he inched toward the tree.

A powerful blow caught his lower back, sending him sprawling onto the hard earth. The flashlight smacked into the ground and went dark, just as a second jab smacked into his side hard enough to crack his ribs. Instinctively, he curled into a tight fetal position.

A gunshot rang out so loud it left a tinny din in his ears. The flash of powder blazed in the night and he heard something fall hard onto the ground next to him. Light shone down, directly into the furry, fanged face with its horrid humanoid features. Wounded, but not dead, it snarled at him, lurching ineffectually in his direction. A second shot slammed into its head and it lay still, staring at Richard with lifeless yellow eyes.

Burke squatted next to him. "Grandpa? Are you—"

The black, clubbed tail shot out of nowhere, slamming into Burke so hard it lifted her from the ground and tossed her a few feet away. Richard spun onto his back to look at the monster that disappeared behind a tree. He glanced at his granddaughter, struggling to lift herself onto hands and knees. From the corner of his eye, in the glow of her fallen flashlight, he glimpsed a dark shadow slinking toward her.

In one motion, he lurched for the gun he had dropped, rose to his knees, and fired. His finger developed a mind of its own, pulling the trigger again and again, emptying the chamber completely. With each round that tore into the hidebehind's body, it jerked again, and when there was nothing left but a hollow clicking sound, it fell beside its mate.

Burke pushed herself up and looked at him. Blood poured from a cut near her scalp, making the right side of her face shine in the faint light.

"Are you okay?" they both asked at the same moment.

"No," they both answered.

Her lips curved into a smile. A tiny chuckle slipped out. It grew into a genuine laugh and swelled up to hysterical, gasping guffaws.

He gaped at her. "Are you mad?"

She pointed at the two dead creatures. With tears of mirth running down her face, she said, "You were so scared!"

"Me?" He planted one foot on the ground and ignored the searing pain in his side in order to stand. "You screamed like a girl!"

She laughed even harder. "I am a girl!" she whooped, falling back against the large oak behind her.

As though her hilarity were contagious, he felt it creep into him and, a moment later, he, too, was panting for breath. He remembered laughing like this with Stanley after killing the bowrow, and he wondered if adrenaline weren't just about as good a drug as laughing gas.

Once they were able to pull themselves together enough to walk, they retraced their steps to the road, each leaning heavily against the other.

The white SUV was there, exactly as they had left it, easy to spot by the glow of the dome light.

The dome light that was on because the back door was open.

The back door was open, and Stanley was gone.

A lingering smell of roses hung in the air.

CHAPTER TWENTY-FOUR

Finn

"Finn. Finn, baby. Wake up."

Sara's voice came to him from a thousand miles away. "Finn. Come on, baby. Back to the land of the living for now."

His eyelids were lead weights. He'd once finished a triathlon. He'd had strength enough for that, but not strength enough to move even those tiniest of muscles now.

Her soft chuckle crawled across his skin and into his ear. "Okay, then. Drastic measures." Her teeth grazed his neck, then tugged on his nipple. Her tongue drew a path across his belly and moved south. Now, at least part of his body was awake and ready to do something. She chuckled again. "Wakey, wakey, Finn O'Doyle." She took him into her mouth and he moaned and arched up under her.

When he lay breathless and spent, his eyes finally opened. His limbs under his control again, he asked, "What time is it anyway? It's got to be after midnight."

"Mmm. Probably." She stretched out on the warm rocks under the moon.

Reality crashed down on him. "Shit! How are we supposed to get back home?"

"Same way we got here, I suppose."

"Run? At this hour?" He sat up and looked around like he might spot an unexpected taxi cab waiting for them.

In one swift motion, she rolled onto her knees, pushed herself up, and slung one leg over his so she straddled his lap, her perfect breasts pressed against his chest. "We could stay here all night, I suppose."

There was an astonishing stirring in response to her words. Good Lord! He'd gone back in time and become a teenager again. He gave her round little bottom a firm squeeze and lifted her off. "You're a temptation, for sure, but we can't sleep out here."

"Why not?"

"Snakes? Scorpions? Coyotes? Because I have a pillow top mattress at home." He stood, and his muscles flexed and moved with newfound strength. "Plus, I'm not tired anymore." It was the truth. He wasn't just awake. He practically vibrated with life. Once, in college, he'd done a line of cocaine and he'd felt invincible. Two friends had to convince him he couldn't fly. But they'd been wrong. He was sure of it. "Let's run."

Her eyes twinkled. "Yes. Let's."

Was there no limit to her vitality? He hoped not. There was no limit to his. He would race her ten miles home and then he would take her again on the pillow top mattress.

The expression on her face convinced him she knew exactly what he was thinking, and there was no doubt in his mind she'd go along with the plan.

CHAPTER TWENTY-FIVE

Richard

DAWN CREPT OVER THE HORIZON, CASTING A SICKLY YELLOW pallor across the world. Richard sat, leaning against the ugly brown headboard of the bed, watching the room brighten. Breathing hurt. Exhaustion pressed him down onto the mattress. His left eye was swollen nearly shut. He couldn't remember hitting his face. Still, for all that, he couldn't sleep. The moment on the roadside played in his mind on an endless, maddening loop.

With one hand on the open door of the rented vehicle, staring at the spot where Stanley had been sitting, the world had shrunk down around him.

The Devil took Stan.
Good. Let her have him.
He got me into this mess in the first place.
This has been the greatest adventure of my life.
There are only twenty-two days left in the moon cycle.
Who will kill the skinwalker?

I'm going to fall.
I need my walker.
I'm too old for this.
Burke almost died.
How would I tell my daughter her child is dead?
She's not dead.
Stan might be dead.
Not dead.
Taken by The Devil.
Will she come back?
How do you fight The Devil?
Oh, God! Burke almost died!
The Devil took Stan!
There are only twenty-two days left to kill the skinwalker!
Burke almost died!
Burke almost died!
Burke almost died!

"Grandpa?" Burke had gripped his arm, gentle but firm. "Come on, Grandpa. Let's get you in the car."

He let her guide him toward the passenger door, but he didn't get in. "I should have never called you," he said.

She smiled, but the corners of her mouth turned down. Her eyes sparkled with tears in the dim moonlight. "Everything's going to be okay. Come on. Let's get away from this place."

They'd ridden back to the hotel in silence. She'd chosen to lay on the bed next to his, rather than in the other room.

"We shouldn'ta left him," he forced the words out into the dark space between them. Speaking hurt a great deal.

"He knew she was coming, Grandpa. He gave himself up."

He pushed himself up, hissed in pain, and fell back against the mattress. "What are you talking about?"

"He planned the whole thing."

It didn't make sense. He gave himself up? Why would he do

that? He'd been running from her for years. Why now, when he was so close to bagging the one creature that had eluded him for so long? "But...the skinwalker."

"He knew that he couldn't fight The Devil and the skinwalker at the same time. He made a choice and gave himself up so she would no longer be a distraction from the hunt."

"So now what? The skinwalker gets away?"

"Of course not. Stanley wouldn't want that."

"Confound it, kid, I don't know what in tarnation Stanley wanted, but he's gone and balled it up good now." Hot anger bubbled up and burned away the sadness. He welcomed his old friend, preferring rage over the desire to curl up and cry like an infant at his mother's breast. "We don't even know how to kill the stupid thing. This one needs a wooden stake, that one needs an iron bullet. What're we s'posed to do? Just start throwin' stuff at it till it up and dies?"

"Grandpa, we have the book. We're the hunters now."

Her words shocked him into silence. His mind, a buzzing hive of urgent questions just moments earlier, was now silent as the grave. Eventually, her breathing slowed and became heavy and he knew she slept.

Blast Stan Kapcheck! Stinkin', smirking, cocky, over-dressed coxcomb! In the entirety of eight plus decades, no other man had made Richard's blood boil so. No doubt, he'd die from an aneurysm and it would be all Stan Kapcheck's fault.

A single tear escaped and made a quick fugitive track down his cheek.

For the first time since Barbara died, he prayed.

BURKE MADE ANOTHER TRIP TO DOLLAR GENERAL AND returned with enormous sunglasses that hid the worst of her bruises, a bottle of Miralax, and a jogging suit for Richard.

He handed the Miralax back to her. "I said prune juice."

"They didn't have prune juice. This will do the same thing."

"It's not the same. Prune juice is gentle. This stuff will tie me to the pot all day."

"Fine. Choose to suffer, then." She tossed the unopened bottle into the little grey trash can in the corner.

"I'm going to look like a fool in these clothes," he said.

She turned to go into the other room, calling over her shoulder, "You'll look a lot more foolish in your boxer shorts."

"Dagnab, smart aleck kid," he mumbled, gingerly pushing himself to his feet. He'd had to swallow three times the recommended dose of Ibuprofen before he'd been able to stand up and walk without wincing. No doubt about it, he'd developed a nasty hitch in his get along. He managed to wash up and dress himself. He stuffed his dirty clothes in the yellow plastic bag and when Burke said it was time, he was ready to go.

He rode in the car, his fingers tapping out an unsettled rhythm on his thighs.

Burke's long nails clicked on the steering wheel.

He forced himself to still.

"Grandpa, Stanley—"

"Stan Kapcheck's a vain old fool who's like to break an arm pattin' himself on the back. Now he's got us both mixed up in this—"

"Stanley saved your life. He's a good man."

With dawning horror, he stared at his granddaughter. "You've got a thing for that old fart."

Her immense sigh could have powered a sailboat. "I do not have a *thing* for him, Grandpa. I can respect a man without wanting to go to bed with him."

He clamped his mouth shut and stared out the window. In his day, women weren't so crass, but he supposed if he said anything about it, he'd be in trouble for that, too.

"Stanley and I talked the night you and I argued," Burke said.

Richard held himself together with wishes and spit. The mention of the argument was a shot straight to his heart. He pressed his lips together, hard. There would be no more tears from him, that much was certain.

"I wanted to leave. Or, well, I thought that's what I wanted after we argued, but I didn't. I came back to the hotel and talked with Stanley."

Stanley was good at talking, Richard thought. If he had a special talent, it was wagging that silver tongue of his. "So, you stayed for Stanley's sake," he said.

"No, Grandpa. I stayed for my own sake. Just like you came on this trip in the first place for your own reasons. You didn't really care about saving some author you never heard of." Her voice had a hard, angry edge to it. She stopped for a moment, and when she went on, her tone had softened a little. "We're not so different, you and me."

Richard studied her, the young, exotic-looking, self-made millionaire, dressed in fashionable clothes and looking forward to another half century of life. Aside from a shared relationship with his daughter, what did they really have in common?

As though she'd read his thoughts, she said, "I'm alone, too, you know. Do you realize that I was the same age when Greg left me that you were when Grandma died?"

He hadn't realized that. He'd not really given it much thought. He'd only met the boy twice. His granddaughter's husband had been rude and abrasive the first time, and the second time, he was a downright horse's backside.

"It's not the same, though."

"No. Not the same. Your wife loved you with all her heart until her very last breath and then left you alone, wishing you'd find happiness again, whereas my husband took the time to tell me I was an insufferable bitch and he hoped my female parts would shrivel up and rot in his absence before he walked out with my favorite set of luggage and set up house with a twenty-two-year-old underwear model from Sweden."

Did he know that's what had happened to the girl's marriage? It didn't seem like he did. He'd been told she was divorcing and made his own assumptions. He'd never bothered to ask why.

"I made a fortune in my twenties," she went on. "The plan was to retire young and stay home to raise my babies, never worrying about money the way my parents worried. So, I retired, and before I got pregnant, I was single. The market changed. Technology changed. What I did was groundbreaking when I did it. By the time Greg left me, what I'd done was as obsolete as vacuum tubes in a television." She signaled and carefully passed a school bus lumbering along in the right lane.

Richard glanced at the speedometer. The needle hovered at just over eighty. He started to point it out, but memory of how frustrating her slow puttering along had been stilled his voice. A higher speed meant fewer hours in the car, and since it was impossible to find any position less painful than another while strapped upright in the seat, he entirely favored a shorter trip.

"I was just like you," she said. "I was sitting in a comfortable chair, entertaining myself to death. The only difference is that I picked books and you picked The Weather Channel."

"Nothing wrong with The Weather Channel," he mumbled.

"Nothing wrong with books," she answered. "A good book is part of a good life, but it's not a good life, all by itself."

She didn't seem inclined to say any more.

Richard shifted, trying to ease some of the pain in his side. Movement only made it worse. He produced the bottle of Ibuprofen from his pocket and took two more. Sitting very still, waiting for the drugs to produce some result, he thought about Burke's words. It was one thing to be waiting out your days when you only had a few days left. Doing the same at her age was a whole different ball of wax. The pity that crept into his heart was foreign. He was used to feeling sorry for himself, not for other people.

Unbidden, Stanley's grinning face came to mind. Where was he now? What was the witch doing to him?

We were good together, Stan had said.

"What if Stanley don't want rescuin'?"

Burke glanced over at him. "Why would you say that?"

"Well, The Devil. She's evil, sure, but she's not too hard on the eyes, you know."

"She's *The Devil*, Grandpa."

"Yeah. There's that." He began to tap on his legs again. "So, what are we going to do?"

"We're going to do what Stanley would have wanted us to do, what Grandma would have wanted us to do."

"Which is?"

"We're going to slay the monster, trap the Devil, and rescue Stanley." When she looked at him again, a smile played across her battered and swollen face. "We're going to live every single day on purpose. We're going to turn our lives into a grand adventure."

The contagious smile caught, and he felt his spirits rise as though they were being tugged up by the curving corners of his mouth. "We're gonna be hunters."

"Both of us," she said, and leaned forward to fish in her huge black purse, coming up with the battered leather book. "Maybe you can find something in here that will help us."

He slipped the glasses from his pocket and perched them on the end of his nose. In his hands, the book fell open to the last written page. On the thin page there was a single entry in Stanley's neat, precise printing.

The Devil is on our trail. She can be held off, but running from her is a distraction from capturing the skinwalker. We will divide and conquer. -SK

Beneath that, in a pretty, looping script were the words, *I am a hunter now. I will slay the skinwalker, but I pray I will not have to do it alone. -BM*

There was a red and white Bank of America pen in the ashtray. Richard took it in his hand and pressed the tip to the paper. His handwriting wasn't what it once was. The tremors of old age had given it a strange, warbling look. Trying his best to hold the pen steady, he made his own entry.

As long as there is strength in my body, I will hunt at my grand-daughter's side. She will not slay the skinwalker alone. -RB

He capped the pen and put it back where he'd found it.

Burke's hand found his arm and gave it a gentle squeeze. They'd probably be killed doing this, but they'd go down on their own terms. Death was going to have to drag them out of this world by force.

He leaned forward and started reading the diary, picking up where he'd left off.

RICHARD HAD NEVER SEEN A TOWN LIKE SANTA FE, NEW Mexico. He imagined that when Coronado pictured the future it might have looked like this pristine city of modern adobe houses with manicured lawns surrounded by snow-capped mountains. If Burke had told him they'd driven into a foreign country, he wouldn't have found it hard to believe. The streets grew more and more narrow and twisted as they approached the center of town and then widened once more on the other side of the city.

He held the book in his lap. He knew what they needed to do. He had no idea how they were going to do it.

They were climbing now, following a twisting path into the Sangre de Cristo Mountains. Burke had told him that Stanley's last bit of instruction was to find Jeremiah's cabin. When she pressed Stanley to tell her who Jeremiah was, he simply insisted that he was a friend who had what they needed to defeat the skinwalker.

Eventually, she slowed to a stop in front of a dirt track that led farther up the mountain. "I think that's his driveway."

Despite the bright cerulean sky above, night appeared to have settled within the close confines of the high desert forest. Shadows ruled the rough little road, dancing like teasing imps before them.

"Reckon we should go up there, then."

Burke tapped the steering wheel. "Yeah." The car didn't move.

"Better to do it before dark," he said.

"You got the gun?"

"It's in my pocket."

"Maybe you should take it out."

He didn't argue. The weight of it bolstered his courage.

"Make sure the safety is off," she said as she pressed the accelerator and urged the car forward.

The light died away as they entered the canopy. The gnarly tips of branches scratched and tapped at the windows, where a thin film of frost formed with unnatural speed.

"This is so weird," Burke whispered, leaning forward over the wheel, her attention unwavering from the path before them.

"Dark as pitch and colder than a witch's tit in a brass bra," Richard agreed in similarly hushed tones. He switched off the revolver's safety.

The road took a sharp turn to the right and led to a wooden bridge so narrow it was impossible to drive across. Burke shut off the engine and the two of them sat staring at what lay on the other side of the deep arroyo.

A cottage with a thatched straw roof stood in a beam of sunlight that shone down on it like a spotlight. Roses climbed the side of the little stone structure. Little decorative windmills and suncatchers, ceramic gnomes, and trees made of old bottles and rebar sprung up in a sprawling garden of vegetables, wildflowers and towering sunflowers. A cobblestone path led from the other side of the bridge straight to the arched wooden door.

"How does he grow tomatoes in this dry, rocky soil?" Burke asked.

Richard turned toward her, agape. "You've lost your danged mind."

"I've been trying to grow tomatoes for ten years. I've got the richest, blackest dirt in North America. The climate is perfect. I plant them and fertilize them and water them and every year they sprout up and die. Those tomato plants are flawless."

Richard rolled his eyes. "No wonder you and Stan got along. You're both a few pickles short of a barrel."

She finally turned toward him. "You don't have to be so critical of a thing just because you don't understand it, you know."

"I understand that any person who looks at that there bit of witchcraft and has gardening tips as the first thing that comes to mind is a few blasted pickles—"

"Short of a barrel. Yeah, yeah." She sighed. "Stay there. I'll come around and help you out."

"Don't need no help," he muttered, but pushing the door open caused a sensation akin to being stabbed in the side, so he waited for the girl to make her way over to him. She reached out her arms and he leaned on her far more heavily than he wanted to, but he managed to get both feet on the ground and balance on those unreliable pins.

They walked across the bridge together, the sturdy planks giving no protest under their feet. Crossing was like walking from the inside of an enormous freezer out into the most perfect of summer days. He realized as their feet touched the cobblestone that they were still clinging to one another. It was impossible to say if he was holding on to her or if she was holding on to him, but, either way, he was grateful for her presence.

The ugliest cat he ever saw slinked out of the bushes and trotted directly toward them, looking up at them with a single yellow eye. Where the other should have been, there was only an ugly scar. It meowed loudly, rubbed its head against Burke's leg, and ran off, disappearing behind the house.

"Curiouser and curiouser," she said.

As if someone inside had heard her voice, the door swung open and a figure that looked perfectly at home in this surreal setting stepped out. The man was tall enough that he had to duck to get through the door. He wore a long robe that resembled Gandalf the Grey's and a black tactical vest. In his left hand he held a long-handled garden spade that he leaned against as if it were really a magical staff. His long, shaggy black beard reached nearly to his belly and little glass beads had been woven into it. They sparkled in the bright sun. Atop his wild mop of hair, a Cleveland Browns cap perched like a bizarre star adorning the uppermost branch of the world's homeliest Christmas tree.

His eyes gazed in their direction, two white orbs with no color at all. "A hunter has fallen?" he asked by way of greeting.

Richard was still standing there with his mouth hanging open when Burke said, "Stanley Kapcheck was taken."

"By whom?" his voice was warm maple syrup spreading over a fresh stack of hotcakes. Introduced to the executives at RCA, he could have given Elvis a run for his money.

"The Devil," Burke said.

The man burst into a fit of hysteria. His laughter filled the glen and echoed from the trees. Tears spilled from his milky eyes. If not for the garden spade, he would have fallen to the ground in hilarity. He gasped and waved a hand in front of him. "Sorry! Sorry, it's just that..." and the laughter began again.

Richard and Burke looked at each other and shrugged.

The man, still bent nearly in half and shaking with amusement, turned his back on them and motioned for them to follow him into the house.

They stepped across the threshold into a warm, airy space that smelled of loose-leaf tea and cinnamon. Colorful, over-stuffed furniture made a cozy seating area around the stone fireplace. A heavy wooden table dominated the space in front of the potbelly stove. One wall sported a single closed door painted with fantastical symbols from top to bottom. The remainder of the wall space held shelves of books. The ugly cat watched them from the uppermost ledge, it's tail twitching slowly back and forth.

"I'm sorry," the man said again, still a little breathless, but apparently under control. He propped the shovel against the counter, took three mugs from a cabinet, and filled them with tea from a pot on the stove. Each was placed upon the table in front of one of the mismatched chairs. "Sit, sit. We have a great deal to discuss and I know enough about hunters to know the two of you are anxious to be on your way."

He moved with total ease and assurance, turning toward the counter once more to retrieve a large metal tin and bringing it to the table. The three of them sat and the man took the lid off the tin and helped himself to a chocolate chip cookie the size of a bread plate. "Help yourselves," he said. "I find there is nothing so good in the whole world as tea and cookies for boosting the spirits."

Richard braced his hand against the table and lowered himself into the chair directly across from the man. He glanced at the cup in front of him. In a bold, looping script it said *Adulting is hard. Tea is easy.* He glanced over at the large black mug already in Burke's hands. *World's Okayest Employee.* The strange man's read *FBI - Female Body Inspector.*

Burke sipped her tea. Her shoulders relaxed as though a

great weight had been removed. "I can't tell you how happy I am to have found you, Jeremiah."

The man guffawed and Richard was afraid he'd fall into another fit of hysterics, but he managed to keep himself together. "I'm not Jeremiah," he said when his laughter had died away.

Burke's hands gripped the edge of the table. "Who are you, then?"

"Name's Nathaniel. Jeremiah's been watchin' over me for a while now. I guess you could say I'm something like a... a..." He tapped his hand on the table. "Whaddaya call it? Ha!" he burst out, causing Richard to jump.

The sudden movement sent a sharp pain through his side and he hissed through his teeth.

"Oh, dear. That does sound bad," the man said. "Here." He patted the pockets of the tactical vest, apparently found the one he wanted, opened it and produced a little red and white mint tin. "It isn't really mints. I mixed it myself and put it in the container. Reduce, reuse, recycle, you know? Rub it on your sore spot and you'll be right as rain in a minute."

Richard picked up the little container and sniffed it. He glanced at Burke. She shrugged.

"So, who are you?" she asked again.

"That's right. I apologize. I got distracted. My name is Nathaniel. I'm sort of an administrative assistant to Jeremiah. That's the word I was looking for."

"Stanley told me to find Jeremiah. He said he had what we need."

"Did he? That sounds like something Stanley would say. Leave it to that old codger to run off with the most stunning monster in town and leave a couple of freshmen to do his dirty work."

"I don't think he ran off with her, exactly," she said. "He was sort of kidnapped."

The man chuckled, shaking his head. "Okay, then."

Richard knew he had never been a patient man, nor a tolerant one. This weirdo and his hysterical, cryptic words were too much for his weary soul. "So, can this Jeremiah help us out or not?"

The man wagged a finger at him. "A hunter must be in control of his emotions at all times."

"You listen to me—" Richard said, pointing a finger at him.

"We need help," Burke interrupted. "Are we in the place to find it?"

Nathaniel chomped down on his cookie, letting the crumbs fall into the tangle of his beard. "I believe you are, Ma'am. This place is nothing if not a haven for the ones who need help."

"So, Jeremiah is here?" she asked.

"He is."

"And he'll help us?"

He cocked his head. "I'm not really sure, but we'll see what we can do." He turned his unseeing eyes toward Richard. "You really should try that balm. It'll do you a world of good. Promise, I'm not a monster. If I was, you'd have been dead ten minutes ago."

"Let me help you." Burke started to rise from her chair.

"Don't need no help," Richard insisted. "I ain't some kind of invalid."

"Everyone needs help sometimes," Nathaniel quipped over the lip of his mug. "The inability to admit that is, in itself, a handicap."

Since everything from the armpits down had seized up and he had no way of getting out of the chair without an undignified amount of groaning and leaning on the table, Richard remained in his chair, scowling at the man. "Fine." He slid the little tin across the table toward Burke. "You can rub that hoodoo on my bruise, if it'll get you off my back, so we can get something accomplished."

Burke came around the table to kneel next to him. She lifted the hem of his shirt, exposing the spectacular bruises there. "Oh!"

"I'm fine."

"Grandpa, this—"

"The salve will help," the man said. "Feel free to use it for your own bruises, as well, dear girl. May I ask what caused all this trouble?"

She opened the little hinged lid. With her long, thin fingers, she scooped a bit out and dabbed it with infinite care along the bottom-most edge of the injury and then began working her way up. "It was a hidebehind," she said.

"Two," Richard corrected.

The man's eyebrows shot up in surprise. "Two? That is rare. Yet, you're both still alive. Stanley chose you well. You obviously have a natural talent. You fought them on your way here? Are they nearby?"

Burke finished, tugged his shirt back down, returned to the table, and accepted a napkin to wipe her fingers. His side didn't feel any better. Greasier, but not better.

"No, they were at the junction of Colorado, Nebraska, and Kansas. There's a small wooded patch there."

"Hmmm..." He sipped at the tea again, making a loud slurping noise. "These are strange times we are living in. Strange, indeed. Keep your eyes out," he warned, pointing a thick finger at no one in particular. "If things ever get normal, it's a good sign the end is nigh upon us."

The hideous cat jumped down with a soft thud. It padded over to them and leapt onto the table, circled the perimeter a few times, sniffed the cookies and then settled down in a tightly curled ball in front of Nathaniel.

While these feline investigations took place, the man said, "Tell me the whole story, please, so I know best how Stanley wanted me to help you."

"With all due respect, sir," Burke replied, "Stanley didn't say he wanted you to help us."

If he was offended, it didn't show. His blind, white eyes still crinkled at the corners.

"I can promise you, Jeremiah is hearing everything you're saying right now."

Richard glanced around nervously. "He some sort of spook?"

Nathaniel's laughter lent a sparkling softness to his tone. "Nothing like that, I assure you."

Burke raised her eyebrows and shrugged, leaving her grandfather to assume that she was letting him make the call on this one.

"All right," he said, "I'll tell you, but I reckon it'll be the *Reader's Digest* version or we'll be here 'til the cows come home."

The cat twitched its tail and watched him with its one golden eye.

He didn't trust that cat.

Truth be told, he didn't trust any cat. Or any cat-sized yappy little dog, either, but there didn't seem to be any of those around. The creepy feline likely chased 'em away.

"Stan saved me from a strigoi back in Michigan. After that one was dealt with, her friends came after us and Stan and I took care of them." He hadn't intended to make himself seem brave or heroic, but he rather liked that he came out sounding that way.

"'Course, I ain't never encountered a thing like that, so I thought...so it was..." he trailed off, not sure what it was, exactly.

"Unsettling, I'm sure," Nathaniel finished for him.

Close enough. "Yeah. Unsettling," Richard agreed. "Stan and I talked. In all that talkin', it came out that he didn't come to that place because of the strigoi. He came for me."

"How unusual!" Nathaniel exclaimed.

"You can say that again."

"How unusual!" he said again, and burst into another round of laughter, not quite as uncontrolled as before. "Ah," he said, running a hand through his long beard, dislodging cookie crumbs. "I'm sorry. Do go on."

"So anyway," Richard continued, "'parently, Stan's been hunting one specific thing all his life and his teacher was after it before him."

"The skinwalker." No amusement colored those words.

"Right."

"And he brought you, of all people, into that hunt? How unusual," he said again.

Richard was offended. "I ain't a helpless little girl."

Burke shot him a look that told him he'd stepped in it again with her.

"Of course not," Nathaniel agreed. "But you said yourself you'd no experience in this field. Hunters are often chosen as children and trained up in the life. Nevertheless, Stanley chose you. I'm sure he had his reasons."

"The skinwalker killed my wife," Richard said.

Nathaniel didn't interrupt again, but nodded. His hands formed a little steeple under his chin.

The cat continued to stare, rudely.

"So, I told him I'd go with him, but Stan said we had to make a few stops along the way."

"A hunter on the move can never resist doing battle with any monster remotely near his path."

"That's what he said, more or less," Richard agreed. "We got as far as Minneapolis and stopped to rest. That's where The Devil found us. We gave her the slip and carried on to South Dakota. Stan thought there was a chupacabra there, but when we went out, turned out to be a bowrow instead. Took us both by surprise and Stan got hurt."

"You didn't exactly come out unscathed," Burke quipped.

"You gonna let me tell it?" he asked.

She lifted her mug and sipped her tea by way of answer.

"There we were in the middle of nowhere, and all of a sudden she was there. I snatched her phone and called for help."

"Well played! You used one of her own tools against her."

"Next thing I knew, she was gone, and we were tucked into a couple o' hospital gurneys. Girl made off with Stan's car, though."

Nathaniel gasped. "She took the Cadillac?"

"Yup."

"Oh, my. That is serious business."

"Well, Stan weren't none too happy 'bout it, but he was laid up with a broken leg so not much he can do, right? Still, we couldn't quit on the skinwalker, so we called my granddaughter to help us out."

Nathaniel inclined his head toward Burke. "And you came. Well done, young lady. The ties of family run deep. Too many of your generation have forgotten that important truth."

Burke directed her eyes to her tea mug and said nothing.

"Stan said we oughta head south. Said we had a job to do on the way. So, we went to Colorado and he sent Burke and me to deal with the hidebehinds. When we got back to the car, he was gone."

"You are certain it was The Devil who took him?" Nathaniel asked.

"Smelled like roses when we got back to the car," Richard answered.

"He knew she was coming," Burke said. "He told me she'd take him as soon as he was alone. He gave me his book and told me we should come here as soon as we could because Jeremiah has what we need to defeat the skinwalker."

Nathaniel stroked the cat curled on the table in front of him. "Jeremiah has it, huh?"

"That's what he said."

The man nodded. "Have you read the book? Do you know what you need to do to kill the skinwalker?"

Richard produced the book from a pocket and placed it on the table. "Says we need to get it under our power by using its real name—the name it went by in life, before it turned bad. Then we have to dismember it in the light of the full moon and burn the pieces to ash before sunrise." He avoided Burke's eye, not wanting to see her reaction. If the girl looked scared, he wasn't sure he'd have the gumption to carry on. "Also says it's faster than a greased pig and smarter than a whip, has a temper that sits on a fuse shorter than a mouse's pecker and it'll rip the heart out of anyone who gets in the way of its plans."

Nathaniel's raised eyebrows disappeared into the tangle of hair sticking out from under the brim of his ballcap. "Is that really what it says?"

Richard shrugged. "More or less."

The joyous, booming laughter filled the tiny house again. "Oh, I do like you two, very much."

"I'm glad you're amused." Burke pushed her chair back and stood up. Like a tiger in a cage, she paced back and forth across the short distance between the kitchen counter and the front door. "Is Jeremiah going to help us or not? Because this is nuts. Nuts!" she exclaimed, throwing up her hands. She stopped and grasped the back of her chair. "We are not hunters. We don't know anything. We have no tools. We have no guide. This. Is. Insane."

Nathaniel sipped his tea. "If you weren't hunters, you wouldn't have been able to get to this place. It's powerfully protected. You know everything you need to know. The only tool you need is a sharp blade." He reached inside the vest and produced a shining blade with a serrated edge. "Take it, if you want. I have more where that came from. And take Stanley's book. He will continue to guide you just as Busar guided him."

Burke sank back into her chair and lay her head down on her crossed arms.

"How are we s'posed to learn the thing's name?" Richard asked. "If that's the magic that binds it, I don't guess it'll have it stitched on its breast pocket."

The other man nodded. "You're right. Creatures of magic guard their real names jealously, but I think Stanley already solved that mystery for you." He gestured to the cat. "This is Jeremiah."

"He sent us to find a darn cat?" The old familiar heat rose into Richard's cheeks, along with the desire to punch Stan Kapcheck's grinning face.

"Don't be silly, now. Stanley didn't send you to find a cat. He sent you to find a name."

"Jeremiah," Burke whispered.

"Why didn't the old fool just tell us?" Richard asked.

Nathaniel shrugged. "Stanley is a great hunter. I'm just a hermit in the woods with an unusually extensive library. He must have had his reasons. I don't pretend to know how The hunter's mind works, but I suspect by the time he gave you this information he was well aware that The Devil was on his trail."

Burke was nodding enthusiastically. "Of course, he wouldn't want her to know the details of what we were doing. The whole reason she was after him was because she didn't want him to kill the skinwalker."

Nathaniel cocked his head as though he weighed the truth of her deduction and found it a reasonable conclusion. "I wouldn't say the whole reason, but it's certainly a large part."

The slurping of the tea and the ugly cat's soft purring composed a cozy melody. A bold little robin lighted on the windowsill and lent its whistle to the tune.

"We should rescue Stanley first," Burke said. "He can help us."

"Did he tell you how to do that? Or ask you to make him a priority?" Nathaniel asked.

"No, but..." Tears glistened in her eyes.

Richard's mouth twisted down at the corners. Whatever she felt for Stan Kapcheck sure did seem like a thing to him. The thought made the tea and cookies roll unpleasantly in his stomach.

"I don't think you have time to help Stanley first," Nathaniel said.

Burke wiped her nose with the back of her hand. "We've got twenty-one days."

"You've got seven days." He reached for a second cookie and nibbled its edge. "Mmm. Peanut butter."

"You're wrong about the days. We're certain because of my wife's death. If the creature is active every twelfth twelfth moon cycle, it will still be hanging around for a good three weeks."

"True," he agreed. "It is active for the entire duration of the moon cycle—"

"But it can only be killed in the light of the full moon," Burke finished his sentence.

Nathaniel leaned forward with his elbows on the table. "Forgive me, dear, if this is too personal, but I wonder, why are you here? You asked for the hunter's knowledge, and you followed the path this far. You clearly care about saving Stanley, but you're conflicted. Half of you is still struggling to believe the existence of what you're fighting against."

A single tear escaped the glistening pools in her eyes and rolled down her cheek. "Stanley gave me purpose. I was so lost until he came along. Now he's gone, and everything that's happened in the past few days seems like smoke and mirrors. If Stanley can get captured, what chance do we have? In some moments, I remember his faith in us and I'm strong. Then my own faith is gone like so much dust in the wind."

Jeremiah lifted his backside into the air, stretched luxuriously, and padded over to Burke. He rubbed the tear away with the wild, silken fur on his head.

Richard was moved. The girl had spoken the words of his own heart. A lifetime of disbelief was not so easily overcome in a single week. He reached across the table and took her hand in his. "We'll find him, kid. It'll all be okay, just like he said."

She gasped. "Grandpa!"

"What?" he replied, startled.

"Your ribs!"

He pulled his hand back and sat up straight in the chair. Not only did the movement cause no pain in his ribs, the old aches in his hips and knees were gone. He couldn't remember being so comfortable.

Nathaniel laughed at their stunned silence. "I told you the salve would work. I might not be a hunter, but even a hermit in the woods is allowed to have a few good tricks, right?"

CHAPTER TWENTY-SIX

Burke

SHE SHOULD HAVE BEEN SLEEPING. IT WAS PAST MIDNIGHT, and tomorrow would be another long day of driving, but here she was, sitting in an enormous, overstuffed armchair reading the hunter's journal.

Nathaniel had been kind enough to offer them shelter for the night. When they'd protested about how little space he had for himself, he opened the door covered in unusual symbols and revealed a labyrinth of rooms, including, so far as she saw, several bedrooms, a library, at least four baths, and what appeared to be a bowling alley, though the lights were off inside that space so it was hard to tell for sure.

Her grandfather slept in the room across the hall, snoring so loudly that, even with both doors closed, she heard him. The sound soothed her. If he was snoring, he was alive.

After she'd studied the pages about skinwalkers until she'd memorized the words, she flipped backward, randomly stopping on page fifty-six.

The xochitl is an aspect of a human spirit that has broken away and learned to live independently of the flesh in which it originated. It should not be hunted indiscriminately. The nature of the spirit is dependent upon the nature of the human from whence it came.

"What does that even mean?" she asked the empty room, and she flipped forward to page sixty-two.

It is most important that one not sever the head of the Hydra, for it will be replaced by two more.

"Well everybody knows that," she mumbled. She'd lived alone for a very long time. There were whole weeks of her life when, if she hadn't talked to herself, she wouldn't have talked at all.

Page seventy-eight was interesting.

A spirit possessing the strength to produce ectoplasm cannot be contained with a salt boundary as lesser spirits most often can. Rather, the only way to destroy such a spirit is to burn the bones of the spirit's human body.

She sincerely hoped she wouldn't be faced with the prospect of digging up a body any time soon.

The dybbuk is similar in most aspects to a low-level demon. However, it is derived from a tortured human soul, which gives it a drive to torture the souls of others. Under assault from the dybbuk, a person will experience flare ups of irrational rage and violence.

Burke slammed the book closed and tossed. "I'm not possessed," she said. "I have a good reason to be angry. There's nothing irrational about it. I'm a freakin' rock star for how calm I stay." She stood and started pacing again, but stopped when she caught sight of herself in the mirror.

It was true that she was a woman of a certain age, but she'd never looked better. She was strong and fit. Confidence straightened her spine. The finest salon in the Detroit Metro area had curled her hair.

"You can be the finest peach in the orchard, Burke Dakota. Some people just prefer apples."

How many times had her mother said that to her over the years?

She remembered being twelve years old and thinking, "But wouldn't it be nice, just for a day, to be an apple and know what it is to have those people like you, too?"

No doubt about it. The only demon who made her anger flare was the one she'd nurtured in her own heart all these years.

"Do all the good you can, for all the people you can," she said to the woman in the mirror. "All the people, Burke. Even the ones who royally piss you off."

In the mirror, the woman gazed back at her with a warrior's eyes.

CHAPTER TWENTY-SEVEN

Finn

Finn stood over the toilet, hacking, waiting to see if the overwhelming force of the coughing would make him vomit. All that came up was a wretched yellow glob that he spit into the bowl. He wiped his face with a wad of toilet paper and tried to catch his breath.

For a long time, smoking had been a social thing, something to do with his hands, in between drinks, when he was out with friends. Back then, time with friends kept him sane. The worlds inside his mind were so vivid and all-consuming, they often seemed more real than the physical plane on which he was forced to exist. Singing karaoke at Big Nose Kate's was therapy.

Then his moderately successful books exploded into a cultural phenomenon. He knew it was true because *Entertainment Weekly* said so. His characters were on HBO now, in movies, referenced by other fictional characters in sitcoms, like that made-up world was an alternate universe where everyone knew each other.

His fans wanted more. His publisher wanted more.

Everyone wanted more, and no doubt about it, there was more for him to give. If he wrote twenty-four hours a day, he'd never have enough time to get all of his thoughts onto paper.

He couldn't manage twenty-four, but he started pushing it from his usual six or eight to a routine twelve. Twelve sometimes became sixteen and, even then, sleep eluded him because the stories banged on the bars of the prison of his mind.

A year ago? Two years? Five? He'd found himself sitting in front of the computer doing nothing. His fingers moved restlessly over the keys, never pressing hard enough to send a signal to the computer. The cacophony in his head was louder than ever. So loud that he couldn't hear it through the haze of exhaustion that had settled around him. Sitting there with his fidgety hands made him crazy. A pack of cigarettes lay on the shelf. He'd dug it out of his pocket and tossed it there so long ago that it was covered in a thin film of dust. Just for something to do, he lit one and drew the foul, stale smoke into his lungs.

Five minutes later, with the filter clamped between his lips, his story started pouring out of him.

He went through at least a pack a day now, even though they no longer worked their magic.

He still ran, convinced the exercise helped work the toxic garbage from his lungs. The only time he really noticed how it affected his health was in the morning. In the mornings, he had a smoker's cough.

This morning, he thought he was going to die hacking up a lung.

Seemed like the moment had passed though. Apparently, today wasn't the day, even if the reflection in the mirror looked twenty years older than it should and had two days' growth of beard where there should have been just a shadow. "You're old and pathetic, O'Doyle."

Sara didn't think so.

The corner of his mouth turned up at the thought of Sara.

She'd reawakened a passion in him he forgot he ever had. No wonder he looked half dead. The girl was screwing him to death.

What a way to go.

"Finn! You're awake!"

Speak of the Devil. He met her eyes in the mirror. "I have to make some calls today. I promised my editor I'd have the first chapter to him by Tuesday morning so I'm already twenty-four hours late, and after blowing off the con—"

Her laughter cut him short.

"What?"

"Thirty-six hours, Finny baby." She danced around in a manic little display that brought back the feelings of discomfort he'd had when he first met her.

"What are you talking about?"

"It's Thursday afternoon, sleepyhead. Guess that little...uh... run wore you out."

He turned to face her straight on with a frown. "You mean Wednesday afternoon. I slept past noon."

"Nope, Thursday."

Her grin struck him as predatory. He stepped around her, into the bedroom, not wanting to be closed in the tiny space of the bathroom with her any longer.

His phone was charging on the bedside table. He picked it up. It was Thursday.

"I slept for thirty-six hours?"

Sara's warm hands slid around his waist and held him tight. "Yeah, but you're awake now. Let's do something fantastic."

He pulled away from her.

"What's the matter?" she asked. The perfect lip turned out and he hated himself for responding to it with a powerful surge of desire. "You don't want to spend time with me anymore?"

"I just need a little space. I—" He couldn't bring himself to tell her to go, and he hated that, hated that he was too weak to speak his mind to a little girl half his age and half his size. "I need to take a shower."

The grin returned. "Sounds nice. I'll join you."

"No." He held up his hands. "Please, I just need a little space," he said again. "You know how it is. Writers and their solitude. I'll be out in a little bit and then we can go have lunch, okay?" Even as he said the words, he regretted them. The thought of food made his stomach turn. After a long run and an even longer roll in the sack, followed by an entire day and a half of sleep, he ought to be on the verge of starvation, but the reality was, he wasn't sure he'd be able to eat at all.

Sara backed off and let him shower.

He took his time, luxuriating in the hot spray. By the time he got out, the bathroom was misty and the mirror was covered by a film of condensation. He wiped it away and reached for his shaving cream, but the movement caused the light to reflect against the silver whiskers in his beard that hadn't been there the last time he looked. "Geez," he whispered. "You really are old and pathetic, O'Doyle."

Fifteen minutes later, he found Sara on the couch, reading one of his novels. "Stephen King is better," he said.

"He's not my type," she said, patting the cushion next to her. He sat down and the soft padding accepted him like it was giving him a hug.

"Ready for lunch?" she asked, but he couldn't bring himself to answer through the thick haze of sleep settling on him. From very far away, he was aware that she was covering him with a heavy quilt and kissing his clean-shaven cheek. "That's okay, Finn. You rest, and I'll stay right by your side."

Or maybe she didn't say that, at all. Maybe he just dreamed it.

CHAPTER TWENTY-EIGHT

Richard

THE SUV GOBBLED UP THE MILES BETWEEN NEW MEXICO and Arizona too quickly. Thoughts and images floated through Richard's mind, flotsam and jetsam on a churning sea. One single certainty rose above them all again and again until he no longer had the strength of will to ignore it, try as he may. It had occurred to him thirty minutes into the drive, something he hadn't given much thought to in the days since Burke showed up in Spearfish. Now, he couldn't let it go.

He finally blurted the words into the silence of the car, "You need to call your mother."

He had expected resistance, anger, annoyance, even maybe a little fear. That he was treading on thin ice with her was apparent. He was completely unprepared for Burke's quiet, "I know."

They sailed past a bright blue sign with a starburst of yellow and red surrounding a gold star. *Welcome to Arizona.* The slow, subtle climb into the foothills of the Chiricahua Mountains began.

"She's going to be furious with both of us," Burke said.

Richard sighed. "Yeah. I know."

"Do you love her, Grandpa?"

Her question astonished him. "Of course, I love her. Give anything for that kid."

Burke flashed a pretty grin at him. "She's a senior citizen, too, you know."

"She'll always be my kid."

His eyes searched the landscape. Familiar, vague, subtle panic nipped at his soul. The sky in this part of the country was too big, the land too rough and alien. He'd always had the thought that most of what lived here was trying to hurt people —from the prickly cactus to the venomous animals, to the rough-hewn, leather-skinned people descended from lawless frontiersmen. Darn hippies tried to make the state into something arty and modern. Peace and love. Ha! Retirees with more dollars than sense came along and built enormous green golf courses in this barren desert, sucking the aquifers dry with no care beyond their own pleasurable final years. They thought this country of eternal sunshine was a paradise. They didn't see the hard truth that had existed in the land for a million years before they came along, that would remain for a million after they were gone. This land was a place of death.

He shivered. Better to return to the conversation with Burke than follow that train of thought too far down the track.

"I was a bad father, but I always loved her."

"You weren't so bad," she said.

"I wasn't so good, either. Your father—he did a fine job. That always stuck in my craw, you know. I grew up in a generation where we were taught..." He glanced at her out of the corner of his eye. Her grip was tight on the steering wheel, her eyes straight ahead. "Well, we were stupid. I've been foolish far more often than I've been wise. I reckon I have a few more lessons I need to learn. More than a few mistakes to make up for." He swallowed the lump in his throat. "But I never stopped loving her."

"She *is* a little hysterical, though."

He snorted, his own laughter catching him by surprise. "Like a long-tailed cat in a room full of rocking chairs! Never met a woman so quick to get bent outta shape."

Her cheeks lifted in a responding smile. "It would be the easiest thing in the world to put off calling her a little longer."

"It would. That's true."

"But what's easy isn't always what's best."

"Almost never."

"Okay then." She leaned up onto one hip and dug a phone from the pocket of her pants. "Call Mom," she said.

Richard jumped. "Now? You're calling her right this second? I thought maybe—"

"Hello?" his daughter's voice emanated clear and loud from the tiny speaker on the phone. "Burke?"

"Hey, Mom. Sorry I didn't call sooner."

"Oh, thank God! Are you okay? Is your grandfather with you? Where are you? Last I knew, he'd been in the hospital and—"

"It's okay, Mom. Grandpa's right here. I'm on speakerphone. He can hear you."

"Dad?" her voice broke with emotion. "Oh, Dad. Thank God! Are you okay?"

"I'm fine, just fine. Calm down."

"Don't you tell me to calm down! In the history of the world, no one has ever calmed down because someone ordered them to. You disappear in the middle of the night without so much as the courtesy of a note. Where in the world have you been? What's going on with you?"

"I—" Panicked, he looked at Burke.

She cut in, speaking in the same quick, firm tones his Barbara used to use when she would accept no further nonsense. "Grandpa was helping Mr. Kapcheck. You know, his friend from Everest?"

His daughter's hysterics would not be calmed so easily. "Helping him do what? Why couldn't you tell anyone where you were going, Dad?"

"He has a friend who's dying, Mom. A best friend. Like a brother. In Arizona. He doesn't have any time to waste and he was afraid to drive alone. He came to Grandpa in the middle of the night because Grandpa had told him he used to live there, and they took off right away because there was no time to waste."

"But they were in the hospital!"

Richard could practically hear the gears turning inside her head, trying to piece everything together into a coherent picture.

"I told you, they're okay, Mom. The doctors were just being cautious. But they still needed a ride, so I offered to drive them."

"Why would you do that?"

"What else did I have to do?"

"You could get a job. I bet there are plenty of nice, divorced men your age in the computer industry."

"First of all, Mom, what the hell?"

"Burke Dakota! Don't you curse at me."

Burke continued as if she hadn't heard the reprimand, "And second of all, the men in the computer industry right now are children. Trust me. Not dating material. Besides, there are men in Arizona."

Her mother huffed into the phone, "Cowboy wannabes."

"Anyway," Burke said in a loud, strained voice. "We just crossed into Arizona, so—"

"Just now? Where have you been for the last four days?" cold suspicion gave her words a sharp edge.

Richard was eight years old, trying to get away with lying to his mother about where he'd been when his school teacher's car got egged. Anxiety forced beads of sweat to pop out across his forehead.

"Well, they're not so young, you know. They need to stop a lot." That part was the truth, and it slid off Burke's tongue so smoothly it was clear that she'd been keeping track of the frequent pit stops.

If he could ever get his hands on another bottle of prune juice, it would save them some time. He'd have to stop just as often, but he wouldn't have to stay at each rest area for quite so long.

"Well, if you were going to Arizona, why were you in South Dakota? It's not at all on the way." She was speaking to Richard now.

He looked at Burke in a panic.

She rolled her eyes. "He wanted to take the scenic route," she said.

"That's right," Richard added. "He'd never seen Mount Rushmore." His tone turned up slightly at the end of the sentence, lending the statement the air of a question.

"I thought he was in a terrible rush to get to his friend," she was louder now, her pitch rising ever higher.

It could have been his imagination, but he was pretty sure that Burke was starting to sweat, too.

"Mom, I—"

"Don't you Mom me, young lady!" Soon, only dogs would be able to hear her. "You two are hiding something from me and I want to know what it is. You're always sneaking around behind my back. Well, I raised you better than that, and I want an explanation right now."

"Mom, calm down. We—"

"I will not calm down! Stop telling me to calm down! You tell me what's going on. Better yet, let this man, Stanley, speak for himself. If you're in the car on speakerphone he must be able to hear this load of horse hockey you're trying to feed me."

"Okay. Fine, Mom. Fine. Of course... Sta.... just... mountain..."

The girl was having a stroke. Richard started to ask if she was okay but she held a finger to her grinning lips.

His daughter was furious now. "Don't you—"

"Hear...must..." Burke continued.

"—hang up on me—"

"Mom?"

"—Burke Dakota, I—"

"Mom? Are..."

"—swear I will—"

"Break.... Up." She hit the red button to end the call.

Richard stared at her with his mouth hanging open.

The girl was a genius.

Her smile stretched all the way across her face. "And that's how it's done, Grandpa. She knows we're safe and she's out of our hair for a while. In two days, she'll call to scold me for being a petulant, ungrateful child."

"That's ridiculous. You're a grown woman."

She cocked her head. "Yeah, well, I'll always be her kid."

He couldn't argue with that.

"Now, tell me something. Once we get the skinwalker in our power by calling its real name, and we cut it into pieces, and burn the pieces by the light of the full moon, how are we going to get Stanley back from The Devil?"

He'd read and re-read the same passage a dozen times. "Well, there's really only one way, so far as I can tell."

"What's that?"

"We have to bind her in the name of Jesus and make a trade."

The pretty smile faded, pushed down by a deep frown. "Like

in an exorcism? I thought that was for possession not...uh... whatever she is."

"No. There's a drawing in here. An octagon with these crazy symbols, one on each side. Underneath it says the symbols equal Jesus of Nazareth. I think we have to make this symbol and get her inside it."

"Make it out of what?"

"Salt, I think."

"Salt."

He shrugged. "I think."

Her fingers clicked away on the steering wheel. "How do we even find her?"

"Well, that's in a different part." He opened the book and thumbed through the pages. "Summoning spells. The Devil. Place an image of yourself in a box made of bone. A communion wafer, stolen from a saint, must be placed over the picture and covered in the blood of an innocent child. Fill the box with graveyard dirt, wrap it in the stole of a faithless priest and bury it in the exact center of a crossroads."

She pinched the bridge of her nose. "That's all, huh?"

"Well, then you say, 'I offer a bargain.' Then I reckon she comes to do business."

"And where, exactly, are we supposed to get all this?" Her voice bore a distinct resemblance to her mother's, but he wouldn't have told her that for all the tea in China.

"From wherever it is, I reckon."

He closed the book and slipped it back into the glove compartment. His stomach made a strange, protesting noise and he wondered if he was hungry or if he needed another pit stop. If it was the latter, he was going to force himself to wait a while. Not for all the whiskey in Heaven would he have asked Burke to pull over just then.

"Grandpa?" her soft voice broke through his thoughts. She sounded so innocent that, for a moment, he could have believed she was eight years old again. She'd been a beautiful child. He'd always thought so, despite her dark skin. He supposed if he said that, she'd be offended. For the first time in his life, it occurred to him that maybe she'd be justified in her offense. He'd been a jackass. He was glad she was willing to give him another chance. Surely, he'd done nothing to deserve it.

"Yeah?"

"Do you think Jesus is real?" she asked.

"I reckon. He's in the history books."

"Yeah, but do you think he's really who they say he is?"

He shrugged. "Ask a hundred men, get a hundred answers. *They* don't know crap from Crisco. How would *they* know who Jesus really was?"

Church had been important to Barbara. In that time and place, it seemed everyone they knew donned their best clothes on Sunday morning and spent an hour or two listening to the preacher talk. Did he believe all the stuff about being born again and loving your neighbor? Some days more. Some days less. But what was the harm in sitting there and listening if it made his wife happy? He would have walked to the front and sacrificed a goat if it made her happy.

"It would seem that The Devil is real," Burke said.

"Yeah. I reckon it does seem that way. She ain't much like the Bible says, though."

She cocked her head to one side. "What docs the Bible say?"

He thought about it. Random phrases, often repeated, jumped up in his mind like so much popcorn.

Repent and be saved.

For God so loved the world...

In the beginning...

Lazarus, come forth!

The way, the truth, and the life.

Hallowed be thy name.

The word of God, for the people of God.

"Guess we didn't talk about him much," he finally admitted. "Or, I wasn't listenin' when we did."

"Her."

"Right. I suppose he...uh...she was just God's adversary. The force in the world trying to trip us up. The one who made bad things happen."

"Seems to me people are the ones who make bad things happen," Burke said.

He couldn't deny that. In his lifetime, he'd seen mankind do horrible things. "Stanley says she's nice."

"That makes sense."

He scratched his head. Noticing the wild tangle of his hair, he tried to pat it down, in vain. It hadn't lain flat since it turned white, half a lifetime ago. No reason it would today. "It does?"

"Sure. Have you ever heard of a con man who was a jerk? They make old ladies fall in love with them. They charm their way past security guards. They dazzle businessmen into fraudulently investing hard-earned fortunes. They're horrible people, but unfailingly nice."

"Huh." He would have to chew on that for a while. He'd always equated nice with good and mean with bad, but maybe he'd have to rethink that. *Bodes well for an ornery old coot like me. Maybe I ain't so bad, after all. Just grouchy.*

"So, if The Devil is real and the name of Jesus will bind her," Burke began, but she didn't finish. There was really no need. He knew exactly what she was saying.

"Yeah. I reckon you're right."

"We might want to rethink a few of our beliefs."

It occurred to him that he had smiled more in the past few days than he had in the last decade. "Your mother will be thrilled if we go to church with her."

She nodded. "She'll think it was because we were won over by her righteousness."

"Maybe we should tell her the truth."

"The whole truth?"

"Nothing but the truth."

They were both cracking up at that thought when she took the sharply descending ramp that led them onto AZ-80. The green sign on the side of the road told them they had twenty-five miles to go until Tombstone.

CHAPTER TWENTY-NINE

Finn

IN HIS DREAMS, HE LAY ON HIS BACK AND WATCHED HIS FLESH rot away from his bones, falling from his arms in chunks like he'd been trapped in a b-level zombie movie. Maggots writhed in the gaping wounds and he tried to scream for help. Sara rode him hard, pushed toward climax by his fear. Against his will, he came inside her and, as his body spasmed, her face became the grinning skull of Death.

He lurched awake.

Sweat drenched his clothes. The heavy quilt still covered him. Sara sat on the floor next to the sofa, one finger slowly sliding up and down an arm, bringing goosebumps rising to the surface there.

"Did you have a bad dream?" she asked.

"Yeah." He pushed himself into a sitting position. Thirsty. His throat was raw. It lent his voice a harsh raspiness. "Could you grab me a bottle of water?" he asked.

She bounced off to the kitchen without complaint and came back with one of the little plastic bottles.

The icy water chilled him, coursed through his veins, tore a shudder from his damp body. "I'm sorry," he said. "I don't know what's wrong. I must have the flu or something."

She pressed a hand to his forehead. "You seem healthy and full of life to me."

"Yeah, well, I feel sick and half dead. My bones ache like I've been hit by a truck." He swallowed the rest of the water and handed the empty bottle back to her. "Maybe you should just go, Sara." The horrible dream was fading and his eyelids were growing heavy again.

Sara pushed his hair back from his forehead and ran her nails gently along his scalp. It felt wonderful. "Don't be silly," she said. "I'm staying right here with you, Finn. Don't you worry about me. I have everything I need. Just rest."

He was too tired to argue. He slid back down until his head found the pillow again.

"Finn?" she asked.

"Yeah?"

"Do me one favor, though, okay? Try hard to focus on the good times, the times when you felt alive and strong. Like when you ran that race in California. Do you remember?"

He did remember. Fire had burned in his thighs as he strained against gravity to get to the top of hill after hill after hill. The cool drizzle that fell on that misty day ran down his face, infinitely more pleasant than running under the wretched desert sun. His lungs weren't so damaged then. He drew in deep breaths and the fresh air coursed through his veins with each powerful beat of his heart. He ran for days like that. He lived for days like that.

"Oh, yes. That's good, Finn. Don't stop," she whispered as he drifted off to sleep again. His last waking thought was that she sounded just like she did when he was making love to her. Strange girl.

CHAPTER THIRTY

Richard

THE GIRL AT THE FRONT DESK OF THE LITTLE HOTEL ON THE hill had hair that reached past her bottom and a habit of shaking her head every few minutes so it shimmered like a thick brown curtain over an open window. A silver name tag with black letters said her name was StellaLuna. Richard had a vague notion of a storybook by the same name. What kind of weirdo named their kid after a book about a bat? He refrained from saying anything and considered his newfound restraint a sign of growth.

"I'm sorry, but I don't have adjoining rooms. I had a cancellation today for a room with two double beds on the second floor. That's the best I'm going to be able to do. It's Wyatt Earp Days this weekend, you know.

"Wyatt Earp Days?" Burke asked.

"Oh, yeah! It's a big deal," the girl said. "People come from all over."

"Come to play dress-up and act like they know something

about guns, and cowboys, and history," Richard mumbled. He'd always loved the wide-eyed tourists who came to Tombstone to experience the Old West, but the ones who seemed to think they were the reincarnation of Doc Holliday or Billy Clanton really stuck in his craw.

StellaLuna narrowed her gaze on him. Burke must have sensed a storm brewing because she was a little too loud when she said, "Sounds great. We really got lucky coming into town during a festival. The room with two beds will be fine." She offered her license and credit card and leaned her elbows on the counter. "Listen, can I ask you something? Kind of girl-to-girl?"

"Sure." The girl popped her chewing gum, a gunshot in the quiet, echoing lobby.

"Well, it's a little silly, but I confess, I didn't know anything about Wyatt Earp Days, but I did come here because I have something of a celebrity crush."

Casual indifference was washed away by gleeful conspiracy. "Dirk?"

A little line formed between Burke's brows. "Dirk?"

StellaLuna waggled her brows at her. "He's *so* bae. I mean, *all* the girls here always knew it, but ever since he had that walk-on role with Will Smith last year...well...now the whole world wants him, right?"

"Oh." Burke lifted one coy shoulder. "I guess I'm too much of a book nerd to know much about movies. I bet he's very handsome, though."

"Ohhhh.... *Now* I get it." The girl was fully focused on sharing her celebrity experiences, leaning forward on the counter, too, chomping her gum like a cow with cud. "You're looking for that author guy."

"Finn O'Doyle. That's the one. Have you met him? Is he as handsome in real life as he is in his picture?"

Beaming with pleasure at being The Girl With All The Info,

she nodded and popped another enormous bubble. "Oh, yeah. For sure. Totally handsome. Kinda grouchy, though. I see him at Joe's every now and then, sittin' and drinkin' and eatin', but hardly ever talkin' to anyone. My boyfriend asked him to play doubles at pool one night, but he said he had to go. Then he sat there for another two hours doin' nothin' but starin' into his MGD."

Burke's eyes rolled up toward the ceiling. Richard continued watching her performance in mute astonishment. Had he ever suspected the girl was an actress? For the second time that day, he was impressed by her special brand of genius.

"Oh, the strong, silent type. Makes me all shivery," Burke gushed.

The girl giggled and straightened up. "I'd rather have Dirk, but to each her own, right?"

"Do you know where he lives?"

"Why? Are you gonna stalk him or somethin'?"

Silly, girlish giggles bubbled up from Burke. "Oh, you know. Not stalk. Just...drive by once or twice. And if he happens to be out front chopping wood with his shirt off, where's the harm in snapping a photo or two?"

StellaLuna's giggle matched Burke's. "He might not be my type, but even I'd click the link for that pic." She handed two plastic key cards across the desk. "All right then, take Charleston Road a coupla' miles out, right? And then you'll go over the big wash and his driveway's on the right side. Good luck catching a glimpse, though. House is probably half a mile off the road down a dirt drive."

Burke beamed. "You're the best, StellaLuna."

A bubble covered her face and was sucked back into her mouth. "Us girls gotta stick together. You're in room two-sixteen. You can park 'round back. Breakfast is in here from six thirty till nine."

Richard followed his granddaughter back to the SUV. "That was good." He couldn't imagine he'd have ever thought to just come out and ask where the man lived. The plan was brilliant in its simplicity.

She gave him a long look before slipping her sunglasses on. "Thanks," she said before disappearing into the car.

"What was that?" he asked once he'd followed.

"What?"

"Your thanks was a little—"

"Surprised?" She turned the key and sweet, cool air filled the little space. Somewhere after Colorado, they'd switched from heat to air conditioning. "Can you blame me, Grandpa? I think that's the first compliment you've ever given me in my life."

Was that true? He tried to think back. A man couldn't be expected to remember every conversation he ever had. "That can't be true."

"Okay, my mistake," she agreed.

Her nonresistance irked him. It's just the answer Stanley would have given. Thinking of Stanley was salt in the wound. "Well, I'm sorry you're stuck in this mess with such a cantankerous old fart."

She pulled into a spot at the far end of the lot. "I'm not sorry, Grandpa. I love you, and I appreciate your compliment. It's more valuable for being rare. That way I know you wouldn't have said it if you didn't mean it."

"Well, I ain't never been one to stick my nose in someone's backside and call it a bouquet of roses."

"I respect that," she said. "We should go inside and make a plan."

"Got one." He'd been waiting for the right chance to tell her. It was a good one, too. He'd been cooking it up for a good hour or more, and he was pretty sure she'd approve.

They carried in their belongings, which consisted of Burke's fancy leather suitcase full of clothes and Richard's plastic grocery sack full of dirty laundry, the bag of sandwiches and chips they'd picked up at the convenience store across the street, the leather book, and the two guns.

Burke had worried about someone noticing the guns.

Richard laughed at her. "In Tombstone, they think you're a suspect if you don't have a gun. You ain't in Detroit anymore, kid."

Once they had the food spread out on the tiny round table in front of the room's one window, Burke asked Richard to fill her in.

He took one more enormous bite before he started. Had food been this delicious before he began this adventure? Even these nasty gas station sandwiches were fantastic. Add to that a miracle—his guts weren't twisted in a knot anymore.

Earlier in the day, he'd spread a thin layer of Nathaniel's magic balm on just about all the parts he could reach. Best decision he ever made.

His guts weren't twisted, his ribs weren't bruised, his hips didn't hurt, and darn if he didn't find a brown hair on his head that afternoon. The sight had been so startling he'd actually felt a thrill of fear. What did this new-found health mean? But he brushed off the fear as quickly as it came. He was getting exercise and fresh air and living life with a purpose for the first time in far too many years. It only stood to reason he felt fit as a fiddle.

"Okay, so we have to get the skinwalker in the light of the full moon, right? But we still have five days until then and we don't want to tip it off that we're looking for it. So we've got time to prepare. I say we get some decent rest and we can drive past this writer's house tomorrow and get the lay of the land. Then we go to Sierra Vista and pick up a few things we'll be needing."

She took a long drink of her iced tea. "I was thinking that, too. We're going to need something...you know...sharp."

"But not a knife. Not strong enough. Maybe an ax," he said.

Her face turned a sickly ashen color. "Yeah," she said in a hoarse, squeaky voice. "That would probably do it."

"But we need some other things, too."

"Such as?"

"Communion wafer, kid's blood—"

"Grandpa!" She pushed her chair back and began pacing, as she had in the little cabin in the woods.

He held out his hands. "What?"

"How are you going to get those things? We can't hurt some innocent little kid! And how do we know if a priest is faithless?"

Self-satisfaction buoyed his already high spirits even further. "I have a plan."

"Enlighten me!" she demanded, hands on her hips.

"Well, you don't have to get all snippy with me."

"Grandpa." The single word carried a threat that he took at face value.

"Okay, okay. So, it's like this, right? We need a communion wafer from a saint. There's a catholic church over on Safford. They have mass every Sunday morning at eight."

"How do you know that?" she asked.

"I lived here for years, remember? My boss, Fred McCurdy, went to mass every Sunday morning. Never missed a week, even when he was sick. Had to confess that he was workin' overtime with that dish of a secretary, if you know what I mean."

She sank down onto the chair across from him. "Let's say you're right and they're having communion there. What are we going to do? Snatch a wafer from some old lady's hand?"

"I reckon that's the easiest way."

She propped her elbows on the table and buried her face in her hands, leaving Richard to speak to the wild mass of curls facing him.

"I figure you can go in and make nice with one of them old ladies. They're all saints, you know. Ain't never done a thing wrong in their life 'cept maybe have an impure thought or two about the milk man. Probably did a thousand Hail Marys and donated a king's ransom to pay for it, too. They always sit in the front row. You can sit next to one and, when it's time for communion, you just follow her up to the rail, snatch the wafer the second it touches her lips, and make a run for it. She'll be too surprised and too old to chase you out of the church."

She dropped her hands to the table. "All right. Let's assume I go along with that bit of lunacy. What about the rest of it?"

"I reckon no one said anything about hurting a kid. Figure we can go up to the hospital and snatch a vial of blood."

"Sure," Burke agreed with a sigh. "That'll be a piece of cake. And the stole?"

He chuckled. "That part's easy. We'll get it at Big Nose Kate's."

"The saloon?"

"Yup."

"Do I even want to know?" she asked.

"Back in the day, the bartender there wanted to earn some extra cash, so he took some kind of six-week correspondent class to become a minister. Made everyone call him Reverend Sam, but we called him Three Cent Sam 'cause he always gave you his two cents worth and a little more. Performed marriages for the tourists. Sixty bucks a pop. Wore big fancy robes that made him look like the pope. Kept a running tally of how many brides he had."

One eyebrow arched up. "You mean how many he married?"

He leaned forward over the table. "I mean, how many he *had*. Man was a legend. Musta bedded more women than Solomon. When he died, they put his robes on a mannequin in the saloon in tribute. It's up on a balcony where nobody sits. If I can get to the steps without being seen, the rest'll be easier than taking candy from a baby. I tell you, that man didn't have a lick of faith in a thing beyond the next glass of whiskey and the pretty girl serving it."

"This is a weird town."

He cackled in joy. "Yeah. You know, I kind of miss it."

CHAPTER THIRTY-ONE

Burke

HER GRANDFATHER HAD BEEN SAWING LOGS FOR AT LEAST two hours, but Burke couldn't sleep. Her body was tired, but her restless mind simply wouldn't settle down. Finally, sometime after midnight, she stood up and padded out onto the second-floor balcony that ran along the front of the hotel.

The desert breeze was soft and fragrant. Very faintly, in the distance, she could just catch the beat of music. Apparently, the wannabe cowboys were night owls.

Her phone rang, startling her so she nearly dropped it over the railing. "So much for the mighty hunter and her nerves of steel," she whispered into the night. She looked down at the caller ID. "You've got to be kidding me."

As if it had a mind of its own, her thumb swept across the green button. She lifted the thing to her ear. "What could you possibly have to say to me?"

"Hello to you, too, Bebe."

If she gripped the phone any tighter, it would crush in her hand. "You don't get to call me that anymore. You can call the underwear model whatever you want, but you don't get to call me by your stupid pet names."

"Come on, don't be that way," her ex-husband crooned. He had a deep, masculine voice that had always made the hairs on her neck stand up in the most delicious way. "We had good times."

The bright moon, a perfect circle with one little slice taken from the side, came out from behind the clouds and painted the world silver. A coyote howled. The music in the saloon played on.

"We did. Then you left."

"Aw, Burke."

"Did you call me in the middle of the night to reminisce?"

"I miss you," he said.

She grunted. "Like Russia misses the Romanovs, no doubt."

"Really, Burke." He didn't say anything else.

She waited, not quite strong enough to hang up on him, but more than happy to enjoy making him squirm.

"I want you back."

"Well, we don't always get what we want, do we?"

He laughed a sexy, low rumble that stirred in her belly. "Okay. I get it. You're mad."

"Do you really think that?"

"Well, aren't you?"

"My God, it's been four years."

"I can't believe we lost so much time together."

She walked the length of the balcony and wandered down the steps, not giving much thought to where she was going. "We didn't lose anything. You threw our marriage away."

"I know. I'm sorry. Let me fix it."

"After all this time you think..." she trailed off. The obvious truth stopped her in her tracks. "She left you."

"It's not like that, Bebe."

It was her turn to laugh now. Sweet, genuine joy bubbled up out of her. "That's hilarious! She left you!"

"Burke." Colder now. Angry. No pet names.

"I'll tell you all about it. Let me come over. I'm catching a flight out of—"

"You can't come over."

"Come on. Just hear me out."

"Okay. Fine," she said, wandering again. A little fire pit in front of the lobby was surrounded by squashy patio chairs. She headed in that direction. "You can come over, but I'm not there."

"Where are you? You're out in the middle of the night? With who?"

She sank into one of the chairs. The cushion, still warm from the day's sun, was soft and luxuriant. The fire pit made a perfect place to prop her feet. It had taken a few moments, but her mind had finally kicked into gear and it was churning out some pretty terrific stuff.

First, came the realization that a week ago she was sitting alone in her house and she probably would have let him come. If nothing else, a visit from her ex would have alleviated the all-encompassing boredom of her days.

None of that bothered her, though, because that was a week ago. In the past seven days, she realized that she didn't need him. For as long as she could remember, she'd doubted herself, her ability to exist in the world without someone guiding her. She had her mother, a force to be reckoned with. Then she had her teachers, protecting the soft-spoken girl who was always at the top of her class. After school, she got married and, while she worked creating software in a quiet office, isolated from the world, he took care of selling her creations and investing the money.

She gave him credit. He had been honest and wise with her money. It had been so carefully managed, in fact, that when he left, she was able to lock the outside world away and spend her days jogging on her treadmill and doing a whole lot of nothing.

But then Stanley Kapcheck whisked her grandfather away from the world of safe and normal and she went chasing after them, and now she was taking care of them. She was on an adventure. She was no longer cowering from the world. She was saving the dang world and, quite frankly, she was rather enjoying it. At least, she enjoyed it during those moments she wasn't beat up, or terrified, or arguing with her grandfather about his special brand of ignorant racism.

"Burke? Are you seriously giving me the silent treatment?"

His voice pulled her out of her thoughts. She'd actually forgotten she was holding the phone to her ear.

"What?" she asked, trying to remember what they'd been talking about. "Oh. No. No, I'm not giving you the silent treatment. I was just thinking."

"I get it, Bebe. There's a lot to think about when it comes to you and me."

"No. There's not."

"But, Bebe," he was getting whiny now.

She rolled her eyes. "I told you not to call me that. I'm not your pet. I'm not your Bebe. I'm not your wife and, thank God, things didn't work out like I planned so I'm not the mother of your children. I tell you what I am, though." A weight lifted from her shoulders and dissipated into the night. "I am completely over you. I don't need you. I don't want you, and I can't think of a single reason why you should ever call me again."

"I get it," whininess turned to ice. "You met someone."

"You know what? You're right. I did. I met someone. He's funny and brave, and kind, and he taught me about the kind of person I want to be, and right now, I need to focus on my friend and what he needs."

"Your friend, eh?"

"Yes. My friend. Look up the word. Learn to be one. Maybe you'll be less of a selfish asshole after that."

"I expected more from you, Burke."

She rolled her eyes again and stood to walk back to her room. "No. You expected less. You wouldn't even know how to handle the woman I am today. I gotta go." She jogged up the steps. "It's late. Goodnight."

"Burke. I—"

She clicked off the phone before she found out what he was going to say. It didn't matter. He was the past and she was focused on the future, a future in which she was determined to do all the good she could.

Snuggled under the covers, she realized her ex-husband had done her a favor. Having talked to him, she'd settled a few lingering questions, and she could finally settle down enough to go to sleep.

She dreamed of chopping up a monster with an ax. The task was gruesome and her heart raced with healthy fear, but she was strong and confident that she had done the right thing. She was a hunter, and the world was better off because of her.

CHAPTER THIRTY-TWO

Richard

THE WRITER'S HOUSE WAS STRAIGHT OUT OF A SOUTHWESTERN design catalog—a low, sprawling adobe-and-glass structure that seemed to have sprouted up from the reddish dirt of the Dragoon Mountains. The driveway twisted between enormous clumps of prickly pear cactus and majestic mesquite trees, their tiny leaves creating a dancing kaleidoscope of sunlight inside the car. In the distance behind the house, cattle ranged on the hillside.

No dog barked at them. No person came around from the back of the house to see who had arrived. The windows showed only a reflection of the high desert landscape, no sign of movement or light. The clearing around the building was tidy, landscaped with rocks and succulents that required little care. A cord of wood was stacked to one side, an ax still stuck in a stump as though it had recently been used.

Burke turned the SUV around without hesitating, keeping up the pretense that they had simply taken a wrong turn off the beaten trail and were trying to find their way back.

Richard twisted in his seat and watched the house recede through the rear window. Oh, the freedom of being able to twist around without pain! He thought maybe he saw the twitch of a curtain behind that inscrutable glass, but it was impossible to tell at such a distance. It could just as easily have been a trick of the light.

CHAPTER THIRTY-THREE

Finn

PHLEGM WAS BUILDING UP IN HIS CHEST, STRANGLING HIM, suffocating him. It hurt to breathe. Every few minutes, little involuntary chuffs burst out of him, hardly enough to dislodge the mess within him. He longed for a good, hard coughing fit, but it seemed he couldn't muster enough energy for that.

He rolled onto his side, huffed and wheezed for a moment at the effort, then settled once more into the soft mattress. "Sara?" he asked. His voice trembled like an old man's.

"I'm here, Finn." She came into view with a pretty smile on her face. Apparently, whatever ailed him wasn't contagious. She looked bright and fresh as a spring daisy. She offered him a glass of water with a bendy straw and he sipped, more out of instinct than desire. "I was just taking a peek out the window. I thought I heard something, but it must have just been some tourists that took a wrong turn. They left right away."

As a young man, he watched his mother waste away and die in the care of doctors. She'd felt a little off. They ran tests that left her exhausted and frightened, gave her a diagnosis that scared her so much she couldn't speak of it without having tears spring to her eyes, and then they treated her with poison that made her vomit and faint. Her hair fell out. Lesions opened on her skin. Then after all that, she died anyway. She died in the hands of doctors.

In all the years since then, he'd avoided the doctor at all costs. Illness rarely affected him and, on the rare occasions it did, he quipped to concerned friends that he'd visit the doctor when he was at death's door.

It was hard to face the truth, but it was harder to continue drifting off to sleep wondering if he would wake again.

Pushing the words out of his mouth was a powerful act of will. "I need to go to the hospital."

Sara set the glass on the table and brushed his hair away from his forehead. "You're so strong, Finn. Much stronger than you give yourself credit for."

"I'm sick, Sara."

"Shhh. None of that kind of talk. You know what I've been wondering? I want to know about the woman who taught you how to make love. She must have been—"

Like lightning striking, his wish was suddenly granted and he was sent into a wild spasm of hacking coughs that ripped through his body.

Sara held the trash can for him to spit into.

He fell back against the bed again. Better. He could breathe now. "Sara, I don't know what's wrong with me, but I'm sick."

"No doctors, Finn," she insisted. "I'll take care of you. I won't leave your side until this is all over. I promise."

She twined her fingers through his. He gazed at their clasped hands, hers young and flawless, his covered in brown age spots that hadn't been there two weeks ago.

"Are you killing me?" he asked. He'd thought of the possibility a few days earlier, but he'd lacked the courage to ask.

Now, whatever was wrong had reached a point where such fears seemed trite by comparison.

"Oh, Finn. I want you to live. I want you to be bursting with life. I love your vitality. You have no idea how much it turns me on."

She's talking about being turned on? She just held a can for me to cough up into.

"Help me up, will you?"

"You're feeling better then?"

"Sure. If you say so. I can't stand the smell of myself. I want to take a shower." He'd just had a bath the night before. Or was it two nights before? Was it even night? What day was it now? Everything was a blur. It didn't matter when it had been. He stank, and he wanted to wash.

She pulled the covers back and held his arms, lifting him to his feet with startling strength. In the bathroom, she started to tug his shirt over his head.

"I can do it," he said, backing away.

"But it's more fun if I do it. I wouldn't mind getting in the shower with you," she said, rubbing one hand between his legs.

Good God, woman. I'm dying! He couldn't say that out loud, though. He simply said, "I can't."

"Oh, but you can," she purred, sinking to her knees.

He could, and he would. He wasn't that sick. He was just exhausted and being overly dramatic. If he was at death's door, he wouldn't be moaning in pleasure. And panting. Panting meant he could breathe.

If he turned just a little, he'd be able to see her in the mirror.

The thought added an interesting flavor to the sensations in his body.

He shifted, but he was careful to keep his eyes on the beautiful young girl in the mirror. The old man with streaks of white hair freaked him out.

CHAPTER THIRTY-FOUR

Richard

THE OLD LADY AT THE HOSPITAL INFORMATION DESK GAVE the impression that she had come there for treatment and, feeling better than usual that day, had decided to come downstairs and socialize a bit. Her steely gray hair was an impenetrable helmet of lacquered curls. She stared at Richard and Burke with watery blue eyes that peered into their souls from behind drooping lids. A permanent frown-crease marked the spot exactly halfway between her thin, spidery brows.

"My father needs to have blood drawn," Burke told her. "Could you point us toward the lab?"

"Follow the blue line on the floor, dear. That will take you to the laboratory seating area. Be sure to register with the ladies there." She lifted her chin a fraction. "You do have paperwork, right?"

"Oh, yeah. Of course." Burke nodded. "Thanks for your help."

They followed the rainbow of colored lines on the floor

around the corner and past an intersecting hallway where the orange and black lines branched off in separate directions.

Richard shivered. "Old biddy reminds me of my fourth-grade teacher. The woman had supernatural sight, I tell you. Put a frog in Susan Morgan's desk one time. Swear that lady was in another room, talking to another teacher, when I did it. Walked in and beat me with a ruler."

Burke laughed. "What did Susan Morgan ever do to you?"

"Didn't do nothin'." Richard shrugged. "Thought I was in love. Just trying to get her to notice me."

She lifted one hand to her heart in mock outrage. "Grandpa! I thought you only ever loved Grandma."

"Your grandma was Susan Morgan's best friend. How do you think I met her? Finally got old Suzie to go out with me for a soda after school."

"The frog worked?" she asked.

"'Course not. That was in fourth grade. I weren't takin' no girls for soda in the fourth grade. Wasn't till years later. Said she'd go, but only if her friend could come and I had to pay for 'em both."

The blue line turned left at the end of the hall, branching away from red and yellow. Two doctors in green scrubs rushed past, paying no attention to them. Burke had fussed about hospital security, but Richard had lived in a medical facility. He was all too aware of the cold truth: It wouldn't be hard for an old man to go unseen in a place like this.

"So, you went on a date with two girls?" she asked.

The memory was enough to make life worth living. How had he come to a place where he'd only thought of the bad things? There were so many good moments to recall. "That I did," he said. "But I only paid attention to one of 'em, and it weren't the one I invited."

"I love the way you loved her, Grandpa. I wish everyone could have that."

"Hmpf." He waved away her words. "Because I was smitten? People are smitten all the time. It's easy to lose your mind over a pretty young girl with legs that go all the way up to her backside. Harder to stay with her when she insists on decorating every room in the house with pink flowers or serving runny mashed potatoes with every meal, or when she gets sick and..." the words stuck in his throat and refused to go any further.

He grunted again. "Love is all well and good, but *commitment* is what's missing from the world today. Look at that fool you married. Loved you just fine. Loved the next thing that came along, too." Oh, it was so much easier to talk about her pain than his, but he wasn't so blind that he missed the stricken expression that flitted across her face. "Man was a fool," he said again. "Had a good thing and not enough sense to hold on to it."

"He called me, Grandpa. Last night. His new wife left him. He says he wants me back."

"You said?"

"I said, after all this time, I finally figured out how to be my own person and I didn't need him to come along and try to undo that."

He nodded his satisfaction. She was as smart and strong as he'd come to believe she was. "You can do better." Hearing the words stirred a memory of saying the same thing to his daughter. Shame blossomed in his heart. He had a lot to make up for.

The sliding doors to the laboratory waiting room hissed open. They stepped through and found two seats a row away from the patients flipping through old magazines or staring at their phones. A white-haired lady in a wheelchair was pushed past them and through the door that apparently led to the rooms where the lab technicians worked.

"Grandpa?" Burke's eyes fixed on the silent figures talking about world politics on the muted television set mounted to the wall.

"Yeah, kid?"

"Thanks for calling him a fool."

Richard knew all too well that Burke's mother had blamed Burke for the breakup of her marriage. She felt that her daughter had pushed her husband away with her independent spirit, that she should have tried harder to please him and make him feel important, that she should have tried to win him back after he left. She'd ranted on about it at every visit for the better part of a year. Not that there were more than a handful of visits in a year, but still.

"Ain't no need to thank me. Just callin' 'em like I see 'em."

A man in a white, short-sleeved uniform shirt that showed off biceps the size of an average person's thighs stepped into the room. "Gerald?"

A man with arms like toothpicks sticking out of his plaid, button-down shirt stood and followed him back into the hall-way. Richard couldn't help but think they looked like cartoon characters walking side-by-side.

"I don't have a crush on Stanley. You know that, right?"

Her words startled him back to the present. "That's what you keep telling me."

"Grandpa, really. I'm not in love with him. He's old enough to be my grandfather." She paused. "Good Lord, he's old enough to be your grandfather."

He didn't believe her for a second. It was good she had kicked her worthless ex to the curb, but surely, at least a small part of that fortitude came from her feelings for Stanley.

"If you say so."

She laughed. "You're really convinced I am."

"Not my place to judge." He still judged. It was hard to break a life-long habit, but at least he'd learned enough in his recent adventures to keep his mouth shut in regard to his judgments.

A sour-looking lady with a bun so tight it pulled her eyes back unnaturally came into the room and called for Joseph. The chosen patient trotted into the hallway behind her.

"Why are you so convinced I have feelings for him?"

"You seem awfully concerned, is all." Not to mention, Stanley had never met a woman who wouldn't let him leave a few cracker crumbs on her sheets. It was unnatural.

"You're concerned about him, too," she pointed out. "Are you in love with him?"

He scowled at her. "That's not funny. He's my..." How to finish that sentence? Stan friggin' Kapcheck was *not* his friend. He couldn't stand the man. Stan was every smug, arrogant son-of-a-gun Richard had ever despised all rolled into one. Not his enemy, though. That was certain. Stan had helped him, and taught him, and earned his respect. There was no denying he was worried. Stan deserved better than being dragged into Hell by The Devil.

The man with the Incredible Hulk arms returned. His voice boomed in the quiet room. "Zachary?"

"Come on, honey." A young woman with dark circles under her eyes and wisps of hair falling from her ponytail lifted a little boy from his seat. The child's eyes were red-rimmed and teary. "No more pokes, Mommy."

"Just a little one, Zackie. They're going to check your blood one more time."

They both followed the boy's progress into the hall. Little Zachary disappeared around the corner and the two of them sat very still, waiting. Magazine pages rustled. Someone coughed. Behind the frosted glass window, a phone rang. In the hall, the child began to cry.

"Now?" Burke asked.

Richard stood, nudged her. "Help me find a john, will ya?" he said loudly for the benefit of those around them.

No one paid any attention. They had their own problems.

"Oh, sure. There's probably one back there. Come on, then." She jumped to her feet and held out her arm. As he had after his hip surgery, he wrapped his arm around hers and leaned hard in her direction. Holding on to her and moving with slow, shuffling steps, he let her help him through the door and into the hallway.

This is how I walked the day I left Everest, he thought. Had he really been such a feeble old man? How had he come back from such a state? Surely, Nathaniel's homemade medicine wasn't responsible for all of this. Did his adventure with Stanley have a greater magic than he realized, or was fresh air and exercise really enough to restore a man's vitality?

They inched past a woman sitting at a desk in the hall, talking on the phone. A young man pushed a gurney toward them. The young woman in the patient room hushed her son. "It's okay, Zackie. Almost done. One more little vial and he can take the needle out. We'll go for ice cream, okay?"

"Excuse me. Can I help you?" came a voice from behind them.

Their pace quickened.

"Are you looking for something?" the woman called.

"Just headed out for some fresh air," Burke shot over her shoulder, gesturing vaguely toward an exit sign at the end of the hall. "Fall," she whispered to Richard.

Richard's fall was spectacular. He hit the floor hard enough to knock an involuntary grunt out of himself and sent a metal tray of instruments crashing against the wall in the process.

"Grandpa!" Burke yelled. "Oh my gosh!"

The woman who'd been calling to them rushed toward him. "Sir! Are you hurt?"

"My hip," he groaned, cringing at the memory of having a real accidental fall and shattering his brittle hip.

The woman dropped to her knees next to him. "I need some help, Logan!"

The man with the biceps emerged from the nearest room and squatted down next to her. "Just be still, sir," he said.

The lady who had been on the phone came jogging in their direction.

From the corner of his eye, he saw Burke take a step backward, making way for them to assist him. "Help him! Please help him!" she said, her voice shaky and panicked. She disappeared from his line of sight.

The big man rolled Richard onto his back. Embracing his role in their little production, he moaned loudly.

"It's okay, sir. We're going to help you. What's your name?"

Burke reappeared and stood over him, a triumphant gleam in her eye.

He pushed to his feet and gave a little bounce on his toes. "Wow! That was a close one. I really thought I was hurt there for a second."

"You're okay, Grandpa?" she asked.

The three medical workers stared at him with their mouths hanging open. "Yeah. Yup. Yes. Thanks, all. Sorry for the fuss. It's not really so bad, after all. I'm fine. Thank you for your help."

Burke grabbed his arm and they took off toward the green glowing exit sign as fast as they could without breaking into a run. They rushed along the blue line, past the fourth-grade-teacher-doppelganger and burst into the brilliant Arizona sunlight.

In the car, Burke looked at him with wide eyes. "Are you laughing?" she asked incredulously.

"Yes!" he wheezed.

She rolled her eyes and shook her head, but by the time she had backed out of the parking space, she was laughing, too.

The last week had held more laughter than the last ten years put together. If he was about to die at the hands of The Devil or her minion, at least he was going out on a high note.

THEY MADE A QUICK STOP AT THE SIERRA VISTA WALMART for an axe and a photo print of the selfie Burke took of the two of them, then they headed back down the snaking path of Charleston Road toward Tombstone. The sun was dipping low on the western horizon. The progress they'd made seemed a small dent in the mountain of Things To Do, but there was no denying the day was slipping away. Days had a way of doing that. Days. Years. Decades.

It didn't used to be that way. He used to be immortal.

Back then, there'd been a starry night when Richard had been so overcome by lust, he'd pulled his car off to the shoulder of this road and made love to his wife right there in the front seat. Well, if you could call it making love. At the discovery that she'd waited for him all day with no panties, he could barely contain himself. It wasn't five minutes after they stopped that they were driving again.

In those days, he'd taken it for granted that they'd live forever. They were so young and full of life, how could they not? Someday they'd probably grow old, but that day was so very far away as to be incomprehensible.

And then she died.

They both turned to stare at the writer's house as they drove past. It was nothing more than a dark smudge against the hillside.

"I'm going to kill that monster," he said.

Burke nodded. "What if it's not him? What if we're wrong? Our evidence is thin, for sure."

Richard had entertained the same thought a dozen times,

but he'd always dismissed it with the same logic. "I don't think we're wrong. It feels right." It was a pathetic argument, but he was certain.

"I think so, too. I want it to die. I want to kill it. I'm afraid of how much I want to."

CHAPTER THIRTY-FIVE

Finn

SARA'S STRONG, SURE HANDS WORKED THE EUCALYPTUS-scented soap into a thick lather in his hair. Her nails scratched his scalp, gently massaging. She washed behind his ears, his neck, and down the entire length of his body with tender care while he leaned against the wall, vacillating between terror and affection.

"Why are you here?" he asked as she pushed the suds in between his toes.

She grinned up at him. "Finn, don't you know how much I enjoy your company? You make me feel alive."

Oh, the irony. Hadn't he wondered how close to death he was just an hour ago?

She stretched to her tiptoes, but couldn't quite reach the showerhead. He grinned.

"It's not funny, Finn." She scowled, with her hands on her hips. The effect was lost, due in large part to the fact that she was naked and wet.

He reached up, took the showerhead down, and handed it to her. "Don't say I never helped you."

"Baby, I promise you, I will never, ever say that." She planted a kiss over his heart.

With the same thoroughness with which she had washed him, she rinsed each individual part. Stepping out of the shower, she snagged a towel from the shelf and wrapped it around his damp shoulders.

"How do you feel?" she asked.

"Better," he said, which was true. Mostly. His bones still hurt. He was fairly certain that if he lay down and covered up, he'd fall asleep again, but he was on his feet and breathing well. "I even have an appetite."

She beamed at him. "Fantastic. Let's go out."

"Okay," he agreed.

The shower had been restorative. Well, the shower and what they'd done before the shower. Maybe some fresh air would help bring him the rest of the way back to himself.

"Still fussed about food poisoning, or can we go to Murphy's."

"Why do you like it there?" he asked.

"They have the best burgers in the state of Arizona, the most level pool table, and the cheapest juke box." She turned toward the bedroom, where she gathered clothes from the bottom dresser drawer.

What the hell? Did she move in while I was sleeping?

He watched the sway of her little round backside as she bent and stepped into a pair of black lace panties. Lord, but he was a mess. Inside and out.

"Plus," she added, "there's a great energy there. It's alive. I mean...really alive. Like...manic...you know?"

"Yeah. All the people in there are on meth. That's what it does to you," he said.

She snapped her jeans and looked at him with her head tipped to one side. "Come on, Finn. Please?"

"Yeah. Okay. Murphy's it is. But if I relapse, it's all on you."

She laughed harder than his comment warranted. "It's a deal. I accept full responsibility."

He brushed his hair and teeth, trying hard not to spend too much time considering the disturbing reflection in the mirror. Moving at a snail's pace, he managed to get dressed, and finally they reached the car. He drove toward Tombstone. The road had a soft, blurred appearance. Was he going blind on top of everything else? If he wasn't totally better by Monday, he was definitely calling the doctor. As much as he hated doctors, it was going to be damned hard to write if he went blind.

They parked on Toughnut Street and walked along the boardwalk toward the restaurant. Fatigue was creeping up on him again and he thought he'd rather lay down and rest than eat dinner.

Sara laced her fingers through his. "Once you eat, you'll feel more energetic," she said as though reading his thoughts.

"Yeah. I'm sure you're right." He hoped she was right. It was a chore to put one foot in front of the other. He desperately wanted to feel more energetic.

CHAPTER THIRTY-SIX

Richard

ON SATURDAY, THEY WOULD STOP BY THE EMPORIUM, a tourist shop with every sort of Old West bric-a-brac, to get a box made of bone, hoping that cow bone would be sufficient to lure The Devil. After that, they could pop over to Boot Hill Cemetery where they would fill a Ziploc baggie with graveyard dirt. Everything was falling into place.

"Maybe trapping The Devil won't really be so hard. We almost have everything we need already," Richard said.

"Why, Grandpa! If I didn't know better, I'd say you're getting downright optimistic in your old age."

"Hmph. Ain't so old. Look at this." He tapped out an enthusiastic jig on the boardwalk. The freedom of movement left him cackling with glee. "Come on, kid. I'll buy you a burger at Murphy's."

He led the way to a narrow establishment with little signage. With the flashy Crystal Palace across the street, historic Big Nose Kate's to the right, and The Longhorn on the left, which advertised a free seventy-two-ounce steak to anyone who could finish it, Murphy's was clearly a local haunt. The tourists probably didn't even notice it was there. It wouldn't have been difficult to convince someone that the rickety old screen door that opened with a rusty shriek was part of the original hundred-and-fifty-year-old building.

"Careful there. Looks like just one step down to get into the restaurant but it's actually two," he said.

Burke peered at the single little step. "Are you sure?"

"Yup. One step down, physically, when you go in and one step down in social status." He cackled again, his laughter ending in a wheezing fit of coughing that did nothing to rob him of his joy. He was an inchworm away from having everything he needed to catch that saucy trollop who had tricked him. He was going to unleash the fury of Hell on the beast that stole his wife away before her time, he'd had a bowel movement for the past three mornings in a row, and he was about to enjoy one of the best burgers this side of the Mississippi.

Burke perched on the edge of a stool in front of a long bar made of scarred pine and coated with a thick patina of ancient grease. She folded her hands primly in her lap. She appeared to be trying very hard not to pass judgement or touch anything. "You look happy," she said.

"I am," he answered, astonished to realize it was the truth. He plopped down on the stool next to Burke. For the first time in forty-two years, he was really and truly happy. He flicked a cockroach off the counter. "Don't worry," he said in response to her little squeal of disgust. "No one ever gets sick here. There's so much alcohol in the air, the germs can't survive."

"If only the same were true of the bugs," she muttered.

"They don't eat much," he said, and leaned over the bar to order two burgers with the works, fries, onion rings, and two beers.

"That it?" the girl at the grill asked.

"Also, an order of fried cheese." She nodded, and he sat back on his stool. "For Stan," he told Burke.

There's no way she could have understand the reference, but she didn't comment. She seemed too busy scanning the shadowy corners for grime.

"How can it be this dark in here when it's still daylight outside and the whole front wall is a window?" Burke asked.

"Part of the charm," he told her.

The girl set two bottles on the counter. "Wanna glass?"

"Drink it from the bottle," Richard advised. "It's probably cleaner."

Burke declined the offered glass, opting instead to scrutinize the lip of the bottle as though she might be able to note any germs lurking on the dark glass.

Richard swallowed deeply, and, in that instant, he was thirty years old. He and Barbara used to come to this little hole-in-the-wall at the beginning of a night on the town. In those days, they'd lived on love and wishes, and they could get two burgers and enough beer to wash them down for five bucks. Then they'd scamper across the street and dance the night away in the Crystal Palace, sharing a single glass of Coke. By the time they got home, they were exhausted and dehydrated and ready to eat again. They'd make love in the small, squeaky bed they shared and snack on peanut butter and chocolate chips.

Two red plastic baskets full of burgers and fries were unceremoniously dropped in front of them, followed by two more with onion rings and a little paper box of cheese sticks.

"Oh, my God," Burke said.

"Amen," agreed Richard, assuming that she was overwhelmed by the beauty of this bacchanalia of crunchy grease and meat. "Looks amazing, right?"

Behind them, one of the cowboys by the pool table fed a dollar bill into the jukebox and stunned Richard by selecting one of his favorite Johnny Cash songs. Life was good. Great.

Fantastic! What a shame he'd wasted so many years believing otherwise.

He took a bite of his burger and moaned in pleasure. "So good," he mumbled, aware of how rude he was being by talking with his mouth full, but too enraptured in the moment to care. "Try it."

Burke held her sandwich like she was afraid it might bite back and took a single dainty nibble from one edge. Her eyebrows shot up in surprise.

"Good, right?"

"It really is," she said before taking another, more reasonable bite.

The squeak of the door rose above the deep voice singing about a ring of fire and they both instinctively turned. The man seemed vaguely familiar. He looked like he'd rather be at home in bed than just about anywhere. Dark circles under his eyes took on the cast of bruises in the dim light of the bar. His clothes were rumpled and hung on him as though he'd recently lost a good deal of weight. The girl holding his hand looked young enough to be his daughter, but he'd have bet dollars to donuts she wasn't. Her jeans clung to her legs. A diamond sparkled in the navel exposed by her bright red, short-cropped t-shirt.

A spider of fear crawled up his spine. The sensation was not lost on him. He'd experienced it before, in the presence of The Devil. There was something more to what he was seeing than he realized. He watched the couple in the mirror behind the bar. The man with his slumped shoulders and five o'clock shadow. The girl oozing sex and power. No wonder he was worn out.

Burke's little gasp drew his attention. In the mirror, her eyes were wide. Her mouth formed a perfect little "o."

"Ghost walk over your grave?" he asked, and immediately regretted his choice of words. Such a thing was entirely too possible in this new world they were uncovering. He shivered a second time.

Something was wrong, but what?

Two guys were playing pool and smoking. The couple was ordering food from the kid with the nose ring. The smell of frying onions filled the air.

Burke whispered.

"What?" he asked. The clamor of the music, sizzling meat on the griddle, pool balls clacking together, and drunken voices sent a wave of feedback through his hearing aid. He fiddled with the volume, knowing from experience no amount of fiddling could truly fix those old ears.

She whispered again.

"Speak up!" he insisted. "Can't hear a word you're saying."

Her eyes flitted to the couple and back to him. She fished in her purse, came up with a pen, and snatched a little square cocktail napkin from the stack on the table. When she finished writing, she rotated the napkin and slid it toward him.

←O'Doyle

His heart stuttered in his chest. If the haggard man was O'Doyle, that meant the girl was the thing that was feeding on him. If Burke was right, they'd guessed well. O'Doyle looked forty years older than his picture—closer to Richard's age than Burke's.

He turned from Burke toward the couple.

The girl flashed a smile at him, warm enough to win a Miss Congeniality ribbon.

She's no girl. She's the monster who murdered my Barbara. His hands began to shake. His heart hammered out a chaotic rhythm of rage.

Her smile faltered. A little line forming between perfectly plucked brows. She cocked her head as though wondering what had come over the poor old man who was suddenly red faced and trembling.

When they started past on their way to the single little table near the back of the bar area, she pulled O'Doyle to a stop in front of Richard.

"Have we met?" she asked him.

He swallowed hard. Words would not come. He would see this thing dead and burned and scattered to the four winds. "You," he managed to whisper. "You—"

"I'm sorry, my grandfather gets a little confused sometimes," Burke said. Her strong hand pressed down on his shoulder. He was not to rise from his seat.

"I gotta sit," O'Doyle said, let go of the girl's hand, went to the table, and slumped into the black plastic chair.

"Enjoy your meal," the girl/monster beamed.

Burke pressed his back. "Time to go, Grandpa," she said, but he didn't budge. Now was their chance. He could take her out right here.

"Grandpa, time to go. *It's almost dark.*" Her words carried a strange emphasis that caused him to look outside.

The creature had to be killed by the light of the full moon. It wasn't even dark yet, and when night came, it would bring a moon still four days from full.

Her hand still pressed his back. She guided him up and out of the restaurant toward the blinding light of sunset. In the distance, gunfire roared. It was time for the dinnertime old-west show at Six Gun City—the dinner show on the other end of the boardwalk. A carriage clattered by, churning little whirlwinds of dust into the air. Families riding, laughed and waved at the cowboys smoking cigarettes on the corners. Life swirled around them in a nonsensical blur of color and sound.

Burke was talking, pulling on his hand.

"We have to kill it," he said.

She prattled on about hotel rooms and the importance of anonymity.

"We have to kill that little girl," he said.

A woman walking by gave him a wary glance and stepped a little faster.

Burke's strong hands descended upon his shoulders. She gave him a single, solid shake. "Listen to me. We need to get out of here. There is nothing we can do against that creature right now. Nothing. Do you hear me? It can kill us, and we can't give it so much as a paper cut. If you want to do what we came here to do, we need to get out of here right now before that thing suspects we are something other than ordinary humans out for a bite of dinner."

He stared into her brown eyes and let the strength of her spirit ground him. "It recognized me." He hadn't meant to whisper, but it seemed that's all he had in him.

Her mouth pressed into a thin line, turned down at the corners. "I know, but we shouldn't panic. It has no reason to suspect that you know what it is. We have to go, Grandpa. We have to *stick to the plan*."

"Yeah, the plan," he whispered. "Right." He turned and went past the big window of the bar, resolutely keeping his eyes forward. The monster's preternatural gaze marked his progress through the glass, or, at least, he imagined it to be so.

Burke jogged to keep up, and when he took a sharp left turn, she kept going for several steps before realizing he'd slipped through the swinging doors into Big Nose Kate's Saloon.

The nighttime crowd hadn't arrived yet, but the dinner group was trickling in. On the stage, a young Asian man in a black AC/DC shirt and ripped jeans unpacked an elaborate Karaoke setup.

The stairs to the balcony were beyond the restrooms, just past the kitchen door. He jogged upward into the darkness, taking the steps two at a time, slowing only as he reached the arched opening where he could be seen by the diners and staff below. Stooping low, he reached forward and grasped the tasseled end of the long stole and tugged. The mannequin wobbled.

For a moment, he was certain the thing would topple, falling over the wrought iron railing and spinning end-over-end to the hardwood floor below. Imaginary screams filled the air when bits of plastic and wood exploded from the broken body, but then the mannequin stilled and a second, gentler tug brought the purple silk sliding down the back of the imitation Three Cent Sam just as Burke tiptoed up to the top step.

With one hand, he shooed her back down, following close on her heels as he wrapped the fabric into a tight ball and stuffed it inside his shirt, under one arm.

Burke stopped in the little hall at the bottom of the stairs and turned toward him. "Grandpa, I know you're upset but—"

"I'm not upset," he said.

Her eyes were wide and panicky. "We have to stick to the plan."

"That's what I'm doing. This is the plan, remember?"

A tiny woman with enormous breasts held unnaturally high by a black-and-red corset pushed through the door and past them, a black tray full of food balanced on her shoulder. "Men's room's on the other side," she said without breaking stride.

"We're going to draw suspicion just standing here. We should go," he said.

For the first time since Stanley first interrupted the evening news, Richard could see the path ahead of them with crystal clarity and he was certain he had it within him to do what needed to be done. Elation was gone, but strength and vitality coursed through his veins. He understood now what had made Stanley seem so strange, what had attracted women to him.

Stick to the plan.

Ha!

Just try and stop him.

He brushed past Burke, not wasting any more time

addressing her silly concerns. Worry was as useful as a spider's fart in a rainforest. Action was what was needed. He allowed the music and noise of the increasingly busy saloon to push him back out onto the boardwalk. A brother and sister in coonskin caps raced by shooting cap guns in the air. The *snap, snap, snap* of the toy weapons whipped painfully across his ears. He scooted close to the wall to let them pass. When he looked up, he met Barbara's beautiful eyes.

She stood on the boardwalk, leaning casually against a wooden pillar. Her hands remained tucked into the pockets of her denim pedal pushers and the diamond in her navel sparkled. Her red t-shirt was so short it barely covered her breasts. The fabric strained across her chest. Moonlight shone on her thick, soft curls. "Thought I recognized you. Have you missed me, Richie?"

Steel bands clamped around his heart and squeezed. The earth tilted beneath his feet.

"Why, Richie, you look like you've seen a ghost." She sashayed toward him and pressed her palms against his chest. Her warm, solid flesh seared him. Spots of light flashed in his oxygen-deprived mind and his body gave a sudden, involuntary gasp so fierce it made his lungs hurt.

Barbara stuck out her lip. "You don't look happy, Richie. I thought you'd be pleased to see me after all this time." She stepped closer, crushing her breasts against his chest, pressing her hips to his. Her pout slid into a knowing grin. "Oh! You are happy to see me. You've still got it after all this time, eh? Color me impressed." She wrinkled her perfect nose. "You stink though, Richie. You've got the reek of hunter on you."

His mind screamed in protest against the assault of this monstrosity that pretended to be his beautiful wife, but his body remembered her soft, strong flesh and every cell responded to the memory. Tears blurred his view of her angelic face. Surely nothing evil could lurk behind those innocent eyes.

"Get away from him!" Burke was there, yanking Barbara's shoulder, trying to wedge herself between them.

Barbara's hand, a flash in the night, grabbed hold of Burke's throat. "Who invited you?" she hissed, slamming Burke against the wall.

A door banged open.

Richard winced and blinked. When he opened his eyes once more, Barbara had vanished.

Burke sagged against the wall.

"Sara?" Finn O'Doyle stood thirty feet away. He turned toward Richard. "Have you seen a woman? Short? Black hair? Looks like a twelve-year-old?"

Did he shake his head no? Was he still standing? How could he still be alive?

"Sara?" O'Doyle called once more and then slumped away around the corner of the boardwalk.

A group of tourists spilled out of The Longhorn and surged in a tangled, staggering, laughing mass of noise across the street to The Crystal Palace. As though cued by the group's entrance, the band started up and music filled the evening.

Burke gasped, a harsh, wet, ragged sound that acted like a slap across the face, waking him from the time-warp nightmare he'd stumbled into.

He reached for her and withdrew; considered putting an arm around her; hesitated; settled for, "Okay?"

With one hand over her throat and tears in her eyes, she nodded. "Let's get out of here," her whisper was sandpaper dragged across fine satin.

"Yeah. Come on." He put an arm around her then and, leaning on one another in a way not so different from the drunken tourists who'd just passed, they made their way back to the car and up the hill to the hotel where they turned on every light, drew the curtains closed, engaged all three locks on the door, and hid from the monsters that lurked in the night.

Lying on the bed with his back to his granddaughter, Richard let the tears spill. When she sat next to him, causing the old bed to creak and sag, he confessed, "I had a moment when I was sure I'd give my soul to hold her again."

"What stopped you?" she asked.

He rolled onto his back so he could see her. What difference did it make if she saw his swollen eyes and red nose? Was it so shameful for a man to cry? "You stopped me. I'd give my soul to be with her, but I couldn't give yours."

She looked away but didn't leave. After a little while, she curled up next to him and he held her just the way he'd held her mother when she was a little girl. Together, they slept, each chasing away the nightmares of the other.

SATURDAY, THEY REMAINED HIDDEN, COOPED UP IN THE TINY hotel room, picking and fussing at each other all day. The only time they'd gone out was to get the box made of bone and the bag of graveyard dirt. In those moments, they'd been quiet and jumpy. Back in the hotel, they found reasons to bicker. It was better to argue than to sit in silence. Silence left too much space for thinking.

Richard wanted to go into Sunday mass with Burke.

"Seriously, if I'm going to do this, I need to know that you're outside with the engine running," Burke said. "I can't rob an old lady of her chance to partake of the Body of Christ and then get stuck with no escape."

"I'll come out and start the car the second communion starts."

She sighed. "Why do you want to come in so bad?"

"I ain't never needed to pray the way I need to pray right now."

"Fine," she relented. "But you sit right next to the door and you scoot at the beginning of the hymn before communion."

He agreed to her terms, and on Sunday morning they entered the tiny sanctuary where three old women and a single man sat waiting for mass to begin. Richard slipped into the very back pew and watched Burke head toward the woman nearest the pulpit. She murmured a few words that he couldn't quite make out and the woman nodded and slid over to make room.

A handful of parishioners trickled in.

He hadn't entered a church since Barbara's funeral. That day, he'd sat in the front pew and stared at the closed lid of the cherrywood coffin and hardened his heart against God. Any being who could create and then put their creation through unspeakable pain didn't deserve his worship. He'd always been agnostic at best. Sitting through his wife's funeral, he believed in God with all his heart, and his belief seethed with festering black hatred. For more than forty years, he'd let that loathing infect every part of his life.

"I'm sorry," he whispered to the figure hanging on the cross in the front. "I was a fool."

It felt good to admit it. Well, not good maybe, but healthy. It was true, apparently, that confession was good for the soul. Is that why these people came here so faithfully, week after week? Did they understand something the rest of the world had forgotten in all its silly busyness?

The worshippers listened in silence as the priest began the service.

Old people. Not a kid in the place. They were strangers, their faces unknown to him.

Faces that could be masks.

They could be exactly who they appeared to be, or they could be the monster stalking him, waiting for the perfect moment to strike. He'd known that before, but the true magnitude of that truth only now struck him. Cold horror raced through his veins, pushed forward by the frantic beating of his heart.

He couldn't trust *anyone*.

The monster could be a pretty little sprite of a girl, his own sweet Barbara, an old lady in church. It *could be* Burke.

Burke peeked over her shoulder at him.

Madness waited at the end of the tracks this train of thought ran on. He had to trust someone. He had to trust Burke.

Didn't he?

It was the kid. Out of nowhere, the thought slammed into him with all the force of a Mack Truck. She'd taken that kid in like he was her own. Fed him after school. Poured over his schoolbooks with him. Let him sleep in their home when he told her his mom had left him all alone. The kid had been at the hospital every day and then, when she was gone, so was the kid.

All this time, he'd assumed the boy disappeared after she died because he couldn't handle the grief. Richard had made no attempt to find him. He'd had enough on his hands with his own child, who'd cried all night, every night, and couldn't yet do even the simplest of tasks for herself.

He glanced around the room again. Grey-haired worshippers. Burke. The priest.

It could be anybody.

Silent as a shadow, he slipped out of the sanctuary and climbed into the driver's seat of the SUV. With the doors locked and the sun baking him through the closed windows, he sat shivering and prayed, "Dear God, help me defeat this evil. Give me eyes to see and the strength to fight. Once it's dead, you can do whatever you want with me, but for just another day or two, help me fight this evil."

Ten minutes later, Burke came racing toward the car and launched herself into the passenger seat. He peeled out of the parking place, sending a plume of dust and gravel into the air.

The car wove a little toward center. He over corrected, hit the shoulder, and pulled it back into the lane. It had been a long time since he'd driven. Had the steering in older cars been so sensitive? Didn't seem likely.

He drove as far as the Circle K at the edge of town and pulled into the wide lot.

Burke held out her trembling hand and showed him the little wafer.

"I guess it's time to call The Devil," he said.

She swallowed hard. "Maybe we should wait until after we take care of the monster."

Richard thought of the wide-eyed kid sitting at his wife's side and suppressed a shiver. "No. We can't do that today, right? But we can do this. We can get Stan back and we'll be three on one. We're gonna kill that thing deader than a lobster in butter sauce, but first we do this."

"Okay." She slipped the wafer into the ash tray. "But first, I need a soda and then you need to let me drive. Good Lord, Grandpa. I thought you said driving was like riding a bike."

"You ain't dead or crashed, are you?"

She gave him a sidelong look and climbed out without saying anything else.

"Smart aleck kid," he mumbled, then opened his door. His feet hit the ground harder than he expected and the jolt shot through his hip. The pain rattled his already shaky nerves.

"Okay?" Burke asked. She'd stopped at his grunt.

"Fine as frog's hair," he answered.

She rolled her eyes and kept walking. He followed, trying very hard not to shuffle his feet.

BURKE POINTED THE CAR TOWARD SHEEP'S HEAD MOUNTAIN and drove until they came to a crossroads so disused that a tenacious little cholla cactus had decided to try making its home in the middle of the lane. Burke edged the SUV to the side of the road.

"Grandpa, I'm just really not sure that—"

"We should do this," he said.

His nerves were shot. His hip still ached—worse now, after an hour of being bounced around like fart in a mitten on these shoddy mountain roads. There was a terrible ringing in his ears. His stomach was a misery. He craved a glass of ice-cold prune juice. Sitting on his hands since their encounter with the monster on Friday was making him crazy. He needed to take action. Any action. Even wrong action was better than more waiting.

"If you don't want a part of it, I won't hold it against you." A rush of oven-hot air pushed into the car when he opened the door. "I gotta do this."

She didn't agree or disagree, but in a moment, she stood beside him at the center of the crossroads, holding the long, wooden handle of a pickaxe and a box of Morton Salt.

Richard had assembled the little summoning kit as they drove. The photograph of the two of them was laid in the bottom of the box. The stolen wafer had been placed over their faces, the vial of blood poured over the wafer, the bag of grave-yard dirt emptied to cover it all, and then he closed it and wrapped it in Sam's stole. He held the package tightly, hoping to still the tremor in his hands.

"Better do this first." Burke laid down the pick-axe, walked to the front of the car and began meticulously drawing the octagon on the dirt with the salt. On each side, she drew the symbols, and when she was done, she started the SUV once more and carefully rolled it forward so the entire drawing lay under the carriage of the vehicle.

She did the physical work of digging a hole in the rocky, sun-baked earth, and Richard bent to place the box in it, both knees popping loudly on his way down and again on his way back up.

In the distance, an engine roared.

They both glanced toward the source of the noise—a car so far in the distance, it appeared as a flash of light under the bright sun.

Moving quickly, Burke pushed dirt over the box.

Richard picked up the pickaxe and tossed it in the back of the SUV.

The car they could hear in the distance was a streak of red flying through the wilderness.

"Can't be," he whispered, more to himself than her.

Burke scanned the landscape. "When does she come? How? Like, in a puff of smoke or something?"

"I'll be a suck-egg mule," Richard muttered. "I think that's her coming now."

"What?" Burke looked toward the car, a mint condition 1959 Cadillac Convertible. "Oh my God," she gasped. Despite the sweat dripping down her face, her teeth began to chatter.

Richard was struck by a wave of gratitude that he'd not been able to find a glass of prune juice that morning, certain he wouldn't have been able to hold his bowels if he had.

The car roared into the intersection and screeched to a stop directly over the freshly turned earth. The door opened, and The Devil got out. She was bare, tanned, muscular legs from her canvas-clad feet all the way up to her tiny denim shorts. The tails of a man's red and white checkered shirt were tied over her breasts. A straw cowboy hat cast a shadow over her face. Her smile was sweeter than a sugar boat sailing on a honey sea.

"Well, howdy, Dick. What can I do for you?"

Burke guffawed. "That's it?"

The Devil turned her attention to Burke. "Excuse me?"

"The Devil Herself? Really? I've been half out of my mind,

having nightmares about how scary you were going to be, and here you are, Jessica Simpson, straight out of 2005. You might be the least scary thing I've seen in the past week."

The Devil laughed with her. "Well, thanks dear. I never understood what all the fuss was about. I'm not such a bad girl. Or...well..." She giggled and cocked a curvy hip. "I am bad, but in all the best ways."

Richard was not amused. Aroused, but not amused. "Where's Stanley?"

"Is that why you called me? To ask about Stanley?"

"I called to get him back from you."

"How do you know he wants to be taken from me?" She stepped away from the car and pushed the door shut behind her. The metallic thud echoed through the empty land. Gravel crunched under her bright white sneakers. She ran a single long red fingernail gently down Richard's arm. "It could be that he's never had more fun in his whole life than he's had since he came with me."

"He didn't go with you. You took him," Burke said.

The Devil stepped back and arched one perfect brow at her. "Is that what you think?"

"It's what I know."

"Based on what?" she asked. "It's not like you've got any kind of relationship with Stanley. You barely know anything about the man. How do you know he wouldn't brave Hell for one spectacular roll in the hay?"

Burke gritted her teeth.

"Stanley loathed you," Richard said.

"Loathed. That's a strong word, Dick, but, since you brought it up, didn't you once wile away your hours thinking about how much you loathed Stanley? There wasn't a single thing about him that you loved. Really, Dick, aren't you better off without all his drama in your life? When you were in Everest, did you ever hurt the way you are hurting now? Hurting in body, hurting in spirit. It's kind of Stanley's fault."

A snake slithered out of the shrubby grass toward the girl and she crouched to stroke it as lovingly as if it were a newborn puppy.

"He would have died in Everest if it weren't for Stanley," Burke said. With her feet planted wide and her fists at her sides, she looked to be a warrior from mythology.

The serpent lifted its head from the earth and The Devil leaned forward so that it's darting tongue could brush her lips in an obscene kiss before she stretched up to her full height once more. She was taller than Richard, as tall as Burke. "Death is part of life on this ball of dust," she said. Her wide eyes held pity for the whole, doomed planet. "God made it that way. Blame him," she said, bringing her heel down to crush the snake's skull. "Your grandfather is going to die, even now that he's out of Everest. And so will you. And so will Stanley. In fact, Stanley is overdue. He had a good run."

Burke took a step forward. "He will, but he hasn't yet? Is that what you're telling us?"

The Devil shrugged. "Any time now. Actually, the longer we talk, the more likely it is it will be sooner rather than later, so if you want to help him, you should tell me why you've summoned me here."

Richard leaned back hard against the SUV. "Sorry," he muttered. "This heat…"

"Grandpa, why don't we sit in the truck? I'll run the air and we can talk out of the sun."

She turned toward The Devil standing in the road next to the body of the snake, flecks of blood on her white sneaker. "Please," she said. "You said it yourself. He's hurting."

The Devil hesitated, then shrugged. "Okey-doke, but just so you know, that little bit of hoodoo under the car isn't going to hold me for more than a few minutes. The name of the

Nazarene has power, but belief is the wire that power runs through and yours is tentative at best." She strode past Burke and slipped into the backseat with the grace of a mountain cat.

Burke reached out to help Richard, but he turned away from her grasp and walked under his own power to the passenger-side door. This wasn't going at all the way he'd pictured. He had imagined a thousand scenarios. None of them involved her knowing their every move before they did.

The Devil stretched her legs and propped her feet on the center console of the front seat, her slim, pretty ankles crossed between Burke and Richard. She folded her hands across her flat midsection. Her hat lay on the seat next to her. "So, kids, clock's ticking. You summoned me and *you*"—she made quotation marks in the air with her fingers—"trapped me. Now what?"

"Give us Stanley," Burke said.

"No," The Devil answered, holding out her nails to inspect them. "Anything else you'd like to talk about?"

"We'll make a deal to get Stanley back," Richard said.

Her hand hung in the air for a moment and then she lowered it. "You're willing to deal? Well, now. That's a whole different ball of wax. What are you willing to offer?"

"We...uhm..." Richard hesitated.

He was studiously avoiding Burke's eye. The book had told him they'd have to deal with The Devil. She didn't do anything for free. But Burke had been so opposed to the idea anyway that he hadn't wanted to give her any further reason to object. For days, he'd been trying to figure out what to offer her in trade. Only one thing came to mind, but now that the moment was upon him, he was having trouble finding the wherewithal to spit it out.

The Devil laughed, a sound as pretty as well-tuned wind chimes on a perfect summer day. "You aren't actually considering offering yourself in trade for Stanley, are you?"

Hot blood rushed to his face.

"Stanley is a powerful hunter, Dick. He's desirable and clever and strong. Poor Dick. You are so tired. You should find a safe place and rest. Don't you worry about Stanley anymore. You just take care of yourself, sweetheart. Surely you've got a few golden years left."

The pain in his legs flared up and he winced as though her words were a physical assault.

Burke jumped to his defense. "My grandfather is a good man."

"Is he?" The Devil asked, sounding genuinely curious. "I thought he was a mean-spirited old codger, the most unpleasant human being you'd ever been forced to share Thanksgiving dinner with." She pulled her legs back and planted her feet on the floor of the car. "I know the thoughts of your heart, Burke, and all I want is for you to be happy. Are you happy traipsing across the country with a man who looks down on you for something so ridiculously biological as the color of your skin?"

"I don't!" Richard erupted.

Both women jumped at the exclamation.

"I'm learning," he said. "I'm not perfect, but I'm learning how to be better and, yes, if you'll take me, I'll trade places with Stanley. The world needs him more than it needs me."

The Devil flinched, a movement so imperceptible he might have missed it if he hadn't been staring straight into those crystal blue eyes.

"No," she said again. "I won't release Stanley. I'm sorry to disappoint you, Richard, but you're going to have to manage a while longer in this life. I know it's hard, honey, but, gosh. You've made it this far. It's all downhill from here." She reached for the door handle, but her arm stopped in mid-air as though she'd smacked into a piece of glass. "Huh," she said, sounding far more curious than upset. "I guess you still have a few more minutes." She picked at a piece of lint on the seat. "I hope

Stanley still has a few more minutes. Otherwise, he'll be lost to us all and that would be a sad day for us now, wouldn't it?"

"We won't kill the skinwalker," Burke said.

The Devil's head snapped up, her eyes wide.

"Burke!" His fear and uncertainty died in an instant under the onslaught of pure panic.

She reached out and took his trembling hand in hers. Her palm was warm and dry, her touch as strong and certain as a mother's calming caress. "It's okay, Grandpa. We have a chance to save Stanley. Revenge won't bring Grandma back. The thing is about to go to sleep for another decade or so, anyway. O'Doyle is as good as gone. You saw him. He looks like a walking corpse. Let's just get Stanley and go home. You don't have to go to Everest. You can stay with me."

"We can't just..." He lacked the capacity to go any further, to express the tangle of thought and emotion in his mind.

"We can, Grandpa. It'll be okay. Trust me." She squeezed his hand hard. Her eyes were steely with resolve. She gave a tiny nod, as though prompting him to go along.

"I trust you." He hadn't meant to whisper, but that's how the words came out.

Burke turned toward The Devil. "Is it a deal? We don't kill the skinwalker. You give Stanley back to us."

With a grin as wide and pretty as an oceanside sunrise, the Devil held out her hand. "It's a deal."

The two women shook.

Tentatively, The Devil reached toward the door handle once more. Her hand moved past the invisible barrier without resistance and she pushed the door open and slid to the edge of the seat. "I'll just leave the car here. Stanley's in the trunk. He's probably quite thirsty, assuming he's not dead yet," she said. "I'd hurry, if I were you." Then she slipped from the vehicle and the door closed with a loud snick.

Burke was racing toward the Cadillac before Richard

managed to get his feet on the ground. She ripped the keys from the ignition and ran so fast toward the rear of the vehicle, her feet slid on the rocky road.

Richard managed to get there just as the trunk popped open to reveal Stanley, bound and gagged, wearing nothing but his boxers and the leg brace. Dirt and sweat covered his pale body. His eyes were closed.

Burke tugged on the gag. "Stanley! Stanley, wake up!"

She managed to pull the cloth from his mouth just as his eyelids fluttered. A pathetic smile touched his lips. "Knew you could do it," he said before fainting away again.

"Help me," Burke said, and together they managed to lift him from the trunk of the car and get him inside the cool, shady SUV. Burke tipped a series of tiny sips of water into his mouth and he took them without protest.

"Better," he murmured, but he didn't fully rouse.

"We should take him to a hospital," Richard said.

"We don't have time for that," Burke answered.

He scowled at her. "After the deal you made, we got nothin' but time."

"No," she corrected. "After the deal I made, it's more important than ever that we get Stanley back on his feet as fast as possible."

"You promised we wouldn't kill the monster," he said.

She grinned and he noticed that her smile in that moment bore an uncanny resemblance to The Devil's own grin. "That's right. I promised that *we*"—she waved a hand between herself and Richard—"wouldn't kill the skinwalker. I didn't say I wouldn't kill it, or you wouldn't, and I wouldn't have presumed to speak for Stanley."

His mouth fell open.

She laughed at his expression.

"You tricked The Devil?" he asked, stupefied that she would have the nerve to try such a thing.

"She deserved it. Did you hear that garbage about knowing the thoughts of our hearts? If she was so smart, she'd have known what I really wanted was to smack that nasty grin right off her face. Now, come on. We need to get Stanley back to the hotel so he can rest. He's got tonight and tomorrow before the full moon, and I'm guessing he's going to need every bit of that time."

She left him in charge of the SUV and climbed behind the wheel of the Cadillac. As he drove, Richard couldn't stop grinning.

CHAPTER THIRTY-SEVEN

Finn

THAT MORNING, FINN HAD BEEN THINKING ABOUT HIS mother. When she had been sick with cancer, the doctor had encouraged them to put her in hospice care.

"Hospice?" his father had been incredulous. "I won't give up on her like that. She's a fighter. Didn't you see? Just yesterday, she felt so good she wanted to take a shower and walk down to the cafeteria for lunch."

Finn remembered pitying the doctor. He looked exhausted and unhappy all the time. His life was full of dying people and their angry relatives.

"It's not giving up, Mr. O'Doyle. Hospice will be able to take measures to keep her comfortable that we can't provide here. If she starts to rally, then, by all means, we can resume treatment. Right now, I just don't see that as a possibility."

His father's incredulity turned into purple-faced rage. "You're not even listening. My wife's not dying! She's getting better! She—"

"Mr. O'Doyle, it's not unusual for patients to have a final

burst of energy near the end. Your wife's vitals have been slipping since yesterday evening. I don't think she has much time left."

Three days later, she died while Finn was at school.

He was convinced Friday night had been his final burst of energy. Making love to Sara, dinner in Tombstone...that was it. His last hurrah. The little excursion into town left him so debilitated he'd slept through Saturday. At least, that's what Sara told him. Sara, who was either a saint for sticking by his side or the sinner trying to kill him. He still hadn't decided what he believed about her. Couldn't really bring himself to care.

When he finally woken up sometime Sunday morning, she'd helped move him to a chair by the window and brought him a book to read. He sat in the sun, wrapped in a quilt, and chilled all the way to his guts. The book lay closed on his thighs. He couldn't read it. The words were no more than filmy black squiggles against the creamy paper. Instead, he stared at his hands. They were old man's hands, with wrinkled, parchment-thin skin. Age spots dotted them. The hair that grew there was white and wiry. Tendons stood out, thick ropes under brittle covering.

All his life, he'd rode horses and done the hard work of living on a ranch. As an adult, he'd reveled in the strength and agility of his athlete's body. So, okay, he'd gotten in a bit of a slump. The cigarettes were bad, but this? This was unnatural.

It has to be Sara, he thought. *I was fine until she came. Have you ever heard of a sickness that ages a man like this? It doesn't exist. She's killing me.*

Another part of his mind shot back, *You're being absurd. That girl is so far head-over-heels, she won't leave your side even when it's the best thing for her. If she was killing you, do you think she'd feed you and nurse you and sit by your side while you sleep, to keep the nightmares away?*

The nightmares.

He had always dreamed vividly, but this was a slow descent into a hellish madness that came upon him every time he closed his eyes. Which was more and more often these days.

At least when I'm dead, the nightmares will stop. There. A silver lining. You're a regular Pollyanna, Finn O'Doyle.

I really should go to the hospital.

Why? What did they do for your mother? If you're going to die, best to die in the comfort of your own home.

Sara came in with a tray of soup and juice. She set it on top of the dresser. "Hey! You're still awake. That's my guy. Can I talk you into eating?"

"Maybe in a little while," he said.

The thought of putting food in his mouth was as appealing as the thought of putting dirt in his mouth. Nothing tasted right. There was no pleasure in eating, and eliminating what he ate was humiliating since he could barely get to the bathroom on his own.

Sara curled up like a cat on the little window seat next to him. "Tell me something," she said.

"Okay," he answered. "I never watch football, except for the Superbowl. Then I read while they're playing and pay attention to the commercials."

She giggled. The sun shone on her thick hair. Her skin was smooth and tan and perfect. "That's not exactly what I had in mind."

"What do you want me to tell you, Sara?"

"Tell me why you write." Light sparkled in her eager eyes.

Reporters and reviewers had asked that of him before and he'd always given some mumbo-jumbo generic answer about how he wrote because he couldn't imagine the alternative. Sitting in that chair, half dead already, it seemed silly to hide behind falsehoods, so he told her what he'd never told anyone, "I write because it makes me feel powerful. This world is a cruel, hard, chaotic gong show. We all like to pretend that we have some measure of control. We guarantee our health by eating organic bean sprouts. We guarantee our financial security by working hard and saving ten percent. We plan each day as though we own the minutes and hours of our lives, but the truth is, lightning strikes at random. In a split second, our guarantees are shattered and we see how small we are. When I write, it's not like that. I'm in control. I say who lives and dies, who prospers or falters, who suffers and who is blessed."

"You're a god," she said, and her voice held all the awe and reverence it would if he'd been Zeus telling her why he ruled from Olympus.

"Only when I write."

She breathed in deeply and shuddered. "Oh, Finn, I do love to listen to you talk. You're so different."

"Different from what?"

"Different from the rest of the world. The world thinks being vivacious means dancing on the bar and singing from the mountaintop. They think the ones who are most in love with life are the ones who burn the brightest, but you"—she closed her eyes and let her head fall back against the wall, sighing in pleasure as though he were touching her—"you smolder like a coal, hot enough to smelt iron."

He pictured that blank white screen with its flashing black cursor. "Maybe I did once," he said.

"Oh, you still do. You live, Finn. You see the world around you and when you don't love what you see, you create new worlds." She met his eye. "Tell me more, Finn. Tell me about a story you never dared to write."

"Haven't you read my reviews?" he teased. "I'm known for writing what others don't dare say."

"But there's more, isn't there? Something that even you haven't put down on paper yet."

He swallowed hard. The story had been in his heart for as long as he could remember. If he didn't tell her now, odds were, it would die with him. "Yeah. There's more," he admitted.

She leaned forward, the most attentive listener he'd ever encountered. "Tell me, Finn. Let me watch you create a world. Be a god."

Fatigue weighed heavily on him, but intensity was enough to carry him forward. "Okay. I'll tell you."

He did. She listened with rapt attention.

CHAPTER THIRTY-EIGHT

Richard

STANLEY WAS A MESS. HE WAS STILL ASLEEP WHEN THEY GOT back to the hotel, but making strange little guttural noises in his throat. He was bright red, but the sweat that had covered him earlier was completely gone. He clutched his stomach as though it pained him, even in his sleep.

Richard turned into the parking space, pulled forward until the SUV hit the concrete block hard enough to make his seatbelt lock, and killed the engine. Burke pulled the Cadillac into the spot next to him. Seeing as how the white line went right under the middle of the SUV, there was plenty of room between the two cars for both of them to hop out at the same moment.

"How's he doing?" she asked.

"I'm not so sure."

He pulled the back door open, but it was Burke who laid her gentle hands on Stanley's bare shoulders. His eyes fluttered open without focusing on anything in particular. Lying there, helpless and mostly naked on the back seat, he looked like the old man he was. It was painful to see. Richard had come to believe that Stanley was supposed to transcend age. He faced demons and hunted wild beasts with a spear and a machete. He was supposed to be above such mortal concerns as wrinkles, and certainly, nothing so mundane as heat stroke should be an issue.

"He's burning up," Burke said. "Let's get him inside."

They managed to haul him out of the car and onto his feet, but the motion caused him to start heaving. Richard tried his best to block Stanley from the view of anyone passing by. What would people think of a wrinkled old man in his underpants vomiting in a parking lot? Even in this town, that wasn't normal Sunday evening behavior.

Stanley clung to them with arms weak as an infant's but managed to stay on his feet. "The Devil calls me Daddy," he whimpered.

Seriously? Richard thought he was going to puke. *Friggin' Stan Kapcheck.*

Burke rolled her eyes. "Okey-doke then. That's just great," she said. "Come on." They walked toward the hotel, each with one of Stan's arms around their shoulders, the mostly naked man with the broken leg staggering along between them.

A woman with a little girl stepped out of her room, saw them, gasped, covered her child's eyes, and headed off in a different direction.

Welcome to Tombstone, Richard thought. *Enjoy your stay.*

They made it to the room and lowered Stanley onto a bed.

Burke hustled off to the bathroom and started drawing a cold bath. "Bring him in here," she called.

Richard glanced at Stan's boxers. He'd faced The Devil to save the man, but he drew the line at taking his drawers off for him. He grabbed him by the arms and pulled him up again, a great limp doll.

Stan hung on him, burning hot and mumbling. His feet stumbled across the floor. "My junk hurts," he whimpered.

"Oh, Lord," Richard groaned. "I didn't need to know that, man."

"What is it?" Burke asked, rising from her seat on the edge of the tub to help them.

"Nothing," Richard said. "And you should thank me for not telling you."

Stan moaned when his feet hit the water and tried so forcefully to back away from the tub that he stumbled on his bad leg and nearly succeeded in knocking them all over.

"Oh, no you don't," Burke insisted. "In you go, and right this instant."

"She's gonna burn me up," Stanley moaned, tears glistening in his eyes. "She won't stop until I burn up and nothing's left."

"The water will put out the fire, Stanley. Into the tub," Burke said.

This particular bit of crazy talk must have made sense to him because he let them lower him into the water, though he arched and cried out like the water itself burned him.

"Maybe the hospital…" Richard began. He refused to say it out loud, but seeing Stanley like this was as terrifying as anything he'd seen since he'd embarked on this crazy adventure. The man was obviously at death's door.

"No," Burke refused to give an inch. "The hospital will keep him for days. They'll ask questions we can't answer. We just have to cool him off. He'll be fine." She soaked a cloth in the cold water and rubbed it over Stan's head and neck. "He's going to be fine. Do you hear me, Stanley? You're going to be fine."

Stanley lay in the water shivering so hard, his teeth clacked like castanets, eyes closed, not responding. Richard wondered who she was trying to convince.

CHAPTER THIRTY-NINE

Burke

BURKE WASHED STANLEY'S BODY AND PRAYED OVER HIM. SHE didn't mind his nudity, though she kept him covered out of respect. It was like washing a child. When they moved him to the bed, she sat next to him and hummed what she hoped was a soothing melody. She'd made a deal with The Devil to save the man who had saved her from herself. She refused to let something so mundane as heat stroke take him away from her. He was a hunter. The greatest hunter in the world. When his time came, he'd go down fighting, not whimpering in a cheap motel room.

"Rest now, Stanley. Get better fast. We have work to do."

He gave a tiny nod and, sure enough, a few minutes later, the shivering subsided and he slept peacefully.

"Grandpa?" she asked sometime later, after Stanley's skin had cooled to the touch and he was snoring softly.

"Yeah, kid."

"You were brave today."

"Easy to be brave when you've got a partner you trust."

She kissed his wrinkled old cheek. "I'm going out for some food. Be back in a few minutes. Keep an eye on Stanley, okay?"

Richard grunted. "Don't reckon he's in any shape to go runnin' off."

CHAPTER FORTY

Richard

STANLEY SLEPT THROUGH THE NIGHT WHILE BURKE AND Richard watched over him. In a pathetic attempt to pass the time more quickly, Burke turned on the TV. One newscaster after another droned on in the background. Neither of them paid any attention.

They could take no action until the moon rose on Tuesday night. That meant two days of nothing but waiting. The thought made Richard's skin crawl. Facing the monster would be a welcome relief from all this sitting around thinking about what could happen when they faced it..

Thinking of the thing stirred up his thoughts from that morning. It seemed the Catholic church service had taken place in another lifetime. Once the idea of the monster taking on various forms bloomed in his mind, he couldn't seem to let go of it and he ended up spending a full two hours watching out the window, certain the skinwalker, looking like StellaLuna, would come crashing through the door and kill them all.

At long last, the sky turned from black to grey and then

exploded into the obscene panorama of color that only seemed to happen in the desert.

Stanley stirred.

Burke rushed to his side.

"Could I trouble you for a glass of water?" he asked. "I'm quite parched."

Richard beamed. The burden of worry evaporated in a warmth of affection. "Welcome back, Stan Kapcheck, you insufferable old fart."

THE THREE OF THEM SAT GATHERED AROUND THE BEDS, JUST as they had that night in Spearfish.

Stanley had dark purple circles under his eyes and his hand trembled when he raised the paper coffee cup to his lips, but he was alive and conscious and sitting up taking nourishment. The twinkle had returned to his eyes, even if it dimmed a little when they asked where The Devil had taken him and what he'd seen there. "We should focus on the task at hand," he had said. "The present has more than enough complexity to hold our interest. The past is over and done with."

With no steering wheel to clutch, Burke tapped her nails on her right knee where it crossed her left knee. Her foot bobbed in time with the chaotic rhythm. "If it knows we're coming for it, won't it just hide? In two days, it will be safe. There won't be a thing we can do."

"No." Stanley set the coffee down carefully on the cheap nightstand. "It's been trapped in whatever purgatory it exists in for twelve years. If you had only twenty-eight days of freedom out of every four thousand or so, would you waste a single hour cowering for your safety?" He sighed and shifted in bed, drawing the covers a little higher toward his chest. Since they'd managed to cool him off, he seemed to struggle to stay warm.

"No. It won't hide. I rather think it will relish the fight. It will prepare for us. Lay some sort of trap. We must be ready for anything.

"Are you certain you know where to find it?"

"We're certain it's latched onto the writer," Burke said. "We've been out to his house, but we didn't see anything out of the ordinary."

"That makes sense," Stanley said. "What would you see? A man sleeping his last days away, his energy robbed by a foul witch. No one would suspect a thing. That's why this beast is so hard to find. Is the house isolated?"

"Very."

"Good. Then we'll go there and do what we must."

"You going to be all right to do this with us?" Richard asked. "You look like you went twelve rounds with both hands tied behind your back."

"Truth be told, I feel much the same, but have no fear, Dick. I'm not down for the count just yet."

Burke planted her feet on the floor and leaned her elbows on her knees. "Tell me we did the right thing, Stanley. Tell me we did what you wanted when we came after you first."

He held out a hand and she moved to the bed and cradled it between both of hers.

"I can't tell you that's what I wanted. It wasn't what I intended. I meant to go with her and be done with this life. I've lived twice as long as I should have. I'm tired, dear girl, and I thought I could just give myself up and die. You two have already proven you're up to the task of replacing me as hunters."

Tears spilled down Burke's cheeks. Richard stared resolutely at the little grey dust ball in the corner of the carpet.

"What I wanted was to move on and leave the work of dealing with the skinwalker and every horrid thing like it to someone else. In short, I wanted to indulge myself like a selfish child."

"I'm sorry," she said through tears.

"Nonsense. I wanted those things because I was an ignorant fool. I was in Hell, Burke, and the two of you saved me. It was..." his voice cracked. He cleared his throat and continued, "It was quite unpleasant. You brought me back to a place where there is hot coffee and good friends and important work to be done. I owe you a great debt of gratitude."

Richard wiped the back of his hand across his nose. "Or maybe we're all just even now."

"Maybe we should stop keeping score," Burke suggested.

"I think you're both right," Stanley said. "Now, if you'll indulge a weary old man, I'm going to take a nap. Burke, dear, would you be so kind as to go into town and fetch me something to wear? I'm not sure I should head out into the world in threadbare underthings."

"Of course," she said.

Richard stood and crossed to the window. Outside, an elderly couple walked toward a car. A young man swam alone in the pool. He could be anybody. The thought came again that not a soul could be trusted. He didn't know what to do with that truth, but he held on to it. It felt important. He mustn't forget it in a senior moment.

Burke leaned against the wall next to him. "If we had a week to let him heal, I'd feel a lot better about this."

He watched the man reach the side of the pool, gracefully flip in the water and swim toward the other end with long, powerful strokes. "If a bull had batteries, his horns would blow."

She sighed. "Seriously, Grandpa. I'm just saying, I wish—"

"Wish in one hand and poop in the other. See which one fills up faster." He had enough doubts of his own. He didn't want to hear hers. "Stan needs clothes. You going or should I?"

He hated the wounded look in her eye, hated what it said

about him. He didn't know why he snapped at her like that. She deserved better. It was just that his nerves were raw and his mind was chaos. His body hurt everywhere. For the first time since he left his walker on the roadside, he missed it. The magic that had carried him along for the last several days had waned, leaving in its wake an exhaustion that sank into the marrow of his bones. If Stan had been living like this for over a century, Richard could hold no fault in him wanting it to be over.

With his shaking hand, he reached out and patted her arm. "Don't mind me. I'm just tired. Think I'll rest a bit, too, if that's okay."

"Sure, Grandpa. You're all right, though?"

"Yeah. Fine. Just tired, is all. After a nap, I'll be fit as a fiddle."

She left, but Richard couldn't sleep. Over and over, he kept thinking how exactly like Barbara the creature had appeared. It could become anyone. Anyone at all.

CHAPTER FORTY-ONE

Burke

TUESDAY, THE EARTH SLOWED. TIME MOVED AT A SNAIL'S pace, and Earth took ten times longer than usual to make the journey around the sun.

Burke inventoried the weapons in the trunk of the Cadillac and surfed news sites on her phone, looking for unusual stories that might lead them on to another hunt. If she had something to think about, something beyond the coming night, maybe she wouldn't feel like climbing the walls of the dark little hotel room.

Stanley chided her. "You must not force the hand of Fate, Burke. A hunter will be led from one quest to the next. If you were meant to know your next destination, you'd know by now."

An hour later, her grandfather barked at her, "Sit down. You're like a one-legged man in a jumping contest, makin' me nervous with all that fidgeting."

She looked at her phone. It was nine o'clock in the morning. "I'm going to the gym," she announced and, without waiting for a reply, left. In a room off the hotel lobby, she found a treadmill and set her pace at a comfortable five miles per hour to warm up her muscles.

Too many days had passed since she'd run, not counting the moments she'd been running for her life. The rhythm of her feet, thumping against the belt, and the soft whir of the motor was fantastic therapy. Her breath came steady and even.

In with the good, clean, and positive. Out with the bad, toxic, and negative.

She increased her speed until she was racing at ten miles per hour, then added an incline. Sweat beaded across her forehead and ran down her neck.

"I am powerful," she whispered. "I am fast. I am strong. I am unstoppable. I am a force to be reckoned with."

After a while, she slowed back to five miles per hour, and eventually to a three-mile-per-hour walk. Finally, she stepped off the machine and spent longer than she ever had stretching every muscle in her body, luxuriating in the strength and flexibility she'd developed in the past few years.

Then she lay prone on the floor, listening to her heartbeat slow to a normal pace, keeping her mind focused on the intricate workings of her body.

With her emotions under control, her fear checked by her sense of empowerment, and her appetite heightened by the exertion, she meandered back outside and up the stairs to the hotel room.

Her grandfather was staring out the window.

Stanley was watching soap operas.

Her eyes fell on the clock. Nine forty-seven. "Oh, dear God," she grumbled under her breath before going into the bathroom to try to kill another thirty minutes in the shower.

Surely, the day would never end.

CHAPTER FORTY-TWO

Finn

SARA HELD THE WATER GLASS WITH THE BENDY STRAW CLOSE to his lips while he sipped. "I might step outside for a bit while you rest, if that's okay," she said. She set the cup down on the nightstand and dabbed his lips with a washcloth before placing a soft, chaste kiss there.

"You don't need my permission. You should go." He hated the sound of his voice, weak and tremulous. It took all his strength just to stand for a single moment or two now. There was no way he'd last more than a few days. There was no point in making her endure his wasting away.

No point, at all, yet he was infinitely grateful when she said, "Don't be silly, Finn. I've told you a hundred times. There's nowhere else I want to be but right by your side." She kissed him again. "Rest. I'll be back in a little while."

Infinitely grateful, he nodded and watched her blurry form move around the room, changing shirts, tying shoes.

"Sara?"

She stopped. "Yeah?"

"You're not poisoning me to death, are you?"

If she was offended, it didn't show in her girlish giggle. "Aw, Finn. Don't be so silly. Why would a girl like me ever hurt a guy like you?"

"Sorry. It was a stupid question."

She leaned over him to give him another kiss. "Rest," she said again, and then she left.

Feeble as he was, it didn't escape his notice that she hadn't really answered the question.

CHAPTER FORTY-THREE

Richard

UNDER THE COLORFUL VAULT OF TWILIGHT, THE THREE hunters made their way out of the hotel room and across the parking lot.

One of them was dressed like Wyatt Earp in high-waisted, button-front trousers, one knee-high boot, a striped shirt and leather suspenders. His other leg was encased in a hard, plastic boot and he hitched along, leaning heavily on a cane.

One of them wore sweats and sneakers and maintained a careful, shuffling gait.

One of them, tall and slender, held her chin high as though daring the world to defy her, and stayed a step behind the other two like a mother hen guarding her chicks.

The two men went to the Cadillac.

Burke turned toward the SUV and stopped. "What are you doing?" she asked.

"Gettin' in the car," Richard said, yanking the passenger door open.

"You can't be serious," she said.

They both stared over the canvas roof at her.

"You've been down the road to O'Doyle's ranch. It's barely more than a donkey trail. The SUV is going to handle it much better than that antique."

"I'm grateful for the transportation your vehicle has provided," Stanley said, "but there's something to be said for style."

"You've got to be kidding."

"Also, there's an army's worth of weapons in the trunk," Stanley said. "We might need them."

Richard had to admire the way he'd played his trump card.

Burke rolled her eyes but offered up no further argument. Rather, she retrieved the ax from the SUV and put it in the back seat next to Stanley. She took the keys from him, moved the can of gas and the box of matches to the trunk, and started the engine.

The powerful V8 roared to life.

"Would you mind terribly putting the top down?" Stanley asked.

"Oh, good Lord," Burke mumbled.

She lowered the top.

"Can we go slay our dragon now?" she asked.

"I'm afraid that isn't possible," Stanley said.

They both turned to stare at him, agape.

"Well, there simply aren't any dragons left in North America. I haven't slain one since I was a boy in England. We're going to have to settle for a skinwalker, I believe."

Burke rolled her eyes again.

"Dang fool," Richard mumbled.

His mood had started low that day and only sank lower as the hours passed. He'd woken from an afternoon nap to find Burke unpacking the ridiculous, old-fashioned clothes she'd purchased for Stanley the day before. She claimed that's all she could find in Tombstone and she hadn't felt up to driving past the writer's house alone to get to Sierra Vista. Of course, there was nothing for Richard, which meant he was stuck wearing the cheap sweats that had been washed in the hotel bathtub.

He'd spent half an hour sitting on the pot with nothing to show for it but feet that were full of pins and needles. As if it weren't hard enough already to walk with some measure of dignity.

After all that, a dinner of greasy chicken strips and fries that had been laid out on the little hotel-room table looked less than appealing. Did no one in the southwest sell prune juice? Or did Burke not care that his belly was swelling up like he was about to enter his second trimester? He was sure he'd asked for prune juice more than once.

To top it all off, after dreaming about her all night, he couldn't close his eyes without seeing Barbara, beautiful, young, vibrant Barbara, wearing clothes made to fit a smaller woman, pressing her warm, soft body against his.

Not Barbara. The monster. The creature that could make itself look like anyone.

He watched the world roll by as they passed through a few blocks of town and took the turn onto Charleston Road. On the eastern horizon, the full moon peeked into view, and by the time they crossed the dry wash, the desert was bathed in silvery light.

Burke made the turn into the writer's driveway and inched the vehicle along at a crawl. They entered the clearing at a pathetic roll, slower than Richard's average walking speed. And that wasn't saying much, at all, these days. She didn't stop until the chrome bumper overlapped the edge of the brick patio.

Finn O'Doyle sat in a patio chair under the night sky, sipping a long-necked bottle of beer. His hair, now more white than dark, fell across his forehead, a mess in bad need of a trim. One elbow rested on a glass top table. Long legs were stretched out, crossed at the ankle before him. His tired eyes watched them draw near, but he made no effort to stand. Richard wondered if he could stand. He looked more like one of the residents at Everest than a man in his prime.

He looked just the way Barbara had in her last days. His heart lurched at the memory. He couldn't wait to see the monster dead.

The monster who could choose any form it wanted.

"That could be anybody," Richard mumbled to himself.

"What are you talking about? That's O'Doyle," Burke said.

"What?" It took a moment for him to realize he'd spoken out loud. "I know that's O'Doyle. I was just thinking about that skinwalker. It could show itself looking like anybody in the world."

"Which means," added Stanley from the backseat, "we can't be sure that's O'Doyle."

They all stared through the windshield at the man. He took another sip of his beer and stared back with raised brows.

"Now or never." Burke threw the gearshift into park and burst out of the car like a scared cat, hitting the ground so fast she stumbled a few steps. Richard and Stanley scrambled to join her.

"Finn O'Doyle, right?" she asked.

One side of his mouth curved up in a crooked smile that had undoubtedly melted more than a few female hearts. "You found me."

"I…" Burke started to speak again and lurched to a stop.

"We've come to mount a rescue operation," Stanley announced. Richard looked over his shoulder to see Stan behind him leaning hard on the axe in his left hand. The steel head pressed against the sunbaked earth—the world's most disturbing walking aid.

"Oh, good," the writer said. He took another sip of beer. The bottle tapped against the glass table when he set it down again. The clatter contrasted sharply against the silence of the night. "I'm happy to know that an old man with an axe is here to rescue me. Thought maybe you were going to chop my door down or something."

"The woman we saw you with in Murphy's last night, she's not what she seems," Burke said.

The muscles in Richard's thighs twitched—his body's way of demanding action. *Run forward and kill him. Run away and find help. Move. Do anything, for cripe's sake.*

Too many choices. He stood there trembling like a daisy in a hurricane.

The author nodded. "Sara. Yeah. She's something else. Definitely more to that girl than meets the eye. See how old I look? I bet I'm no older than you, but I'm pretty sure she's trying to kill me. Probably too late to do anything about it now, though. Should have listened to my gut two weeks ago, the day she showed up the first time."

Richard wiped his sweating palms against the soft cotton of the sweatpants.

Stanley hitched past him to the edge of the patio, using the axe for a cane. "I wasn't going to mention it, but you do appear to be a bit under the weather."

Finn shrugged. "Women."

Richard watched the bizarrely polite exchange with growing incredulity. Did Stanley and Burke not realize that a man his age could drop over and die at any moment? Especially when his heart was pounding out a rhythm to beat the band. He couldn't take much more of this. The kid was still young enough to think she had forever, but Stanley ought to know better. Time was precious. Wasting it by pussyfooting around like this was sheer nonsense. "Could be your little girlfriend isn't poisoning you. Could be you look like hell 'cause the witch is a demon from Hell," he blurted.

O'Doyle regarded him, showing no sign of offense. "Could be." He finished the beer. "Women," he said again. "Can't live with 'em. Can't kill 'em."

"We'd like to speak with her, please," Stanley said. "Would you be so kind as to call her out here?"

The writer folded his hands across his stomach. "Three strangers show up at my house in the night, carrying an ax, and ask me to call a young lady outside to speak with them. Would you do it, if you were me?"

CHAPTER FORTY-FOUR

Finn

AT SOME POINT AFTER THE FIRST TIME HE WET THE BED, FINN had decided to go along quietly when death came. What was there to live for anymore, anyway?

The next deadline? He was washed up. His world-building days sold to The Devil for a place on the best-seller rack.

The next race? He could barely walk. There would be no marathons in his future.

The next girl? No point thinking about the next when he probably wouldn't survive the one he had now.

But, as he stirred in the bed, trying to alleviate the pressure on his aching buttocks, he heard voices outside and they woke a hope in him he'd been sure was dead.

Help!

"Help me!" he shouted into the dark room.

They couldn't hear him, of course. *Get up, you fool. This is your last chance. Get up now or you die.*

The palsy in his hand made it difficult to grab anything, but he latched onto the edge of the blanket and tugged it off to the side. Grunting with effort, he sat up and swung his legs over. It took a moment to stop the room from spinning, but dizziness passed and he gained his feet.

In his first marathon, he'd hit a wall at twenty-one miles. He'd been certain that taking another step would leave him dead at the finish line, just like the poor bastard who started the insane tradition. His lungs were fire. Bile rose in his throat and he'd been certain he was going to vomit. He knew there were five miles to go. Five miles at nine minutes a mile would be... He couldn't think. The numbers swirled around his head like so many dainty bluebirds in a Looney Tunes production. He tripped and nearly fell. Saved himself by throwing the next foot forward.

That's all I have to do, he thought. *I don't have to run five more miles. I can't do that. It's impossible, but I can throw my foot forward one more time.*

A little less than an hour later, he crossed the finish line, dozens of spots behind the lead, but far ahead of everyone who'd quit along the way.

He used the same philosophy to get to the door. He hadn't walked the entire length of the house in days. He knew he couldn't do it. He was far too weak, but he could put one bare, bony foot in front of the other one more time. And then, maybe once more again, after that. He could, because he suddenly, fiercely, very much wanted to live.

CHAPTER FORTY-FIVE

Richard

BURKE INCHED TOWARD THE FRONT OF THE CAR. "MR. O'Doyle, we have reason to believe you're in terrible danger. This sickness that you have—you're absolutely right. She is causing it."

"I'm not calling her out here," he said. His voice carried a hint of amusement. "You have an axe," he pointed out once again.

"Then, as sorry as I am to say it, we'll be forced to draw her out by our own means," Stanley said, and raised the axe as though preparing to throw it.

In Richard's mind, he saw a machete fly through the air and sink into the earth on the edge of a muddy riverbank. Could Stanley really kill the thing at that distance? There had to be a good twenty feet between them.

The heavy wooden door of the house opened and Finn O'Doyle stepped through. "Please help me. I need help," he said in a hoarse, breathless voice.

Richard's poor battered heart skidded to a stop and jolted forward once more.

"Holy shit!" Finn O'Doyle scrambled out of his chair and stood facing the man in the door.

The man in the door stared, open mouthed, at the man by the table. "What the..."

"I knew it!" Richard said. "I just knew it was gonna pull something like this!"

Burke edged along the front of the car toward Stanley, putting distance between herself and the two O'Doyles. Kid had the right idea. Run for the hills, girl!

You can't run, Richard reminded himself. *Man up!* A weird little whimper squeaked out of his throat. His feet refused to budge.

Stanley remained firm. The axe head thumped dully on the bricks as he hitched another step away from the car. "If whichever one of you is not the true Mr. O'Doyle could be so kind as to reveal himself, it would be very helpful," he said. "We've no desire whatsoever to kill a human."

Both men stared at him while he spoke. Both looked back to the other. Both faces grew wide-eyed and panicky.

"Kill?" Finn O'Doyle asked.

"How can this be?" Finn O'Doyle asked.

"What the Hell is happening?" Finn O'Doyle asked.

"I'm Finn O'Doyle," the one by the table said. "I have no idea—"

"I don't know who the Hell you are," the one by the door said, "or what exactly you think you're doing here, but—"

Burke obstructed Richard's view of the arguing O'Doyles when she drew next to Stanley and wrapped her right hand around the handle of the axe, just below Stanley's left hand. "Jeremiah! Reveal yourself," she demanded.

The O'Doyle by the table twitched and grunted as though punched in the stomach. "I'm Jeremiah," it choked out in the instant before its features melted like hot wax. Then it vanished, leaving nothing but a shimmer in the air—just another heat wave rising from the desert sand. Almost immediately, the good-for-nothing ex-husband stood in place of the fake O'Doyle. The author's clothes stretched tight across his muscled form. "Burke, baby, don't hurt me." He reached out and stepped closer to her.

"Bad choice of form, demon," she growled and lunged toward him with the axe.

Without his makeshift crutch, Stanley wobbled. Richard's legs finally hitched into motion and he managed to catch Stan's elbow before the old geezer fell and broke his hip. Richard looked up just in time to see the air shimmer where the cheating bum had stood.

Burke made a strangled grunt as the axe swung down hard on empty air. The momentum carried her forward and she fell to her knees on the patio in front of the pretty little table.

Richard sensed motion near the wood pile to their right and turned just as a towering Black man rushed by with a thick tree branch in one hand. The bludgeon struck the back of Burke's head and sent the girl sprawling face-first across the bricks. Her attacker spun to face Stanley and Richard, a triumphant smile on his face. "I did it! After all these years, I found the beast, Stanley. All because you helped me. Here." He reached into his pocket and fished out a silver lighter, tossed it across the expanse toward Stan. "Get the fire started. I'll take care of this part. I've been waiting my whole life to do this." He bent and retrieved the fallen axe.

Stanley's hand automatically flashed through the air and caught the lighter, but no other part of him moved. Richard felt the trembling of his arm, still in Richard's grip.

"You gotta do something," Richard demanded.

Stanley shook his head in a series of tiny little spasms.

The skinwalker lifted the axe over Burke's body.

Richard lunched toward his unconscious granddaughter. "Jeremiah! No! Don't hurt her!"

The creature froze. Melting features, a shimmer of heat, and then it was gone again. The axe clattered onto the patio once more.

Warm arms wrapped around Richard's waist from behind. "Protect me, Richie," Barbara pleaded and pressed her chin against Richard's shoulder as she had so many times before. "Please don't let them hurt me."

His vision swam. His hands and feet grew numb and cold.

Her arms tightened around his midsection. "You couldn't possibly hurt me, could you?" she asked.

His breath grew ragged and ineffective under the crushing pressure of her arms. His lungs had no space to expand. His ribs sent flares of fiery protest to his mind under this assault and still, she squeezed tighter.

"Don't worry, Richie. We'll be together again soon," she whispered.

The world grew black around the edges and she bent down with him as he fell to his knees. Burke's limp body filled his vision.

Warm moisture splashed across the back of Richard's neck. Barbara's grip released and Richard landed hard on his side on the bricks. He looked back and up. A knife handle protruded from his wife's neck. She staggered back, blood pouring down the front of her black, button-front shirt and dripped on the light beige bricks. Miraculously, she seemed only slightly injured.

"You can't kill me without killing him." She pointed toward the open doorway of the house. O'Doyle. Richard had nearly forgotten about the poor sap. The man was on his knees, clutching his neck, gasping.

Stanley's shadow flowed across the three injured humans as he limped in front of the Caddy's headlamps to retrieve the fallen axe. "He's as good as dead already." He raised the weapon, but with lightning speed, the skinwalker yanked the blade from her neck and sank it deep into Stanley's chest.

Stanley's eyes widened. His mouth opened in a perfect O.

Barbara vanished, leaving a shimmer in her wake. Or maybe the distortion came from the tears in Richard's eyes. "No!" he gasped, scrambling to gain his feet. Waves of pain shot through him. The hunter's eyes fixed on something off to the right of Richard before he slumped down like a ragdoll with inadequate stuffing. His braced leg protruded pitifully to one side.

Barbara stood there, leering at him as she never had before. "Sorry, Richie. Girl's got to do what a girl's got to do."

Tears burned Richard's eyes. He'd failed. To live with failure this immense would be a fate worse than the Hell that surely awaited him.

He closed his eyes and awaited the death blow with a wild mix of terror and relief pounding through his veins.

"Jeremiah! Freeze!" Burke rasped.

Richard opened his eyes.

Barbara jerked once and then froze.

Burke pushed herself off the brick floor. Her thick curls were matted with blood. One side of her face was scraped and bleeding, but her eyes shone like lamps in the moonlight. "Reveal your true form, Jeremiah."

The pretty young girl before him grew tall. Her fair skin darkened and whiskers sprouted. A sneer that revealed a row of picket-fence teeth replaced her lovely smile. Jeremiah stood before them, a man as wretched and pathetic in appearance as any homeless bum he'd ever seen on a street corner. Still, the beast continued to change. Its skin opened in wide, seeping sores. The eyes mutated into yellow luminescent spheres. The jagged nails grew long and pointed. No longer man, but demon encased in flesh. The scent of rot emanated from the foul creature that stood there, frozen, with hatred burning in its hideous, deformed face.

Burke spun and landed a solid kick in the middle of the freak's chest. The monster staggered backward and struck the front left corner of the Cadillac.

"Go back to the hell you came from," she growled. She lifted the axe once again and deftly removed the monster's head from its shoulders. The gruesome skull thumped to the earth between Richard and Stanley, mutant mouth open in an unvoiced scream, eyes blazing with fury, still lucid and now panicking.

Not aware that he'd moved, Richard found himself staggering away from the aberration.

Burke grunted and an arm fell to the ground. Again, the axe flashed. The body toppled and landed in the dirt next to the car, sending a puff of dust into the headlights.

Burke swung, again and again, a nightmarish lumberjack driven by demons of her own.

"Open the trunk," she shouted.

Richard looked toward the writer, who thrashed about on the patio in front of the house as though in the grip of a seizure.

He looked at Stanley, still and pale, his lifeblood glistening in the car's headlights as it pooled on the hard bricks.

A hand clamped around his ankle. A hand, separated from arm and body. "Argh!" he screamed and staggered backward. He caught himself on the glass-top table. With his other foot, he stomped on the abomination until it let go. He kicked it away, then scrambled to fetch the keys from the ignition.

The hard *thunk, thunk, thunk* of the axe kept time to the grotesque scratching of the sentient pieces of the skinwalker, attempting to rejoin one another.

Miraculously, he managed to keep his hand steady enough to get the key into the slot and the trunk popped open with a screeching of springs. His battered ribs roared in painful protest to the effort of lifting the heavy red plastic gas container.

"Hurry!" Burke called breathlessly.

A horrible caterwauling filled the night and he was certain his bowels would let go. He shuffled back to Burke and saw that the thing's head had reattached itself to its neck, giving it voice once more.

The grisly axe came down again, once more severing the connection.

He unscrewed the cap with the intention of pouring gas on the maimed bits scattered around his granddaughter's feet.

"No!" she screamed. "I have to do it."

"What d—"

She snatched the canister from him and splashed its contents in every direction, grabbed the matches from his hands, struck one, and set the night on fire.

The blaze was bright as the sun and hot enough to blister his skin. The paint on the Cadillac bubbled and hissed. Could be they'd all be blown to kingdom come before the night was over. He rapidly backed away and saw Burke do the same, kicking the remaining pieces of the monster into the flames as she went.

He hustled to where Stanley lay, bent down, wrapped his arms around him, and pulled with all his strength. He managed to drag him ten or fifteen feet farther from the flames before he fell to the ground between him and the body of the real O'Doyle. Stanley's skin was the color and texture of used waxed paper.

Richard reached for the handle of the knife that protruded from his chest but thought of the gaping wound that would remain if he pulled it free and hesitated.

"Stan Kapcheck, you old fart. Don't you die!" he shouted at the body in his arms. Bile rose in his throat. The world needed

Stan Kapcheck. If The Devil showed up in that moment, he'd beg her to deal—his life for Stanley's. His soul. Anything she wanted.

Why would she take such a bargain, though? She'd already told him Stanley's life was worth more than his own.

A sob welled up within his bruised chest.

Burke knelt beside them, filthy with blood and dirt and soot. She smelled of smoke and gasoline. Her breath wheezed in short, ragged gasps. "Pull it out," she ordered.

Richard wiped the back of his sleeve across his stinging eyes, started to protest, then saw his granddaughter reach into her pocket and produce a breath mint tin.

Hope pushed through despair. "You think?" he asked.

"We have to try," she said.

Steeling himself, he lowered Stanley flat onto his back, grabbed the knife with both hands and pulled. For a moment, it resisted, as though Stan's body were holding on, reluctant to let it go, and then it slid out so fast and smoothly, Richard nearly fell again. Blood bubbled through the wound and streamed down Stanley's sides.

Burke already had a glob of Nathaniel's salve on her first two fingers. She pushed her fingers into the wound and wiggled them around.

Richard gagged. He sent up a prayer. *Please don't let me puke right now.*

She scooped more of the stuff up and pressed it into the wound. A third scoop scraped the sides of the container clean, leaving nothing but a silken residue. This was smeared across the surface of the gaping cut. She tossed the tin aside and pressed both hands to his chest as though she were a faith healer. "Come on, Stanley. Come on. Fight."

Sirens wailed in the distance. The sound, like a splash of icy water, brought Richard fully back to the moment. The fire had burned down to a handful of smoldering coals. Ash drifted on the breeze like so much powdery snow. The writer lay still and silent to Richard's left, his face hidden by a dark shock of hair.

"Burke," he tapped her shoulder and motioned toward the man.

"Is he—"

"I don't know."

He left her there, still compressing Stanley's wound, and approached the writer. His lambasted joints popped in protest as he lowered himself and pressed two fingers to the man's neck, just under his jaw. A slow, strong, steady pulse beat within him. Richard's relief was so immense he thought he might swoon like a girl. "He's alive," he called over his shoulder. "Unconscious, but alive."

Not only alive, but young again, with a dark growth of beard along his strong, pale jaw.

Burke sighed. "Thank God.

"Don't thank God, darling. This isn't over yet."

The Devil stepped out from behind the wood pile. Her body-hugging white dress seemed to glow in the moonlight. She picked her way carefully across the gravel drive and crossed the patio in spikey heels that added six inches to her already impressive height. She took a seat in the chair the skinwalker had used earlier and crossed her shapely legs. She pointed one long, slim finger at Burke. "You broke our deal."

"I didn't," Burke said.

"Oh, but you did. I have an excellent memory, sweetheart. I let Stanley go, just like you asked, but here we are. My pet skin-walker is so much dust in the wind. I think the only fair restitution is that I get Stanley back, plus the old man and the writer, too. I mean, Stanley rightfully belongs to me. The writer should, by all accounts, have been dead in a few more days, and the old man...well...he took my iPhone. That's just uncalled for."

Richard sweated like a whore in church.

The sirens drew closer. He noticed a phone on the patio near O'Doyle's hand. He must have called for help.

Burke's steady calm was as impressive as anything else he'd seen her do that night.

"The deal stands," she said.

The Devil laughed. "Are you really going to fight me, dear? You are a spunky one. Maybe I'll take you with me, too. I think you could learn to be a great asset to me."

Swirling red lights turned toward the long driveway.

The pavement beside The Devil split, opening a crevice from which an eerie red light escaped, along with the gut-wrenching wails of people crying for help across an impossible distance.

"The deal stands," Burke repeated and stood.

The Devil rose to her feet.

The smoking abyss separated them. Heat waves gave the impression that he watched them through a shimmering curtain.

Burke held her ground. "The deal stands and you need to go."

The Devil's angelic face took on a cold, hard cast. She clamped her teeth together so hard it made a muscle in her jaw jump. "How dare you contra—"

"The deal was we wouldn't kill the skinwalker," Burke cut her off. "Get it? *We* wouldn't kill the skinwalker. I promised we wouldn't, and we didn't. *I* killed the skinwalker. *I* claimed command over him by using his name. I cut his disgusting, unnatural body into pieces with an axe that I paid for with my own money. I dowsed him with gasoline and I watched him burn in the moonlight. *We* didn't do anything. I killed the skin-walker. I killed him. I did it." As she spoke, her voice rose higher and higher. If she'd unleashed a war-cry of victory it would have been a fitting end to her speech, but she stood there, feet planted wide, shoulders square, chin high, and faced The Devil in stony silence.

For a split second, Richard was certain The Devil would leap across the chasm and tear his granddaughter limb from limb, so great was the rage written on her features, but then she threw her head back and laughed—a melody so harmonious and appealing, flowers must have burst into bloom somewhere nearby. Roses, by the smell of it.

The swirling emergency lights lit the world around them in flashing reds and blues. "Well played, hunter. Well played."

The chasm sealed shut and the Devil stepped over the seam toward Richard. She leaned in so close he could feel the warmth coming off her shapely body. With a slow, intimate gesture, she slid her hand down his chest and deep into the pocket of the ridiculous sweatpants to pull out her phone. "See ya 'round, cowboy," she said and gave him a kiss on the cheek that had a powerful effect on his old, beat up body. That was proof enough that he wasn't dead yet.

Doors slammed and boots hit the ground. "What's going on here?" a tall officer shouted.

Paramedics raced toward Stanley and O'Doyle.

The Devil was gone, the earth as solid and unbroken as ever. Burke stepped away from Stanley and let the medics gather over him.

The young woman in blue coveralls kneeling over O'Doyle called out, "As far as I can tell, this guy is just sleeping the soundest sleep in history."

As if confirming her diagnosis, O'Doyle snored loudly and rolled onto his side.

"He's lost a lot of blood," Burke said to the men checking Stanley.

"From where?" one asked.

They'd ripped open his shirt. Thick streaks of congealing

blood covered the skin all around the smooth, unblemished center of his chest.

"Are you okay?" the officer asked Burke. "Are you hurt?"

She blinked up at him. "I bumped my head," she said.

His eyes traveled slowly down her filthy, blood-covered body. "You bumped your head?" he asked, incredulous.

She nodded. "Pretty hard," she added.

"Right," he said. "What about you, old man?"

Richard puffed up his chest, affronted at being addressed so gruffly, but the act of puffing sent spasms of pain through his body. "I...um...I fell and I think I hurt my...uh..." He took a quick mental inventory. "Everything," he said.

"You hurt your everything?" the officer asked.

"Sit down," the woman medic told him. He did as she said, grateful for the gentle touch of caring hands. *Please, God, don't let her sprout wings unless they're of the angelic sort*, he prayed.

The officer said, to no one in particular, "Take them all to the hospital and keep a guard posted. I want to know what the hell happened here before any of these folks are released back into the general public."

A genteel British voice answered, weak and tremulous. "I'm afraid it's going to be rather difficult to explain. But I can assure you, no laws have been broken."

Richard wept.

CHAPTER FORTY-SIX

Finn

FINN WOKE IN A WHITE ROOM. CRISP WHITE SHEETS COVERED him. He wore a thin blue hospital gown and, by the feel of things, nothing else. A clear tube disappeared behind a piece of tape on his arm.

It's a hospital.

He remembered voices outside his home, remembered wanting to live, remembered stumbling out the door. After that, memories turned to nightmarish flashes of images. A man who could have been his twin, just as old and sick-looking as him, with his own blue eyes and crooked mouth. An old bald guy with an axe. Men and women he didn't know shouted at one another and moved too fast to track.

Someone stabbed one of the girls and, after that, the situation got truly bizarre. Then he suffered some sort of spell where he couldn't draw breath. His vision went dark around the edges and then there was nothing but oblivion.

Now he lay in a hospital.

And he was starving.

He fumbled around until he found the little call button and pushed it. Less than a minute later, a nurse entered, a doctor close behind.

"Welcome back, sleepyhead. I think you might have set a record."

Finn rubbed his eyes. Now that she mentioned it, his eyes were gritty. Gritty, but clear. "I can see you," he said.

The doctor and nurse exchanged a look.

"Does that surprise you?" the doctor asked.

"I..." he trailed off, not wanting to sound like he'd lost his mind. "My vision's been blurry lately, but you look clear to me."

The doctor pulled an instrument from the wall and shot a bright pinpoint of light into Finn's eyes. "Everything looks fine, Mr. O'Doyle." He snapped the instrument back into place. "We do have some questions."

The nurse reached for Finn's arm and wrapped a blood pressure cuff around it. He looked down at the wide band as she pumped it tighter. Dark hair peppered his skin. There wasn't an age spot in sight. He fought the urge to laugh. "I'll try my best to answer them, but it's been a weird few weeks."

"Weird, how?"

"I wasn't feeling well, I guess," he hedged. "This girl...well..."

Sara. He hadn't given a thought to Sara.

"Has anyone been asking for me?"

"Half the world is asking about you, Mr. O'Doyle. You've got quite a fan following," the nurse said, ripping open the Velcro on the cuff and tucking it back into the little basket.

"No, I mean a girl. Sara..."

I don't even know her last name.

"No one by the name of Sara, so far as I know. The folks who came in with you have been asking after you."

"Came in with me? The ones who called for help?"

The doctor gave him a sidelong glance that told him the

psych ward was still not out of the question. "*You* called for help, Mr. O'Doyle," the doctor said. "You don't remember?"

"No." He frowned, trying to piece together the events. "No, I don't remember."

"How do you feel?" the doctor asked.

"Like I'm about to starve," Finn said.

The doctor nodded. "By the sounds of your digestive system, you haven't had a proper meal in some time. You were quite dehydrated, as well. Have you been using any kinds of drugs? Prescription or otherwise?"

Finn shifted. Of course, that's what they'd think. It made sense, didn't it? Maybe Sara had been slipping him something? If so, he'd never be able to tell them what it was. He settled for the easiest answer, "No. Nothing like that. I mean, I smoke, or I did. I've quit now," he announced, startling himself. He liked the way that sounded. It was a good plan to stick with. "I've been really sick for a few weeks, but I feel fine now. Really. Just very hungry."

The two examiners seemed to accept that. "Very well. I'll let you order some soup and crackers. Keep that down and we'll go from there."

Finn agreed without complaint.

"As far as I can tell, aside from the lack of nutrition, you're fit as a fiddle, Mr. O'Doyle. I'd like to keep you overnight for observation. If there are no complications, we'll have you back home in twenty-four hours or so. I'll be back in the morning to check on you. If you need anything in the meantime, just press the call button and a nurse will be right in." He headed toward the door, too busy with people who actually needed his help to worry about an author who didn't eat properly.

"Doctor?"

The man paused and looked back. "Yes?"

"You said something about people who came in with me?"

"Yes, two elderly men and a lady about your age. They were treated and released."

"Who were they? Is there any way I can get in touch with them? You know, to thank them for their help?"

The doctor shrugged. "I'm not sure. You could check with the police."

Finn nodded his thanks. The two left the room and he lay back against the bed, so wide awake it felt like he might never sleep again.

CHAPTER FORTY-SEVEN

Richard

THE THREE OF THEM SAT AROUND A TABLE IN THE O.K. CAFE. A woman with hair as red as a fire engine stood over them with a pad and pen.

"Wha canneye getcha?" she asked around the wad of gum in her mouth.

"Two eggs, over medium, with bacon and toast," Burke said.

"I'd like to try your fried chicken and waffles with some of those famous fried cheesy potatoes," Stanley said when it was his turn.

"Can I just get a grilled chicken breast and a side of apple-sauce?" Richard asked.

"Sure thing, hon. Anything to drink?"

"Do you have prune juice?"

"Sure. That all?"

Richard smiled. "Yes, ma'am."

She took their menus and weaved through the crowded restaurant toward the kitchen.

"A rather bland meal, old chap," Stanley said.

"I'm overdue for some bland and boring," Richard retorted. "Too danged old for all this adventure and wild eating. My insides were stuck in neutral 'til that nurse at the hospital gave me something. Don't need to go messing up what's been set to rights again."

Stanley chuckled and sipped his coffee. He was pale and his hands shook, but he had assured them repeatedly that he felt as fine as ever.

"So." Burke leaned forward and propped her elbows on the table. "Seems like Chief Suspicouspants can't find a proper crime to pin on us. The famous author called and sang our praises, promising to dedicate his next book to us. What do we do now?"

Richard stared at his hands, folded on the table. What did they do now? He was tired. His body ached everywhere. He still had a room at Everest with an adjustable bed and an electric heating pad. Still, the strigoi had been there. Would he be able to sleep in a place where something had tried to kill him?

"I don't want to go back to Everest," Stanley said. "I only ever went there to find Richard."

"Where did you live before that?" Burke asked.

The question made Richard look up with interest. He'd not given much thought to Stanley's life before they met.

"I moved around," Stanley said. "Hunters aren't much good at settling down."

The waitress came with the prune juice. Beautiful, angelic, wrinkled old waitress. Richard sipped the blessed beverage. No fine wine had ever tasted better.

"We could go back to my place for a while. Hang out, you know. Get healed up a bit before we make any decisions," Burke suggested.

"You would take us in?" Richard asked. The idea astounded him. His own daughter had never offered anything of the sort.

Decades had passed since he'd lived with family. It sounded sort of nice.

"Of course. We're a team now, right?"

"I'd be honored, Mrs. Martin," Stanley said.

Burke nodded. "Okay. That's settled. We'll rest and heal. Maybe learn a hobby or something. Relax for a while."

"Toast to it," Richard said, lifting his glass. Something about the word relax picked at his mind, but he pushed it aside and forced a smile.

The juice glass and coffee cups bumped together with a satisfying clunk.

Two young men passed the table. A snippet of their conversation caught Richard's attention.

"...coven in San Diego. If we get there before Solstice, we can..."

Burke and Stanley sat very still and straight-backed in their chairs.

"Probably just kids being stupid," Burke said.

"Most likely," Stanley agreed.

A vague scent of sulfur wafted in the wake of the boys.

"Where's your house again, Burke?" Stanley asked.

"Michigan."

"Right." He nodded. "It's nice there in the spring. Quite green."

"Very," she agreed.

The waitress brought their food. They all tucked in, carefully avoiding eye contact with one another.

Richard forced himself to remember the weeks between his admission to Everest and the strigoi attack. Anger had ruled him. He'd embraced it. Anger, as tough and bitter as it may be, was far more palatable than soul-crushing loneliness. It was easier to swallow than admitting your days had no purpose. Easier to spend time being angry than doing nothing in the name of relaxation.

"You know, just having family, us taking care of each other, that ought to be enough," he said.

"That's true," Burke said. "Loving each other gives our days purpose."

"Indeed," Stanley agreed.

Richard picked up his fork and poked at the bland chunk of chicken. "I've never seen the Pacific Ocean," he said.

"Really?" Stanley grinned at him. "And all these years, living so close to it?"

"We could make a little side trip," Burke offered. "On the way home, I mean. Just to check it out. It would add a few days to the drive but, really, we don't have any reason to hurry back, do we?"

"None that I can think of," Richard said. He took a bite, chewed, swallowed. "Hear there's a good zoo in San Diego."

Stanley nodded. "I've been there. It's fantastic."

"We should go," Richard suggested.

Burke's expression grew serious. "Grandpa?"

"Yeah?"

"Are you sure you're up to...you know...the zoo. That's a lot of walking. Who knows what conditions will be like. You know...with all the...um...creatures... that could be there."

"Hospital gave me a new walker and a bottle of pills that seem to do the trick. Think I'll be all right."

She looked to Stanley. "And you? We came close to losing you twice in the last week."

He waved away her concern. "I'm told close only counts in horseshoes and hand grenades. Besides, I haven't seen Death in ages. Last I knew, he had a condo in Manhattan."

They both stopped eating and stared at him.

Stanley swallowed a bite of his cheesy potatoes.

"Are you serious?" Burke asked.

"I know, right? I asked the same thing. He could have gotten a place twice as big in Jersey for half the rent."

Richard scowled. "Don't be yankin' my chain, you old fart."

Stanley laughed.

The joyful vitality of the sound warmed Richard's heart. "California then?" Richard asked.

"California," Stanley agreed.

Burke's smile was radiant. "California or bust."

SNEAK PEAK AT THE NEXT MONSTERS AND MAYHEM

Some Legends Never Die

E A COMISKEY

BLURB

Kill the monster, not your mother

Ornery octogenarian Richard, his associate Stanley, and his granddaughter Burke are world-class hunters of all things supernatural. They've faced monsters of every ilk, even overcome The Devil Herself, but now they face the most frightening challenge of all—spending the holidays with family.

Richard's daughter is determined to return him to the safety of a senior care facility. She wants to send Stanley with him, and she has plans to make a match between Burke and a young IT engineer she ran over with her car. Little does she know that hunters are invariably led to the hunt.

There's a rogue monster in the neighborhood and Burke's blind date lands her in the middle of a battle between two powerful gangs of supernatural creatures. Now Richard and Stanley need to find a way to rescue her and stop the battle before it grows to truly galactic proportions, but can they do it with a meddling daughter and her quirky neighbors watching their every move?

TRADEMARK ACKNOWLEDGEMENTS

Coca-Cola
Little Anthony and The Imperials
Shelby GT
Paul Anka
Oreo
Cadillac

CHAPTER ONE

Cobwebs dangled from splintered windows that dotted one side of the rusty trailer. Screams emanated from behind the thin, poorly constructed walls. Near the front door, a tall, thin man in a dark tailcoat shouted above the joyous rumble of the crowd, "Come one, come all. Take a journey through the afterlife. Mingle with spirits, dance with monsters, but don't stay too long, or you may forget your way out of the Tomb of the Dead."

Richard rolled his eyes at the carnival barker. Kids spending an hour's income of their parents' wages for the privilege of three minutes of being scared by plastic skeletons and rubber spiders. Little brats had no idea what really peered out at them from the shadows at night. How could they? He hadn't known. For more than eight decades he'd gotten along just fine, more or less, thinking humans ruled the prime spot in Earth's food chain. Then Stan friggin' Kapcheck, his neighbor at the Everest Senior Living Facility, got him mixed up in monster hunting and he hadn't trusted a dark corner since.

Today, though, he clung to his determination to enjoy the moment and ignore the world of monsters. He tuned out the nonsense going on at the carnival "fun house," and focused his attention upon the masterpiece before him. That particular corndog rivaled anything ever created by some over-bred, high-falootin' French chef, and he'd go to the mat to defend that opinion with anyone who dared tell him otherwise. This lumpy, slightly misshapen masterpiece bore no resemblance whatso-ever to any factory-made frozen food-like product. He'd watched the kid with purple spiked hair jam a stick in a hotdog and dunk it into a clear plastic tub full of creamy batter before dropping it into the basket of bubbling oil. When it came out, golden crust gleaming like the life-giving sun, Richard knew he'd won the culinary lottery. The kid then proved he was a genius in freak's clothing when he scooped a handful of fried onion petals into a paper basket and laid his creation upon that glorious bed of grease.

Richard asked for a Coke to go with it, paid roughly the same amount as he had for a week's groceries back in his lonely widower days, and shuffled across the blacktop to the picnic table Burke and Stanley had staked a claim to. He had to weave his way through a crowd that included a ten-foot-tall Uncle Sam, two enormous peanuts with legs, and a frazzled-looking woman with a troupe of children bouncing along in her wake like a row of over-sugared ducklings. Finally, he reached the table and set his treasures on the rough wooden tabletop. All the while, the rich, heady aroma of fried cornbread and onions rose from the flimsy basket, teasing him with promises of flavor to come.

Too eager for lunch to care about dignity, he used his right hand to hoist his leg over the bench, plunked down on his bony butt, used both hands to get the left leg up and over, and swiveled into a proper seated position. He neither knew nor cared how he'd ever manage to extricate himself from the table and its attached benches when the time came. That first bite made it all worthwhile, crunchy on the outside, moist and steamy on the inside, with the salty meatiness of the wiener in the middle. He mashed it up between ill-fitted dentures, struggling to stifle a moan. The second bite held more meat and less bread and contained a surprising little burst of delicious grease.

When he lifted the tab on the can of Coca-Cola, it popped with a satisfying hiss and a snap that sent an effervescent spray of icy soda raining down to settle like so many dewdrops upon the white hairs of his forearm. The sweet, tickling liquid sowed a row of cold satisfaction down his throat.

He closed his eyes and sighed in pleasure while Little Anthony and The Imperials sang over the loudspeaker about tears on pillows and someone revved the engine of the 1968 Shelby GT they'd brought to exhibit in the classic car show. When he opened his eyes, he found Burke sitting directly across from him, eyebrows raised just above the rims of her enormous mirrored sunglasses. Her cheeks lifted in a smile that displayed the freckles on her tawny brown skin.

"Why you grinnin' like a possum eatin' a sweet potato?"

She selected a peanut from the cup on the table and used her manicured pink nails to break it open. "I just don't think I've ever seen anyone enjoy a meal so completely."

Richard popped an onion petal into his mouth. The crunchy tang highlighted the other flavors, overwhelming none of them. The culinary lottery, for sure. "Now it's a crime for a man to enjoy his lunch?"

Unaffected by his gruff tone, she ate her peanut and reached for another. "I think it's nice that you are so happy."

"To truly, thoroughly enjoy a meal is considered by some to be a high form of meditation, capable of bringing a man into communion with the gods," Stanley said in his fancy British accent. He sat on the tabletop, his perfectly shined black shoes propped on the bench. He wore slim fit blue jeans and a bright white starched shirt with the top two buttons open and the sleeves rolled up to the elbow. A newsboy hat protected his bald head from the bright Alabama sun.

"Why can't you sit on the bench like God intended?" Richard asked.

Miss Peanut Festival strode past in impossible sparkly silver shoes. Her tan legs flexed and stretched beneath a pale-yellow skirt tossed about by the gentle breeze. Golden locks hung in ringlets nearly to her slim waist. Her eyes lingered on Stanley a moment and a smile kissed the dimpled corner of her full, wide mouth.

Stanley tipped his hat in her direction. "The view is delightful from up here, Richard."

Richard harrumphed into his corndog. "I ain't some dirty old man." But he couldn't quite keep his eyes from following the princess's progress as she sashayed around a corner and disappeared.

Paul Anka took over the music and started crooning for his girl to put her head on his shoulder and whisper in his ear. A group of teenage girls on a ride screamed high above their heads. "It ain't a bad little festival," he admitted.

"Indeed," Stanley agreed. "Did you know that most of the carnival companies in America aren't actually operated by humans at all but by—"

"Stop it," Burke said. "I don't want to know. For half a year I've been chasing hidebehinds and fighting shapeshifters. If the ride operators here are all descended from Big Foot, I don't want to know. For one day, I just want to sit here and eat these peanuts and not worry about what might be looking to eat me."

"They don't eat people. They—"

"Stanley Kapcheck, I swear to God, I will pistol whip you if you try to finish that sentence."

Stanley chuckled. "I don't often see the resemblance between you and your grandfather, but at moments like this, there is no doubt in my mind." He waved at a troupe of silver-haired cloggers clad in impressively supportive tights and leotards, and bedecked with all manner of red white and blue spangles and fringe. The taps on their shoes click-clacked against the pavement, creating a ruckus akin to the wheels of a steam engine rattling along a rusty rail. The ladies blushed and waved back.

Richard rolled his eyes and focused on enjoying the last of the corn dog. An unsettling weight pressed against his ribs but another sip of Coca-Cola carried the pressure away on the wind of a long, low belch. Several of the cloggers' smiles turned to dirty looks flashed at him. He shrugged, unapologetic. Everybody burped. If some people wanted to pretend otherwise, well, he couldn't stop anyone from being as uppity as they chose to be.

When the noise from the cloggers died down, the paper basket was emptied and the peanuts reduced to a pile of empty shells, Stanley said, "You know, at some point, we're going to have to decide whether or not we have the collective courage to face this challenge."

"Stanley," Burke said, a warning in her voice.

Stanley shifted so he could more easily see Burke. "I know you've no desire to discuss the hidden dangers of the world today but, honestly, isn't that why we stopped here? To take some time to evaluate what we know and proceed with prudence."

"You might be the expert hunter in this group," Richard said, "but you don't know about this. Not the way Burke and I know."

"Once you enter her world, it's nearly impossible to get out again," Burke said.

"She'll suck at your soul until you start praying for death," Richard added. He shuddered at the memory of sitting in his room at the nursing home, waiting for his body to realize his life had ended long ago. Those were the days before Stanley had dragged him into the whirlwind of a monster-hunting existence. He'd been blind to the wonders, both good and bad, hidden in plain sight all around him.

"She's protective of her offspring, but she'll turn on them, too, given the slightest provocation," Burke said.

"Then we must be exceedingly careful not to provoke her," Stanley said.

"She draws you in with tears, makes you feel sorry for her so you aren't expecting when she moves in for the kill," Richard said.

"We shall remain on guard against all forms of emotional trickery," Stanley said.

"She's clever. She'll try to separate us. Divide and conquer," Burke said.

"No one goes in alone. That's just good hunter sense," Stanley said.

"That nest of vampires in California was downright open-minded by comparison," Richard said.

"I cannot force either of you to face this, but the connection between her and you is powerful and I don't believe you'll rest well until this matter is settled. You two will not dissuade me from my opinion. Together, we are strong enough to deal with her," Stanley said.

Burke wrapped the end of one long braid around her finger. "You don't have anything like her in your journal, Stanley."

Richard sucked down the remainder of his Coke. "She's got these pointy little fingernails and they make this noise—"

"It'll destroy you from the inside out," Burke finished for him.

"Surely you both exaggerate. In all this time fighting monsters—"

Burke leaned forward on both elbows. "What will you do if things go south? We can't defeat her by stabbing her with a silver dagger or shooting her with lead bullets."

"Salt won't keep her away. She thrives on the stuff."

Stanley cocked his head and regarded them in silence for a little while. On the loudspeaker, a low southern voice announced that the greased pig contest would start in thirty minutes. A teen boy walked by lugging a stuffed monkey as large as himself. A banner flapped against the wall of a nearby building. In big red letters on a white background, it announced "Coleum Corp, where there's space for all." At last, he said, "She's your family. Your daughter. Your mother. And since you are the closest thing I have to family, when she calls and asks that we come for an early Thanksgiving, I say we ought to go and eat turkey and pumpkin pie. And no amount of chatter from the two of you will convince me that the woman is some kind of demonic entity."

Burke dropped her head onto her folded arms. "She's going to try to hook me up with someone horrid," she mumbled against the tabletop.

"She'll try to get me back in the nursing home," Richard said. "She thinks I'm old."

"You *are* old, Dick."

Richard scowled. Lord, but he hated being called Dick.

Stanley just chuckled. "Come on, you two sourpusses. It's a festival. Let's enjoy it."

"I *was* enjoying it until you insisted we have this conversation," Richard said. Already, his stomach had begun to send out distress signals, but no matter what came, the glorious delicacy had been worth it.

"There's a greased pig contest," Stanley said, lithely hopping down from the tabletop.

Unnatural. Even if he didn't have aches and pains, which he ought to have at his age—well, technically he should be dead at his age, but all things considered—he still ought to have the decency to move at a certain accepted and expected pace. To do otherwise served no purpose but to brag. Pompous old peacock.

Richard carefully hoisted himself out of the picnic table with a fine and proper amount of grunting and crunching joints, as befitted a senior citizen.

Burke collected their trash and dropped it in a nearby bin. "What exactly is a greased pig contest and why are we going to see it?"

Stanley ambled through the crowd with his hands in his pockets, face tilted slightly up toward the crystalline sky. "They grease up a pig and set it loose and try to catch it. There's a skill to it. Not everyone can manage."

"No doubt," Burke replied.

"This year, the organizers of the race wanted to get more bang for their buck."

Richard's guts squirmed. After six months with Stan Kapcheck, he understood this sensation had little to do with his gastric worries and more to do with the pending announcement that death and destruction loomed in their near future. With Stan, there was always a pending announcement of death and destruction in the near future. That was Stanley's stock in trade.

"They sought out the fastest, most powerful pig they could find," Stanley said.

Burke's glasses remained pointed straight ahead, her lips pressed into a thin, tight line.

"They selected a real doozy. Not just an average pig, but a saehrimnir."

"One day, Stanley. Just one day of hanging out at a festival," Burke said.

Stanley pulled one hand from his pocket and lifted it in a gesture of surrender. "Festivals are tricky. Like I tried to tell you. More often than not, the carnivals are run by—"

"Just tell us what the devil a saehrimnir is," Richard snapped.

"They are pigs destined for the tables of the Norse gods. If anyone here dares slaughter one, the wrath of the gods could well wipe Dothan, Alabama, right off the map." Stan winked at a redhead in a pair of teeny tiny shorts and a crocheted halter top that served little purpose beyond keeping her just this side of a public indecency citation.

The woman winked back.

Richard burped and immediately felt a little better. "They're just going to catch it though, right? Not like they'll tear it limb from limb."

"Well, that's true," Stanley agreed. "They won't slaughter it right now, but once it's been caught it goes back with the other pigs."

"So?" Burke asked.

"What do you think happened to the little piggy who went to the market fair, my dear?"

"So, we need to steal a pig and set it loose?" she asked.

Stanley nodded. "Precisely, but we need to be quick about it."

"Why's that?"

"Because, as I tried to tell you, the carnival is run by—"

"Forget it," she said, holding up a hand to stop him. "Forget I asked. I seriously don't want to know."

"Great. We save the pig and then we head north to eat turkey," Stanley said. "I can't wait to meet your daughter, Dick."

"Maybe we can just stay here, eating pork chops and bacon, until the gods come to kill us," Richard said.

Stanley laughed. "I love that you're developing a sense of humor, old boy."

Richard harrumphed again. Who said he was joking?

✵

THE PIG DID NOT ENJOY BEING SAVED. COVERED IN GREASE, terrified, and approximately the same size and weight as a female bodybuilder, it had allowed itself to be stuffed into the backseat of Stanley's 1959 Cadillac convertible only because Burke lulled it with Oreo cookies. She also crooned to it like a baby, but the pig clearly saw the cookies as the real enticement. Unfortunately, what goes in a pig must come out, and when Stanley pulled to a stop to release the animal near the banks of the West Fork Choctawhatchee River, they all burst forth from the vehicle, desperate to escape the stench.

Burke, still angry about being denied her day at the fair, seated herself upon a rock next to the shallow, murky water and announced that she would stay right there until Stanley had the mess cleaned up. Covered in fairground dust, pig drool, whatever lubricant had been used to grease the pig, and a good many Oreo cookie crumbs, she sat with her back ramrod straight. She folded her hands in her lap, brushing the end of one broken thumbnail against the pad of the other thumb. Her long black braids cascaded over her shoulders, the ends just reaching the place on her arm where she'd attained a six-inch-long laceration wrestling the pork chop of the gods past a wire gate.

Richard longed for Stanley to challenge her at that moment but, alas, among the good many descriptors he could use for the old Brit, "stupid" had no home.

"Well, old chap, you and I will take the Caddy to clean her up and—"

Richard broke forth in a wheezy laugh that brought tears to his eyes and tottered toward the riverbank. "We'll expect you upon your return," he said, easing himself down onto the rock next to his pungent granddaughter.

A muscle twitched in Stanley's jaw, but he made no protest. With a nod, he turned away and left them. The powerful purr of the Cadillac hummed to life and faded into the distance.

Richard's eyes met Burke's and they both burst into laughter.

He'd laughed more in the last six months than he had in the past six years combined. Heck, maybe in the past sixty. Something about running headlong toward death took away the weighty seriousness of staying alive that he'd labored under for most of his adult life.

"We should walk into Mom's house just like this," Burke said.

He wiped his eyes and rubbed his aching knees. "We'll tell her the whole truth and nothing but the truth."

"And she'll listen and say, 'How absurd. There is no such thing as Norse Gods. Any fool knows there is One God and Jesus is Lord. Now go wash up, Burke Dakota. No respectable man wants a woman who smells like swine. I swear, it's no wonder you couldn't keep the one you had.'"

"Speaking of that, you heard anything from Dim Ditty Dimwit lately?" he asked.

She stretched her legs out in front of her, letting the toes of her boots fall to the sides.

Richard wondered when she had given up her fancy high-priced girlie shoes for boots with reinforced toes. The change signified by the difference in wardrobe struck him as indicative as something far deeper than clothing. They'd seen the face of true evil in the past half year. They'd waged war and come out still standing, more or less.

"He called me a while back, when we were in Texas. The divorce from the underwear model is final. He's thinking about joining an Ashram in Colorado."

"He called just to tell you that?"

"I think he wanted me to understand he's no longer begging me to come back. He's seeking enlightenment now."

Richard blew a raspberry.

Burke laughed. "Exactly."

Across the river, a doe and her fawn emerged from thick green foliage with watchful caution. The mother deer led her offspring to the water's edge and they lapped up their fill while Burke and Richard watched, silent and unmoving. If they'd had a mind for it, they could enjoy venison for months.

Richard wondered how often humans, like those deer, went about the business of life completely unaware of the still presence of a watchful predator. Only the luck of good timing kept them off some creature's dinner menu. If people really knew, they'd be too scared to function.

The animals returned to the lush green cover of the forest.

"We've put this visit with your mother off for too long," he said.

She chewed on her lip.

"She's been worried sick, you know."

"Yeah, I know."

Richard shifted. He had more than enough padding around his middle and none at all on his backside. Rocks did not serve as adequate seating for a man whose ninetieth birthday loomed just the other side of the horizon. "She's got a good heart. Wants the best for us both. Always has."

"Undeniably," Burke agreed.

"So, you're ready for this visit, then?"

"Nope."

"Me either."

"She'll have some loser lined up for me to meet—an accountant or an architect looking to impregnate me quickly before time runs out."

"There will be brochures for a new nursing home. One more recreational than Everest. She'll say, 'They have a pool, Dad. Didn't the doctor say swimming is good therapy for your hip?'"

"How is your hip, anyway?"

He chuffed. "Well, I ain't usin' a walker no more and I ain't fell over yet."

Comfortable silence settled between them once again. Their shadows stretched long across the river's tumbling current as the sun slipped down the western slope of the sky. Nature's choir, punctuated by the bass of a bullfrog and the high, chirping soprano of a little yellow goldfinch, sent up a song of birth, death, and the sheer joy of living the moments in-between. If he'd had the luxury of a well-padded chair with a footrest, he'd be sound asleep by now.

"Grandpa?"

"Hmm?"

"Don't let her talk you into living in a nursing home again, okay? Not even a really nice one with a pool." She slipped one strong brown hand over his pale, arthritic fingers.

Richard squeezed her hand, keeping his eyes resolutely fixed on some distant point on the other side of the river, lest she see the waterworks welling in his eyes. Weren't no reason to be sitting in a forest, crying like a little girl. "You got it, kid," he said.

Stanley made it back just before the sun dropped below the horizon. Both he and the car had a freshly scrubbed shine and smelled faintly of citrus and chlorine bleach. "I figured we'd had enough fun for one day and rented us three rooms at the Wyndham. Tomorrow we can head north."

Burke rose and stretched long limbs toward the sky. "Is it run by goblins? Staffed by vampires? Are the housekeepers all witches? Do demons live in the sewer lines under the building?"

"Demons would never deign to live in a sewer. They're quite proud," he replied.

Her gaze remained steady.

"Only humans, so far as I noticed," Stanley told her through his grin.

She held out a hand and Richard allowed himself to be helped to his feet. He waited until the blood flow returned to his legs before releasing her hand.

"You know," Stanley said as they hiked back in the direction of the road. "Just because there are no monsters at the hotel doesn't mean it's perfectly safe. I've seen a good many humans who were much more frightening than any monster."

Burke grinned. "Oh, I know. By this time tomorrow, you'll be eating turkey with one of them."

To learn of the release of Some Legends Never Die and other great Scarsdale Publishing releases, sign up for our newsletter at www.scarsdalepublishing.com

www.scarsdalepublishing.com

Made in the USA
Middletown, DE
20 September 2021